Dark Shadows

Erica Richer

DEDICATION

This book is dedicated to my family, friends and especially my husband and children. You help me to see the light on my darkest days. I'd be lost without you.

CONTENTS

ACKNOWLEDGMENTS

I would like to acknowledge my husband and children. Only with their patience and support did I get to bring this story to life. Special thanks to my friend, Jenn, for letting me talk "book" to her.

CHAPTER ONE

Rose

As I lean back against my headboard, a strange yet familiar feeling begins to wash over me. All the energy I had moments ago quickly dissolves into fatigue. My eyelids become impossibly heavy and I struggle to keep them open and stay awake.

Oh, not again. I think as I try to push myself to fight through the exhaustion. If I can only make it to the kitchen, a can of pop will be a quick fix.

But that's all the way downstairs. I can practically hear my own whiny voice inside my head and it's not exactly supportive.

I barely move my laptop off my lap when I realize that my attempts are useless. I let out a sigh and lean back while my eyes close.

Here we go again. I think to myself before I'm engulfed in a darkness that chills my bones.

The darkness begins to melt away almost as quickly as it came. I can see a red glow through my eyelids as my skin warms and I reflexively open my eyes. I'm not surprised to find myself in exactly the same place as I was the last several times I was forcibly pulled into this dream, in the middle of a dirt road, flanked by thick trees.

The first time I was here I couldn't get over how beautiful it was. I just stood in one spot and looked around at the green grass, the thick trees, and the beautiful blue sky while the sun shone down on me. It felt like hours had gone by but when I woke up, I realized it had only been thirty minutes.

The many times in between I'd only marveled at the view for a moment. I'd set off down the dirt road, but I never seemed to get anywhere. I walked for what felt like hours, but I didn't come across any houses, intersections, signs or anything. It didn't matter what direction I went in. It was so annoying.

Now I'm here yet again. *Awesome*! I'm so not in the mood to be stuck in a dream, I have plans. I wasn't even tired until a minute before I passed out. *There is definitely something wrong with me.* I think to myself while I look around.

I look from the trees on my left to the trees on my right. I know the road leads nowhere so it's time to go off-roading. I cross the ditch and start into the trees on my right. I'm sure I'll get somewhere this time.

As I push through the trees and brush my skin begins to prickle and itch slightly. It feels like I'm having an allergic reaction to something, but I don't know what. Not to mention, I don't have any allergies that I am aware of. I look at my arms in the dim light but I see no sign of redness, inflammation or any other sign of an allergic reaction but my skin continues to prickle and itch. I keep moving forward carefully pushing twigs and branches away from my face until something happens.

The prickly and itchy sensation gets worse and my whole body begins to burn. I trip over a root and drop to the ground in frustration. *What's happening to me?* I wonder as I pull my knees to my chest, willing the feeling to subside. A few tears sneak out as I sit on the ground. This has never happened before. Why do dreams have to feel so real?

After some time, the pain gradually lessens until it disappears all together. Finally, I can get back on my feet. My legs tremble under my weight, threatening to collapse when I push on. I don't know what that was, but I don't want to find out. If I never experience that pain again, I still won't forget.

When I push through a thick set of branches, there's a familiar smell lingering in the soft breeze. I feel like I should know what the smell is from, but I just can't remember. The smell gets stronger as I keep moving and the trees become denser, slowing my pace.

I come to a stop at what seems to be a solid wall of trees and brush. Call it intuition but I believe I need to get to the other side. *There must be a way.* I tell myself.

I raise my hands to my face and bravely plunge into the trees. It's dark inside the brambles and branches, not a ray of sun finds its way in. I keep moving forward, tripping over roots and other growths, feeling a little more claustrophobic with every step.

Honestly, it feels like I've been walking for days. My stomach begins to cramp with hunger and my throat is scratchy and parched. I've never been so hungry and so thirsty at the same time. *Stupid life-like dream*!

I fall through a final wall of branches, shrubs, leaves and everything else you find in the woods, and stumble to my knees.

I'm in the open again. I can feel the breeze on my face and the grass between my fingers. *Thank god.* I say to myself as I take in my surroundings. I'm in a cemetery.

As I look around, I decide that it's not the local cemetery just behind our house. I don't know where this one is supposed to be, but it's completely deserted and surrounded by trees. The breeze picks up and cools down in a matter of seconds. I look up and watch as dark gray and black clouds move in and hide the sun and the blue sky. I wait for the thunder and lightning to start but it doesn't. An unsettling calm sets over the entire area like a blanket and puts me on edge.

I don't like this at all. I tell myself even though it doesn't help my situation.

I climb to my feet and make my way between the graves. Looking around I notice that there isn't a single person or animal in sight, this place is just *dead.* I shiver at my own thoughts.

I'm still carefully making my way around the tombstones when I catch the scent in my nose again. I still don't know what it is but maybe it's something I can eat or drink. I keep walking until I come to the opposite side of the graveyard. Just on the outskirts of the cemetery, on a small hill stands a mausoleum, and the stone doors are open. I stare at it in disbelief. I consider going in, but I hesitate. Every fibre of my being is telling me not to go in, and the decrepit tree beside it doesn't help.

If this were a horror movie, I'd be yelling at the character playing me to smarten up and go the other way, but it's just a dream, right? I try to convince myself to ignore the foreboding feeling I'm getting because my curiosity is going to win out and I know it.

I move closer until I'm standing in the doorway, staring down into the dark. The aroma begins to sting in my nose in an almost unpleasant way. I reach out for the wall with one hand and begin my descent. *I'm an idiot!* I tell myself as I move further down the stairs. I turn the corner where a lantern is lit to reveal a marble floor.

In the middle of the room lays a man, blood spills out of his neck and cascades along the marble towards me. I want to scream...To yell...To do something but I can't. My body refuses to react in that way even though I'm horrified at the sight before me.

A man I don't recognize enters from the adjacent room, he stops and looks at me. There is a look in his eyes that strikes me as a longing I could never understand. *Why?*

"My sweet Anastazija, I have been waiting for you." He says softly to me.

I stare at the man in confusion and fear. I don't know him. My name is Roselyn. *He's mistaken and I shouldn't be here in this damn dream that doesn't make sense.* It feels too real.

"No. I don't know you." I say with a shaky voice.

Panic and fear get the better of me and I turn and run as fast as I can up the stairs but as I reach the top, the doors slam shut. I'm trapped in here with a probable killer and a dead guy. *It can't get any worse.* Or so I believe until my skin begins to burn, my stomach cramps up, and my throat feels like sandpaper. I scream out in the dark from the frustration, fear, pain and repulsion that courses through me. All I can think about it the blood spilling from the guys neck. I want it.

I'm disgusted that I'd been attracted to the smell of what I can only assume was death. My breathing grows labored like there's a mass crushing my lungs and slowly suffocating me. The darkness begins to swirl around me, and my consciousness becomes hazy. The cold, dark takes me.

When the darkness lets me go, I wake up on my bed with a sharp intake of breath. *I knew it was a dream, it always is.* I say to myself to calm my breathing.

I started having the same dream three weeks ago but some how it's different each time. When I wake up it's like I can still feel it. Like right now my throat feels dry and my lungs ache. It's just weird. All I know is that I can't stop it unless I get a massive dose of caffeine right away. I don't know who the guy is or where I was, it could all just be a crazy nightmare, but it feels so real.

My best friend Hannah knows all about my messed-up dreams. She's in Europe until school starts but we e-mail and text each other every day. She already thinks that the dreams have something to do with witchcraft or something and she says it's exciting. *It's so not.* Maybe I'd feel differently if she was the one having them but she's not. Unfortunately, I am. I'm already a weirdo at school, having witchy abilities will only mean total social suicide.

I'd love to talk this all out with my best guy friend Morgan but lately he's been like a second brother. He's just less overbearing. *For now.*

And I don't dare tell my brother Alex about it. He's already overprotective and paranoid, besides it's just a dream. *What else could it be?*

So right now, I'll just have to deal with this myself. I can do that. *I hope.* I fall back across the bed and sigh. There are so many thoughts going through my head right now. I need to go somewhere I can make sense of this mess or at least de-stress. *And I know where.*

I jump off the bed and grab my cell phone. I slip past my brother who has passed out on the couch with the television on and I slap a sticky note on the back of the door as I leave. I head off into the fading light.

A while later I glance at my phone. It's 8:30 on a beautiful summer night and I'm spending it walking through a thicket of trees and brush, but it's worth it. I'm on my way to one of the most secluded, tranquil places I know. I won't have many more nights like this, it's already the end of August. *Not that it matters.* I will trudge through the snow just to get to my hidden pond, that's how much it means to me. Even if I can't explain the pull it has over me. It's the only place where I feel like I can breathe.

My name is Roselyn Parker, but my friends call me Rose. Well the few friends that I actually have, do. I'm seventeen but I'm probably not your typical teenager. I know I'm different in ways that even I can't explain. Other people my age, are most likely off at a party, drinking under age, doing drugs, or doing some other moronic activity that will only compromise their brain cells in the future. Not me though. I'm the kind of person who walks through woodsy areas alone at night just trying to find some "me" time to sort out the weirdness. *No wonder I'm a social leper.* For a seventeen-year old I am surprisingly responsible, and I have my priorities straight. I suppose my personality does set me apart from a crowd of seventeen-year old's, but my physical appearance is not so unique. I'm 5'3" which everyone knows is under the average height for females. I have bright green eyes, and long, dark brown hair. I'm not a total lost cause but I'm nothing special.

Other than my freakish, trance-like dreams, being short is probably the most annoying quality ever. It causes me all kinds of problems. I know short people can relate. But I did inherit most of my physical features from my mom including my height, or at least that's what I've gathered from the photographs. I wouldn't be able to tell you that seeing her is like looking in a mirror because my mother's dead. So is my father. It would be better if my parents hadn't been so camera-phobic. I don't think I could find one decent picture of them if I tried. But even the shitty photos mean everything to me, it's the only way I can check to see whose nose I have or whose lips. I know it seems idiotic but when they aren't around, you really begin to wonder these things. I still have my brother Alex even if he is worse than a parent sometimes. He's a little more than three years older than me and I've been living with him since I was fourteen. Which already feels like a lifetime.

Our parents died when I was one, my brother Alex was four going on five at the time. We never really got a straight answer regarding what happened to our parents. All we know is that there had been a horrible accident that claimed both of their lives. We spent years in and out of foster homes not knowing if we'd still have each other in the morning. So once Alex turned eighteen, we both moved into the house that our parents had left us, and Alex took on the role of the guardian to his little sister. Sometimes it bothers me that he still treats me like a child, because I strongly believe that despite my clumsy tendencies and lack of coordination, I can take care of myself, especially in the small town of Bradford, Ontario. Despite the town being located just north of Toronto it has never seen any crime, well at least until the sudden death of our parents. I guess I have some sense of understanding for Alex. However, in my sometimes-teenage mind there is no excuse. Especially, when it makes me feel like I am nothing more than a prisoner in my own home.

Anyway, my life is pretty good. I have Alex, Morgan, Hannah and my pond. I am where I am meant to be right now. Where I like to think angels watch over me, including my mom and dad. *I love you guys*. I whisper to the night.

CHAPTER TWO

Rose

The clearing where the pond is looks so beautiful at night. The stars shine down and the moon illuminates the water. There's lush grass covering the ground and even though no one cares for the grass, it doesn't get long or unruly. The trees that surround the clearing give its visitors complete privacy. *It's just so magical.* I love this pond. I'm drawn to it. I feel safe and comfortable here. It's the one place where I feel like I truly belong.

It's known as the pond of angels, or at least that's what all my hard research turned up some time ago. Whatever the story may be, it's a wonderful place.

I should check the exact time, but I don't want to. This place is too mesmerizing to ignore. Besides Alex is probably still sound asleep on the couch. He doesn't understand the power this place has over me, especially on such a gorgeous night. The sky is as clear as can be, which isn't very common. The stars give me a strange sense of calm knowing that they're watching over me as the water glistens.

As I sit down at the edge of the pond, I can't shake the feeling that I am being watched. I can't explain how I know. I just do. *It's strange.* A nervous, sickly feeling creeps into my stomach and I'm left without a doubt. Someone is watching.

I slowly glance around and see nothing. Even the trees are still, like they're made of metal. Nothing moves or makes a sound in the darkness. I seem to be the only person around for miles. I take a deep breath and slowly release it. I'm getting worked up over nothing. *God I'm such a girl.* I chastise myself for being a wimp. I don't feel threatened, I just feel uneasy. Even as I dangle my feet in the cool, refreshing water I feel the urge to look around. Of course, no one's there and my imagination seems to be getting the better of me. I keep trying to reassure myself as I stare at my feet. I'm moving them just enough to cause a small rippling effect in the water. As the ripples

7

stretch out in the pond, I watch as the perfect reflection of the stars and moon appears to dance on the water's surface. It's an incredibly entrancing sight.

Snap. I hear the twig break on the other side of the pond and my head shoots up. My eyes scan the area directly across from me and my breath catches in my throat. Just to the left of a tree, above a bush, I can see the faint glow of a pair of silver eyes. They look right at me not blinking or moving. It feels like forever while our eyes are locked. It seems neither of us dares to look away.

I don't try to scream or run. *I doubt I could if I wanted to.* All I can do is watch and wait. The longer I watch, the more I realize that it must be an animal. People don't have eyes like that. *Unless they're wearing costume contacts.* But they wouldn't likely waste their time watching me.

Just as I consider the possibilities, a gust of wind comes out of nowhere and blows crap into my eyes. *Perfect!* My eyes slam shut and begin to water like mad. I struggle to reopen them, but they don't want to. The dirt or whatever is still irritating them. When they clear enough to open, I immediately take in my surroundings. The animal or person seems to be gone.

Most of me is positive it was an animal, but I've never heard of an animal having a staring match with a person before. Not to mention an animal that can appear and disappear in complete silence.

I take a moment to rub fiercely at my eyes as the remaining gunk comes out. At least now I can properly see but I was rubbing so hard that my eyes are burning. I glance around again to be sure that it's still gone.

I carefully replay the strange situation. I realize, had it not been for the twig snapping, I probably wouldn't have looked up. I also remember how fast the eyes had disappeared without a sound. It was eerie. It was like they vanished into thin air, which I know isn't possible. Still, why break a twig unless you want to be noticed. After all, it could have appeared as quietly as it disappeared, or maybe I should say they?

I find myself strangely more curious than afraid of what I've seen. I know that I won't be able to talk to Alex about the events of tonight. If I even mention it, I'm going to find myself spending the rest of my summer with an armed escort. It's not exactly an appealing thought to be followed by anyone reporting back to my brother.

"Shit." I say rather loudly. I know I left the house at eight-thirty, but I bet it's nearing midnight now. Time has a way of slipping away when I'm here.

I am so dead. Alex is going to murder me. I reach into my pocket and pull out my cell phone. I quickly check the time and realize that it's eleven forty-four, which isn't a good thing. I check my missed calls and not surprisingly, I have missed seven calls all from my brother. I should have known better than to have my phone on silent. *Curse the creator of that function.* I was just looking for a little peace and quiet. Instead I've managed to screw myself when I get home because Alex is going to tear me a new one.

I shove my shoes on and head towards the overgrown path that will lead back to the road. As I stumble through the path, I pull my cell phone back out to see if he left a message. He did. I hold the phone lightly against my ear as the message starts.

"Rose, why aren't you picking up? I hope you're safe but if you are, you better have damn good reason for not answering. I am on my way to you now, you know I can't stand not knowing." Alex practically screams into the phone with a combination of worry and anger.

Typical. This is just like him. He's always so paranoid, it's a wonder he has all his hair. It's the summer for crying out loud and I'm seventeen. I don't know anyone else who has a ten o'clock curfew set by their brother. *It's so stupid.*

As I stagger through the path, I do my best to get his behavior. The more I understand his crazy mind, the better my chances are at talking my way out of this mess. I'd be a liar if I didn't admit to sort of understanding him. All we have left is each other, we have no other family. So, it's not an overly strange concept to want me safe. He obviously feels like my well-being is his responsibility. I almost feel bad. *Almost.* It's my opinion that he takes the whole big brother, guardian thing a bit too seriously.

I tuck my phone safely away in my pants pocket and continue towards the road. Its pitch black and I still suspect that I am being watched even if I can't see anything. I can feel it.

I emerge from the trees slightly breathless and I see my brother pulling over on the side of the road in his '67 Camaro. At first, his presence brings me a sense of warmth with everything that's happening. When I get closer to the car and see his face, I'm no longer relieved. In fact, the thought crosses my mind to run back in and hide. Right now, I'd rather deal with the creeper than my brother. I know he's already seen me and that I'll have to deal with him eventually, so I maintain my walk of death to the car. Alex leans over and unlocks the passenger door when I am close enough and I grit my teeth and slide in.

At first, he says nothing. I don't really know what to make of it, but as soon as my seatbelt is fastened, he aggressively pulls the car back onto the road and I know he's going to lay into me.

"Okay Rose, correct me if I'm wrong but I am pretty sure you have a working cell phone. I also recall buying it and paying your ridiculous bill every month. So, I think you owe me the common courtesy of answering the damn phone when I call you." He says angrily.

He's beyond pissed. I can tell. He usually doesn't resort to sarcasm unless he's been pushed over the edge, and he is definitely using it now to make his point. He's angry and annoyed with me. It can be felt in every word and I can feel it to my core. A twinge of guilt surges through me but it's overpowered by my own teenage angst.

"Alex I'm sorry. I had my phone on silent and I was distracted. I didn't realize how late it was and I didn't mean to lose track of time. I'm really, really sorry!" I plead guiltily.

It might have been naïve of me to think that my excuses would stifle his anger at least a bit, but I really should have known better. We've been fighting so much this summer and I have no idea why, but it seems like he disagrees with everything I do. I just can't win with him.

"It's always excuses with you Rose. You have no idea what it's like to wake up and find your little sister gone. Do you enjoy torturing me? I thought girls were supposed to mature faster than boys, but you don't seem to be in that boat." He spits the words at me.

I don't know what to say. I'm completely blown away by his attitude. Alex is sinking to an indefinite asshole status in my books. Even I'm amazed by his low blows and cheap shots.

"What the hell is your problem? You're being a bigger dick than usual. Seriously Alex, what are you so angry about? I don't sneak out at night to meet boys or party. I'm not crying to you about being knocked up. You're lucky that I'm so mature and you don't even realize it." I say in retaliation.

Great! Now I'm angry but can you blame me? He's being totally unreasonable. There's something else pissing him off and he's taking it out on me. He can't do that. As far as teenagers go, I'm pretty sure I'm one of the tame girls, and I've seen some untamed ones. Hell, my best friend Hannah is one. So, he needs to smarten up.

I'm turning eighteen in five months and I was hoping that being classified as an adult would make him back off, but I'm having doubts. The older I get, the worse he seems to get.

He lets out a deep sigh and I can physically see him relax.

"Rose. I'm sorry. Maybe I'm overreacting but you were still wrong. The truth is I got a really bad feeling, so I called you. When you didn't answer I panicked and thought the worst. I just worry about you." He says honestly.

He means well. I can tell. I can sense his genuine concern for me, I just don't understand the reasons behind it. I doubt he'll tell me if I ask and I really don't want to push my luck anymore tonight. Not to mention I'm keeping my own secrets. So, sitting in a sharing circle wouldn't be ideal.

"Well, I'm sorry that you thought you had to come and get me, I know you have to work early tomorrow. It wasn't my intention to scare you." I say apologetically.

I mean it. I don't try to make Alex miserable. I do feel sympathy for his life, after all he works at Crowley's, which is a local construction company. Alex took the job right out of high school because a study job means food in the fridge and paid bills. These are two very important requirements when you're dealing with child services in the hopes of having your younger sister put in your custody.

"Forget about it. I'm just happy you're going to be home safe. Maybe that'll give me peace of mind and a goodnight's sleep." He says tiredly.

I know it sounds weird, but I don't find his words very convincing. There is just a strange tone to his voice that leads me to believe that he's waiting for something bad to happen. Like even though I'm sitting right next to him he somehow doesn't think I am really and truly safe. I don't know what to say or think. *Why?*

Alex and I are quiet the rest of the way home. I spend the time reading between the lines and trying to further understand what's going on in Alex's head. I guess it's always possible he is just overtired but it's weird. *What is he so afraid of?*

I think I'm overtired now. Perhaps I hallucinated everything that happened tonight. Maybe the moonlight had played tricks on my vision, and in turn my mind. I badly want to believe that it had been my imagination, but there is a powerful feeling in my stomach telling me that it was real. Somewhere deep inside I know the truth, I also know it's just the beginning.

My thoughts are cut off when we pull into our driveway. I watch as our beautiful Victorian era home comes into full view. It's elegant, classic, and it's nestled in a tree enclosure. It's the same kind of house that kids are too afraid to visit on Halloween. In fact, it wouldn't surprise me to find out that people spread rumors about our house being haunted. I don't care, this house means the world to me. Every day in it is a reminder of my parents. The house represents them. In my eyes it's the most beautiful thing I've ever seen followed closely by the pond. The house has original hardwood floors and it's decorated to match it's time and style, courtesy of our parents who had left it to us fully furnished.

I could stare at our house forever taking in every detail, if it weren't for Alex climbing out and slamming the door. I get out and walk towards the porch behind him. Alex opens the door but stops in the doorway and looks out across the lawn. I look out to see what he's watching but there's nothing there. At the same time, I feel it again. We're being watched. It's an eerie, unnerving feeling.

When we get inside Alex doesn't hesitate to lock the door. When he turns back around, he has the strangest expression on his face. I want to ask him about it, but it is past midnight, and we're both exhausted. I try telling myself that now I'm being paranoid, but it isn't working.

"I'm going to bed Rose. Try to stay out of trouble please. Goodnight." He says groggily.

"Night." I reply.

I watch as Alex heads down the hallway to his room and I look up the stairs towards my room. The shadows on the landing send shivers up my spine. I watch Alex walk out of sight and I start up the stairs. The floorboards creak as I put my full weight on them, the sound only adds to the already uneasy feeling building in my gut. I quickly open my bedroom door and flip on the lights. I carefully look around and when I am sure there are no intruders I stroll over to my dresser.

I slip on a tank top and shorts and climb into my inviting bed. I turn off the lights and curl up against my pillows. When I close my eyes, I try to forget the unnerving events of the night, including my brother's abnormal behavior.

I feel myself floating in and out of sleep because I can't make my body relax. I keep envisioning the eyes from the pond, almost as though they have me hypnotized. When I dream of the eyes, I go directly towards them in the hopes of seeing the body that owns them, but as I get closer the eyes darken to black and then disappear. I can't get close enough, quick enough to see the person. I don't know why I feel so compelled to see the being who spied on me, I guess my curiosity is getting the better of me.

I finally allow my subconscious mind to forfeit the adventures to see my "stalker" because morning isn't far off. And it's like I said, I know this is only the beginning.

CHAPTER THREE

Rose

Before I know it, the morning light wakes me up. I was right about it being here quickly. Even though it's nearing the end of August, I can hear the remaining birds chirping in the tree outside my window. The sun is shining brightly throwing a warm glow throughout my bedroom. I begin to sit up feeling tired still, despite it being nine in the morning. I lift myself up and listen to the sounds in my house. I know Alex will already be at work but secretly I was hoping I'd hear him shuffling about downstairs.

I swing my legs out from under the blankets and over the side of the bed. I feel a cool breeze dance on my legs which causes me to quickly finish waking up. At that moment I become very observant of my surroundings. I look across my room and see that my window is in fact open. It isn't a trick of my mind or my imagination. I know I didn't leave it open last night because I hadn't opened it yesterday. I doubt my brother had opened it this morning considering how he behaved last night. *Why is it open? It shouldn't be open.* I say to myself.

I nervously sit on the edge of my bed, waiting. Waiting for what exactly, I don't know but windows generally don't open themselves. Several minutes go by and I start to relax. Surely something would have happened by now if it was going to at all.

I walk across the hallway to the bathroom and begin my daily beauty rituals with no more thoughts to the window. I'm in the process of blow drying my hair when I hear my phone ringing in the other room. I quickly jog back to my room holding my towel to me, only slowing down when I nearly trip over my own feet. I admit that I'm not always the most coordinated or graceful person, but I make do. *I'm such a klutz.*

The phone rings for like the fifth time and without even looking at the display screen, I already know who is calling. I answer the phone and am instantly proven to be right. It's Morgan. *Of course.* I'm not psychic but I was

13

expecting his call at some point this morning. He calls me every morning. He is predictable because he is one of my best friends after all.

He's been my friend for as long as I can remember. Even during the brief time that I spent in and out of foster homes, he always found a way to visit me. He knows what it's like to have no parents. Although technically he does, they're just never around. Hell, I've never met them. They're always travelling on business Morgan told me. He was raised by many different nannies, I met a few of them. They were nice enough but it's still a shit situation to be in. *Oh well.* He's always welcome at our house. He knows that.

I lift my cell to my ear.

"Hello." I say.

"Hey Rose, I'm guessing your brother found you last night." Morgan says with a chuckle.

It's not surprising that Morgan knows all about the incident, I assumed Alex would have called him the minute he couldn't find me. Common sense says to call the best friends, right? At least Morgan isn't lecturing me into an early grave.

"Yes, he found me alright. He made it out to be a bigger issue than it actually was though. Anyway, I'm pretty sure he left my dignity back at the pond, it was humiliating Morgan. I swear he's getting worse by the day. Don't you think?" I say waiting for him to back me up.

I notice Morgan appears to be hesitating with his reply. *I can't believe it!* It's getting really annoying having to constantly defend my actions.

"You have to understand Rose, you're all he has left. He would never be able to forgive himself if anything happened to you. He's your big brother." He says confidently.

Oh my god! Morgan is actually defending my brother. My best friend has just sided with the enemy, or at least that's how I'm playing it out in my head. As my best friend he's supposed to side with me, no matter how ridiculous or immature I'm being. That's part of the deal.

"I can't believe you Morgan. You know I'm tired of him treating me like a child when I'm not anymore. I'm smarter than he gives me credit for, and you know it. It seems to get worse every year. I'm going to be eighteen relatively soon and he can't keep trying to protect me from everything. He needs to let me grow up." I say angrily.

This conversation is very frustrating for me and it's starting to really upset me. I don't like how Morgan is basically telling me that I'm wrong and Alex is right because he's not. I'm not being petty. I know I'm right about this. And I'm not just being emotional because I'm a girl.

Morgan is quiet on the other end and for a brief moment I feel like Morgan is going to jump to Alex's defense again, but he doesn't. I'm glad he backed off because I'm already on the verge of tears. I feel like I'm a small child being patronized by an adult. Then again, what teenager doesn't feel this way when they're judgment is in question?

"Look Morgan, I don't want to argue with you right now. I've already got too many things on my mind, and this isn't helping." I say honestly.

It's not a lie, I'm feeling completely overwhelmed with everything that has happened. I am beginning to get really stressed, but I'm also a bit angry that he defended Alex.

"Do you want me to come over? We can talk about it." He asks kindly.

"Not really. I think I'll call Hannah. She'll understand me better." I say rudely.

Now that was a downright lie. Hannah is awesome but nobody can understand me as well as Morgan and I know that. I just want to be hurtful right now and I know I can trust Hannah to side with me no matter what.

"You're impossible Rose." He says with a knowing tone.

Morgan knows exactly what I'm trying to do so it's not going to work. Instead of hurting him, now I just look petty. *Damn it.*

"I'll talk to you later Morgan, bye." I say guiltily.

Before I manage to hang up the phone, I can hear Morgan give one of those loud, dramatic sighs. You know, the one where you can practically hear their eyes rolling. So even though I was downright rude with him I feel like I lost that conversation.

I toss my phone back down on the bed and stalk back to the bathroom to finish my hair. When I finish, I head back into my room to get dressed and make my call to Hannah. I pull on a pair of blue jeans and a shirt, nothing fancy since I don't have any plans today. I notice that the breeze from this morning has become a bit chilly and I can see dark clouds rolling in. *Yet another sign that summer is coming to an end, that means "bye, bye" sun and "hello" winter hibernation.* I grab a sweater to keep the chill off and as far as I'm concerned, I'm good to go.

I drop onto my bed grabbing my cell phone in the process. I start to dial Hannah's number, but I stop before hitting send. I don't think I should call Hannah because she's in Europe right now and if I make that kind of long-distance call Alex will probably take my phone away.

Hannah comes from a wealthy, prominent family and she spends every summer in some exotic place. This summer it's Europe with her folks where she'll be pampered and spoiled as their only child. She won't be back until the day before school but the more I think about it, the more I realize that a long-distance phone call is unnecessary and over dramatic. I guess I can send her an e-mail now and eventually we'll discuss it, but I really wish we could talk.

I take the few steps to my desk and fire up my laptop. It had been a gift for my sixteenth birthday from Hannah. It's probably one of the most expensive belongings I own, which I think had been her goal at the purchase.

Despite being spoiled, beautiful, and popular, Hannah is very thoughtful and amazingly unselfish. She always tries to give me the things I really want that Alex and I can't afford. It surprises even me, that my friend is so amazing.

I pull up my e-mail and start writing. I write about almost everything, but I choose my words carefully since I don't want to worry her. The e-mail ends up being a couple of pages long because I also make sure to ask her how everything is going for her. I don't want to come off as totally self-absorbed. When I'm satisfied with the message I hit "send" and hope beyond hope that my drama won't ruin what's left of her summer vacation. Soon she'll be able to offer me some insight into my crazy business.

As I shut down my laptop, I can hear the familiar rumble of Morgan's Ford F350. It's a very common sound to hear in a community as small as Bradford. I head down the stairs, open the front door and step out onto the porch and watch as Morgan steps out of his truck. Leave it to Morgan to come over even after I specifically tell him not to. I try to hold on to the anger I felt earlier but at the same time I'm happy he's here and I'm not alone anymore.

Morgan is as tall as my brother, around six feet, I think. He has an athletic build and the sexy-shaggy brown hair look. All in all, Morgan is the kind of guy that all the girls drool over at school. Even I'll admit that he's an attractive guy, in that preppy just stepped out of an American Eagle ad kind of way. He'd be completely out of my league if I was interested and if he wasn't like a brother to me. He isn't really my type, or he wouldn't be if I had a type. He's not really like me, not to mention high school superstar athlete, academic genius, popular and a-shoe-in for home coming king. Basically, he's everything I'm not. Roselyn Parker. Clumsy, quiet, weird, few friends, and fades into obscurity most times. I am comfortable with who I am, even if it's not what people expect. It's familiar.

My guess is that everybody at school questions my friendship with Morgan and Hannah. Hell, I don't blame them because I'm just so different it seems. Even I don't really understand it. I love them both and I'm glad they're in my life. I've just grown up with them and I wouldn't change a thing, I can always count on them.

There must be a very confused look on my face as I ponder these thoughts because just then, I am flashed a brilliant white smile and greeted with a laugh.

"Hey Rose, welcome back to planet earth! Are you done being mad at me?" Morgan jokes.

I want to tell him I'm still angry but it's almost impossible to be mad at him in person. It's his presence, he just makes me feel happy. I won't let him know it though.

"Maybe. It depends, are you done being an ass?" I say with mock anger. *Typical.* Of course, he doesn't verbally answer my question, instead he walks past me into the house smiling smugly. I turn on my heel and follow him in trying not to give anything away. He drops down on the sofa and I sit across from him, he looks at me with an all "business" face.

"Alright, let's hear it before you explode." He says calmly.

I can't help but smile at him. Leave it to a guy to get right to the point and avoid the pointless chit chat. I knew I keep him around for some reason.

"Ok, it's about last night. I know Alex called you looking for me and when he figured out that I was at the pond, he came to get me. What he doesn't know is that I don't think I was alone. Something or rather someone was there, and they were watching me from the shadows." I say quickly.

I spit it all out quickly hoping he won't focus on any one part. That and saying it out loud makes me sound just as crazy and paranoid as my brother.

"Okay wow! Well Rose, you do know that's not a good thing, right? You should probably talk to Alex about it because I'm guessing you haven't yet." Morgan says.

Secretly I was praying that Alex wouldn't be the solution he came to. In my mind my brother is more of a problem than a solution.

"Are you insane? He will put me on house arrest for who knows how long. I can't spend the last few days of my summer locked up. It's not fair." I whine.

I can only imagine how bratty I sound, in fact the moment after I speak, I regret it. Now my only defense is to pretend it doesn't bother me that I sound immature.

"He's only trying to protect you and you know that. You should be grateful that you have family who cares so much about you." He says bluntly.

The anger I had felt towards Morgan earlier is coming back full force. It's so strong now that it's turning into a giant bubble of rage. Once again, my friend is standing behind my brother and I'm left standing alone feeling winded. *Traitor!*

"Morgan how can you sit here and say that to me? You're starting to sound just like him, and that is not a compliment. Even you aren't usually this passive about it, what the hell is going on? God! Do you even care about my feelings anymore or are you all about making Alex happy?" I say as my voice gets louder.

"Rose, I'm sorry. I just worry about you…You're so much more important than you know, and I just don't want you to get hurt." Morgan says sadly.

I've had enough. I am tired of everyone acting like I am made of glass. Contrary to what they think I'm not some fragile little angel and I don't need them treating me like one.

"Whatever, go home Morgan." I say rudely.

I'm so aggravated that I don't wait for his reply. I head straight out the door and walk around the house to the back. I hurry forward into the trees knowing the cemetery is merely three kilometers behind us. If I walk in a relatively straight line, I should be there in a while. I've done it before, I usually walk everywhere. I don't have my license and it's not weird. I don't have a car and there is no way I can afford one so, I don't really see the point in getting my license. So, if I really want to go somewhere, I walk.

I've only walked a few yards into the woods when I turn around to see if Morgan is following me. Surprisingly, he isn't. In fact, I can hear his truck leaving. *Jerk!* I hate fighting with him.

"Good!" I say it but I'm not sure I mean it. I didn't even get the chance to tell Morgan everything before he pissed me off. I guess I'll have to wait until Hannah gets back from Europe if I really want to discuss this whole thing.

After a long while, I finally emerge from the trees. The sky is gray, it has darkened considerably while I was under the cover of the trees. I'm guessing it's still sometime in the morning, but time doesn't matter here. I walk between the rows towards the center of the cemetery. There's a big tree just behind my parent's grave, it makes it easier to find them. They have a shared tomb stone, so I get to visit them both.

I approach the headstone and read the familiar inscription. "Here lies Daniel and Karen Parker beloved parents. 1965-1989." Every time I read this, I hope it will change, leaving me with more information on them but it never does.

I sit down on the ground in front of their grave. Tears begin to fall from my eyes. I don't remember them at all obviously, I was barely one when they died. I have a feeling that things would be so much simpler if they were still around, then Alex could be a typical twenty-year old instead of the acting adult. I bring my knees to my chest and hug them tight while warm tears streak down my cheeks. All I can do is stare at their names engraved in the stone.

Today is kind of like déjà vu, asides from the fact that they're different cemeteries. Plus, this one doesn't have the creepy ass mausoleum, so I figure I'm not at risk of my dream becoming a reality. I start doing what everyone does at a grave site, I talk to them.

"It's not fair that you're dead. I need you both to be here and so does Alex. I feel so alone. Alex is keeping secrets from me. I know he is. Morgan is starting to take his side. I feel like I can't trust anyone. Mom. It's not supposed to be like this, you're supposed to be alive. You're supposed to be here taking care of me and Alex." I say to the rock.

I stop talking to the grave as the tears fall harder. I feel stupid talking to nothing, where-ever they are, I doubt they can hear me. At the same time, I take comfort in speaking to them when I need someone to listen.

"I love you mom and dad. So does Alex."

I return to sitting in silence and just imagining that I'm sitting in front of my real parents. It may sound silly but if you were me, you'd do it too.

As I continue sitting in my own pit of emotions, staring at the stone that can't bring me more comfort. I have a similar sensation that I had at the pond. I feel like I am being watched. I look around sure that I will see the eyes again, but I see nothing. The wind picks up and the sky darkens. A rumble nearby alerts me to just how bad the weather is getting. I see a series of flashes and hear the ensuing rumble.

Suddenly, something in my peripheral vision moves at an impossible speed, all I see in the distance is a blur. I know I must be crazy, but I swear the blur had been as tall as a person. If it hadn't been for the inhuman speed, I'd be sure of it.

My chest grows tight and I begin to feel dizzy. My heart is in overdrive, I feel like it's going to burst. I twirl around looking in every direction, but I don't see anything. I'm terrified because my vision is starting to go in and out of focus. If someone attacks me, I won't see them until it's too late. I grab my cell phone and clumsily dial Morgan's number hoping he won't ignore my call. It rings and rings, but he finally picks up.

"Morgan, something's happening." I say hurriedly.

I pretty much scream into the phone before he can say anything. I guess I am more afraid than I thought, and I am way past being rational about what I see. I just want to get the hell out of here.

"Rose...can't...you...Where...you?" He says cutting in and out.

Oh my god, I can't believe it. Of all the times my cell chooses to have bad reception now. It's impossible. I've never had signal problems here.

"Morgan, I'm at the cemetery. The cemetery. Please come get me, something's not right. I'm scared!" I say through tears.

I'm hysterical now, I don't know how much of my message he had actually heard, but I hope he caught where I am. There are way too many weird things happening. I don't even want to think about what is going on.

"I'm...co...find...y...Rose!" He says as the static takes over.

I turn with my back to my parent's grave, breathing heavily. I look out towards the woods. I don't know why but I quickly regret it. I see someone moving just beyond the brush. My hand slowly falls with the phone firmly in it. The figure comes rushing in my direction at a blinding speed. A blur is all I see. The figure stops about ten centimeters from me, but I can't see them. My vision is blurring and darkening, I get dizzier, my heart throbs in my chest and I feel like I am going to fall. I feel so weak. The only image I make out is their eyes, a silver-grayish color. *Are they the same eyes that I saw at the pond?* I think to myself. Suddenly, I feel my body start to fall backwards and at the time I can see nothing.

I feel a stabbing pain in the back of my head as my body hits ground and I stop falling. My hair begins to feel wet where my head hurts. I open my eyes to see white and dark blurs and that's it. I close my eyes and I lay there.

I can vaguely hear Morgan's voice, but I forget that it's coming from my phone.

"Rose? Rose? What's happening?" Morgan screams.

I subconsciously make a mental note that the reception appears to be fine now. Naturally. I don't know, nor can I tell if that person is still standing near me. It doesn't even feel real. I try to think about the person but all I can recall from memory is trivial things. They had piercing silver-grayish eyes and what looked like black hair, but I suppose a lot of people do. I really hadn't been able to focus. I lay still feeling like I've been drugged when I think someone touches my cheek. Their hand is warm, and it's gone as fast as it was there.

I lay awake for a minute before it feels like I'm being pulled into a black hole. I am afraid to fall into the dark hole that won't release me, it reminds me too much of the dark inside the mausoleum. Even though it had been a dream, it had felt so vivid at the time. I remember that after the door had shut, I had felt the cold on me like a thousand fingers. My burning skin is forgotten in my mind momentarily. I felt fear and I could hear the dead souls crying. It was incredibly upsetting to know that all those people could feel no peace, only terror and agony. I don't want to remember the emotions anymore. I want it all to be over.

I feel the dark pulling on me as my eyelids are forced shut. I allow myself to fall into the abyss where my mind goes dark.

CHAPTER FOUR

Rose

When I open my eyes, I'm in the mausoleum again but this time I'm prepared to see the dead man bleeding on the marble floor. I walk down the steps and turn the corner once again. This time is different, it's as though time has progressed in this dream world. The body on the floor is no longer relinquishing blood along the marble. Instead the blood pool appears to be dry and crusted over. The body itself resembles that of an old, debilitated corpse that has been decomposing for months if not longer. This once living person is now a heap of decaying flesh and bones. This perturbs me slightly, how long has it been? Why have I come back here? *Why am I punishing myself?*

I stand waiting for the man to enter the room for the second time, but he does not. I choose to enter the adjacent room in search of him. It might seem like an idiotic and suicidal choice, but it is only a dream. *I don't believe you can die in a dream.*

When I walk through the doorway, I unsurprisingly see a sarcophagus in the center of the room. I don't know whose body rests in there, nor does it seem important. What is important, is that the man whom undoubtedly murdered the man in the other room sits in a large chair with his eyes closed. I don't believe he has noticed my arrival, but I don't want to assume anything. I stand transfixed in place, as I watch this man. His body seems lifeless however I will not be betrayed into a false sense of security. There is no dilemma in my mind that this man is substantially dangerous.

"Anastazija, I knew you would come back to me." He says, his voice just barely a whisper.

It's become clear that this is no ordinary man as he speaks to me. I glance around to see if there is another person with us. Unfortunately, we are alone, so I know that he is speaking to me, although I know he is confused because I'm not who he thinks I am.

"I am not this Anastazija you speak of, I'm Roselyn Parker and I have no idea where I am." I say timidly.

I decide that it can't hurt to chat with this mysterious, imaginary man. After all he's not real and I can't open the imaginary stone doors.

"You are my sweet Ana, maybe not in appearance but in heart and soul. I have been waiting centuries for your return." He says calmly.

It's becoming painfully obvious that not only is this made up man a murderer but he's delusional, probably even psychotic. It makes me wonder why I would create this kind of person. *What's wrong with me?*

"I don't understand what you're talking about, I'm only seventeen for god's sake." I say nervously. My voice rises slightly, and I worry I may push this man over the edge.

"You only believe you're seventeen dear Roselyn because you don't yet remember, but when you come of age you will remember whose essence lives in you. Then you will come to me of your own desires rather than being incarcerated in this horrible dream state." He says while his eyes open and linger on my face.

For the first time I'm properly able to see his face. His skin looks flawless and his features are all proportionate. He's actually quite fetching physically. He's wearing black dress pants, black dress shoes and a simple black cotton t-shirt. I presume he is in his late twenties or early thirties, but no older. He has a mature, distinguished air about him, and it gives me the illusion that he is much older than he looks.

"You claim to know me, but who the hell are you?" I say rudely.

I realize he absolutely has more patience than I have, so I guess I will play into his little game to move things along.

"I am Lord Dalibor, and I have been waiting many lifetimes to become reacquainted with you my dear." He says sadly.

I am suddenly aware that this man means me no harm, it appears quite the contrary. He seems to be in love with me, which I don't quite comprehend. My thoughts flicker back to what this Dalibor guy said about my "coming of age", whatever the hell that means.

"I promise I don't know you! This is all just a weird ass dream." I say confidently.

He laughs a silent chuckle, and his smile reveals abnormally pearly white teeth that are perfectly straight. It's not what you'd expect from a guy sitting in a crypt.

"Oh, young one, you only assume this to be a dream because you don't know any better. The truth has been kept from you but not for long. I will not give up on you, in a few years you will be awakened to a world of possibilities, a world in which you're meant to be a part of. You will come to learn of beings that you once thought were imaginary and nonexistent. You shall be my princess and we shall control the other world together. And you will be mine again and once again have faith in the meaning of my name."

He says with longing in his eyes.

I don't understand a word this guy said, not to mention the weird way he speaks. He seems to speak with a knowledge and insight that I don't have. He has an understanding of something that I can't even imagine.

"What exactly does your name mean?" I ask.

I don't know why I'm asking. I should just keep silent until I wake up because the more we speak, the more I become comfortable with this room, and that makes me nervous. It seems almost familiar though I swear I've never been here.

"My name child means "far away" and "to fight". He says proudly. "You once believed it to mean that I would travel to the depths of hell and back to battle for you. I have and I would do it again for you my love. Just believe that I mean that with my heart, and trust that I will wait for you." He says lovingly.

I knew it! I shouldn't have asked. I can never turn off my damn curiosity, even when I know it will be in my best interest.

"Look Lord Dali-whatever, I don't want to be here, I just want to wake up and forget all about this, and you. No offense, but you've got the wrong girl. I don't want to feed your illusions anymore, I'm Rose, a plain, boring, teenage girl. I can't ever be this "Ana" that you speak of and I would refuse to. So just go away!" I say to him.

Ah yes. The sweet satisfaction of being a brat. What teenagers won't say to psycho killers when they're in a mood, I don't know? I'm sort of regretting my whole rant, he looks unhappy.

"Ms. Parker, may I recommend that you change your attitude. I am being very patient with you so I would appreciate a little courtesy." He says menacingly.

I'm not a genius but I know a threat when I hear one. I don't care how delirious this guy sounds. I don't see a need to egg him on. I'm quiet for once and I won't lie, I'm petrified. There was something sickly and twisted in his tone when he threatened me. Now it has me chilled to the bone. As he watches me intently, I believe I see regret and guilt in his eyes but I'm probably imagining it.

"Poor dear, I didn't intend to frighten you. I just wish for more respect even though you don't yet recognize me. Soon your life will truly begin, very soon! Until that day I will wait for you. Now go!" He says.

In a split second I feel the world disappearing beneath me. The cold slithers away while my energy seems to return.

I wake up to a loud beeping. I assume it is my god-awful alarm clock, but it shouldn't be on. I reach over to turn it off, but I don't feel it. I open my eyes reluctantly and look around. I'm not in my bedroom but I am almost a hundred percent sure that I'm awake now.

I'm in a small cream-colored room, and I'm lying in a small bed but I'm not alone. To my left I can see a bathroom, and just to the right are a small sofa and two chairs. Both chairs are occupied by my brother and Morgan. They are both fast asleep, sitting up. I recognize exactly where I am almost immediately after that. I'm in our local hospital.

I will admit to being a bit scared and more than a little confused. I hear the beeping increase in frequency as I maneuver myself into a sitting position in the bed. It is obviously the heart monitor that I had mistaken for my alarm clock. I don't remember what happened to land me in this hospital bed, but I feel like I have been sleeping forever. A sharp pain shoots to the back of my skull and I reflexively lift my hand to my head and feel with my fingertips. I can feel a bald spot, and in the center of that bald spot are stitches.

My heart rate increases again, more because of the bald spot than the stitches. I can't remember what's happened to me. All I remember is that Morgan had pissed me off, so I'd walked to the cemetery in a huff. After that, it all disappears. I close my eyes tight and try to think back and remember anything else that occurred. It is like walking through a thick fog though, my memory is so cloudy. A few seconds later and it hits me like a ton of bricks. I remember the figure, his hair, his eyes and my failed phone call to Morgan.

I don't know why my head hurts though, and I can't remember who it was that found me. I send out mental fingers to the rest of my body, I want to make sure the rest of me is intact and functioning. After a couple of minutes, I'm sure that other than a few bumps and bruises, my body seems fine.

I'm curious to know if the guy had still been with me when someone found me, or perhaps if he had been the one to get help. How much does everyone really know about what happened? I'm not even sure that I know what happened. I do know one thing though, if I tell anyone about the guy having inhuman speed I'll end up in a very different hospital. *The loony bin.* I'm still having difficulty comprehending what I had seen. It just isn't possible! Not to mention that dream was all new levels of weird, even for me.

I sit in the bed contemplating everything and finally I decide what to tell everyone. No doubt they're going to ask me a butt load of questions once they realize that I'm awake, and I need to be ready to answer them. I wonder how long I've been asleep. Apparently long enough for them to stitch me up, and it even feels like it's beginning to heal. Alright, I guess it's time to face them, one at a time would be preferable.

"Morgan? Morgan?" I whisper in his direction.

I'm trying to keep my voice low enough, so that I don't wake Alex, but it's proving to be more difficult than I anticipated.

"Morgan." I say louder as he begins to stir.

"Rose you're awake!" He says excitedly.

He doesn't yell it, but he does punch Alex in the arm on his way to my bedside. It wakes him right up. So much for my one person at a time idea.

Alex wakes with a start and looks over at me. He smiles and rushes to my side. He throws his arms around me and gives me one of the biggest hugs he's ever given me. Then again, he hasn't given me many. Suddenly I feel moisture on my shoulder soaking through my gown. I pull away from Alex with concern that I am bleeding but I realize that Alex is crying. *I can't believe it!* I pull him back to me and hold him tight. I start to get teary eyed myself because it's just so comforting to be hugging my big brother. I look over his shoulder and see that Morgan looks like he is on the verge of tears too. Alex pulls away to look at my face, and I decide that now would be a good time to ask a question.

"Alex, what happened to me?" I ask, with confusion.

I'm hoping he doesn't know everything, but I have to find out somehow. Morgan is pulling the two armchairs closer to the bed. Alex and Morgan both sit. I look at Alex and I can see fear in his eyes, mixed with his own confusion. Every second of silence is agonizing to me. I need to know what they know.

"Rose, you were at the cemetery. Morgan found you. You were unconscious and your head was bleeding. He found blood on the corner of mom and dad's headstone, we're guessing you fell and hit your head." He says in a shaky voice.

He stops there clearly giving me the opportunity to fill in the blanks and digest what he has said. What he says makes sense, at least as far as what happened after I blacked out. I look up into his eyes and he looks like he's fighting the urge to cry again. I don't blame him because this situation is very emotional for all of us. I watch as he takes a deep breath and continues.

"You called Morgan, and he said you sounded terrified. He couldn't make out everything you said but he remembers you saying some things not right. What did you mean when you said that? What was happening?" He questions me.

I think long and hard before deciding the less they know the better. I don't want them to think I'm losing my mind, so I need to word my response carefully.

"Well I don't remember a lot but, I remember it got really dark out with lightning, thunder, and a nasty wind. I thought I saw someone." I say.

Ok so that may have been an outright lie. I know I saw someone, but the rational and logical part of my brain keeps telling me that it just wasn't possible. I shake off my own confusion and focus on explaining the rest of my made-up story.

"What do you mean you saw someone? Who? Did they touch you in any way? If they're the reason you've been in a coma for over a week, they'll be sorry." He says angrily.

"I've been in a coma for a week?" I ask in shock.

I watch while Alex's face changes as he studies me while I consider this new information. When he was asking me questions, he looked pissed. Hopefully he doesn't go around beating up any guy he sees.

"I don't know who it was. I don't remember anything about them. All I know is I saw someone, and it scared me." I admit, half-truthfully. "My heart was beating too hard. I was getting dizzy and my vision was fuzzy. I really don't know what happened." I say apologetically.

I spit the rest out hoping Alex and Morgan will put it all together and assume I'd had illusions that were panic induced. They don't say anything which makes me nervous. They're both watching me with a strange look, and I'm not sure what to make of it. It's like they can read my thoughts and they know I'm not telling them everything. It's a very awkward silence, and I hope someone will say something soon.

Morgan gets up and heads for the door. He stops at the door and turns back to us.

"I'm going to go grab a coffee. I'll let the doctor know she's awake on my way." He says.

With that Morgan walks out the door. My brother turns to me and it looks like he is going to tell me something big. It reminds me of one of those movies where the patient is about to be told that they're dying. His expression gets all serious and for a moment I'm concerned that death will be my fate.

"Rose, I've wanted to tell you something for a while…I haven't b…" He starts saying before he's interrupted.

Alex stops mid-sentence and the doctor enters the room. *Son of a bitch.* I'm so pissed, I think he was going to tell me something he's been keeping from me before he was conveniently interrupted. He's not likely going to tell me now. He's just been saved by the doctor.

"Hello Ms. Parker, it's good to see you're up and talking. How's your head feel?" The doctor asks.

The doctor is young, maybe twenty-seven years old. He has blond hair and dark brown eyes. He's handsome for an older guy. I'm not checking him out, which under normal circumstances I totally would. I'm just giving him the death stare because he interrupted what was probably the most important conversation I'll have for a long time. I'm still aggravated with him but he's my doctor so I may as well talk to him.

"My head is fine and who are you?" I say curtly.

My attitude is definitely uncalled for but in my mind, he totally deserves it. After all, I'm seventeen so naturally I'm going to have an attitude with or without reason.

"I'm sorry. My name is Dr. Warren. I've been tending to you since you got here. I've come to discuss your situation with you and your brother." He says kindly.

Alex is giving him his undivided attention. Clearly, he holds this doctor on a pedestal, which isn't surprising given what's happened. After all, the man may have saved my life for all I know. I guess I should be the last one to be ungrateful.

"Rose. Can I call you Rose?" He asks but doesn't wait for a reply. "Ok well your vitals all seem normal and the wound on your head is healing beautifully and much faster than we anticipated. Your tests all came back with good results, and we should be able to release you today. However, you must remember that you suffered a rather large concussion and you might have some amnesia associated with your head trauma. That is normal in this situation, but it's important you're not alone. Also try to avoid any excessive stress." He says seriously.

I'm not paying much attention to what he's saying, besides Alex is probably taking notes. All I care about is that I get to go home today, which is awesome.

"She won't be alone doctor, that much I can guarantee." Alex adds determinedly.

Of course, Alex just has to voice his opinion. I can hear the determination in every word, and I can practically see what Alex is thinking in his mind. He has probably given it some serious thought and knows that won't be an issue. If he remembers correctly then tomorrow will be Sunday which means I go back to school on Monday. Whether I like it or not, I won't be able to use the bathroom without one of them nearby.

Okay, so hopefully I'm just being overdramatic, and he isn't actually thinking all of that but in the event that he is, I vow to be the biggest pain in his ass.

The doctor is busy talking to Alex near the door and Alex's "promise" that I won't be alone has me a little freaked out. It also has me thinking of another promise Alex made to me years ago.

I remember it like it was yesterday. I was only thirteen and I had just been admitted into a really shitty foster home. Alex was seventeen going on eighteen in a few weeks and he was already basically independent. Anyway, he promised me in that same determined tone that he was going to get our house back and get me out of the foster care system on the day of his eighteenth birthday. He kept his promise and he's been taking care of me ever since. It was the happiest day of my life the day he turned eighteen, because there he was at the door with a social worker, dad's 67 Camaro, and the keys to our home. He didn't give me a hug though, just a big smile. Alex always comes through for me when it matters most. I guess I owe it to him to cut him some slack.

When I look up, I see that Alex appears to be finished speaking with the doctor because he heads out the door and Alex turns to me. Part of me hopes that he'll finish the conversation he started earlier, but I know it's unlikely. Instead he just looks at me sitting in the bed, as if I'm the most precious thing in the world or so that's how I am beginning to feel. I rationalize the thought in my mind and decide I am probably a little drugged, and as Morgan would say, I'm "over thinking" things.

"Rose, why don't you get dressed, grab your stuff and meet Morgan and me in the hallway." Alex says, breaking up my thoughts.

I try to muster up a smile before he leaves the room but I'm just feeling too overwhelmed and disappointed right now.

I know it is going to take me a bit to get my stuff together and get dressed. Not that I have much stuff here but there are a few flowers, and some get well cards, not to mention I hurt all over like I've just been hit by a truck. I remove the monitor clip from my finger and slide to the side of the bed. I notice a giant teddy bear with a card attached. It says "Rose, I hope you wake up soon. We all love and miss you, and we need you!" Signed Morgan.

Leave it to my best friend to put a smile on my face, even when I have been in a coma. I'm just so happy to be going home that I don't even think to ask if I have a clean change of clothes, being that the ones I came in wearing have been removed and likely taken home. I don't look long before I notice some clothes sitting on one of the tables. I put on the clean under garments which I am grateful for, and then happily put on my jeans and pink shirt that my brother had obviously grabbed. As I look around to make sure I have everything, I can't help this strange feeling coming over me. It feels like every thought of going home is suffocating, as though the prospect of my home frightens me. I try to ignore it because I have no reason to not want to go home. While I was trapped in that damn dream, all I'd wanted to do was go home. I take one last glance around the room and head towards the door to find my brother and Morgan.

CHAPTER FIVE

Alex

I left Rose in the room to get changed because all I want to do is take her home, where she belongs. I know it doesn't matter where we are, that Rose will never really be safe. It doesn't change how I wish things could be.

She's so special, more so than any other person in the world. I'm probably biased being her brother but I'm not the only one who feels this way. She means the world to me as my family, and I would give my life to save hers any day. There are others who would die for her too. But. There are also those who would die to kill her.

Sometimes even I can't understand why it has to be Rose, my little sister. She's already been through so much more than anyone should have to go through, and I just want to be here for her. She'll hate me when she discovers the truth, even if I'm the one who tells her. She will blame me for keeping such a huge secret all these years from her. It doesn't matter what my intentions are. I honestly don't think I could blame her. I would be pissed off too.

Everything is so complicated when it comes to Rose because the thing is, Rose isn't entirely human. She's a new breed, a Halfling. Part vampire, part enchanter. I wish it wasn't true, but it is and ignoring it won't help. *I've tried!*

I've known for years but I thought it best not to tell her. That was my decision. They've only been discovered in the last handful of centuries. There isn't a large amount known about them, only that they are incredibly powerful. Only in the last hundred years have beings like her been given a name. She is a ženski melez and she doesn't even know it.

As a ženski melez she is more powerful than most creatures. She has the ability to wield magick as well as physical force. That is, she will be able to do these things once she transitions. The transitory age is between nineteen and twenty-one, but the male counterpart of her species tends to wait to age, generally at twenty-three. No one knows why, it just is. Males aren't as powerful as females for some unknown reason, but this is a well-known problem. I say it's a problem because many ženski melez are hunted and killed before they can transition. This makes Rose a big target because she also carries royal blood. Needless to say, many things would love to kill her, or worse control her.

I don't know a whole lot about bloodlines or the other world, just enough to get by on. Her abilities are mostly unknown because all ženski melez are different. I already know that her senses are more sensitive than a human being's, but I don't think she's noticed this yet. *Who am I kidding?* She's smarter than I want to acknowledge. More than likely, she has noticed things, but she can't explain them.

I keep telling myself that it's better that she doesn't know, only because I have no clue how to tell her that she's being hunted. Hell, I don't even know which creatures are hunting her in the first place. Besides that, the other world that she belongs to is so fantastical how could I make her believe me? Occasionally I don't even believe it. If it weren't for Morgan I wouldn't know as much as I do. There's nothing special about me, I'm only human.

My worst fear is telling Rose that she's going to be immortal and live forever, but that I'm going to grow old and die. I won't always be around to help her and that hurts me. I mean how do you say that to someone you love? I just can't find the right words.

I take a break from my incessant string of thoughts and look up to see Morgan across the hall, arms crossed, and holding a coffee in one hand. He's no doubt been waiting for me to talk to him. He knows about my concerns and fears, we've discussed them before. I still want to believe that I'm doing the right thing. I really don't want to talk about this here but no one else is nearby. *So why not?*

I stop right in front of him reluctantly, I'm tired of having secret talks. I wish Rose already knew everything. It would be easier on me. I can see in his eyes that he's tired, it doesn't surprise me. Morgan may pose as a seventeen-year old, and technically he is. But with everything he has gone through, he feels older. Keeping this secret from Rose is also hard on him. He's not a halfling but an enchanter or a carobnjak. To me both are just fancy ways of saying he can control magick.

Morgan has no parents. They were murdered trying to help our parents. That's when Morgan's future was decided for him. Even as a child he was aware of his future. He has been through training and he knows more than any man should know. He swore a vow of protection to Rose when he sensed what she was. He's been both a blessing and a curse. He constantly pesters me to tell Rose. He wants to start training her but every time I find an excuse not to. I don't know how much longer I can keep him quiet though.

"So, Alex, in light of everything that's happened, you still feel that it's in

Rose's best interest to keep her in the dark?" Morgan says tiredly.

Morgan is concerned for her, I understand that. I know how he feels. He's been a part of her life almost as long as I have, but I am still her big brother.

"No. Yes. I don't know. Look Morgan I am doing the best I can with her. I don't know what would be best but I'm doing what I think is best. There are no rule books for how to raise a halfling and in case you haven't noticed, our parents aren't here to help. At least through ignorance she doesn't know the horrors that exist." I say defensively.

Honestly, I was going to tell her everything before Dr. Warren came in, but the interruption gave me a good excuse to procrastinate and I took it.

"Alex, I understand that you want to protect her. So, do I. I can't pretend that I can fight off every single thing that the other world throws at her. I just think that maybe if she knew who she really was and what she is capable of then she'll be able to come with me to train. Hell, she might even be able to learn how to protect herself. There are others here, I can sense them. If they've found her, it's only a matter of time before they get her." He says sensibly.

"Morgan, I know it's going to get worse before it gets better. You swore to protect her and that's what I expect from you. Your obligation ends there! Her safety and interests are my concern because I'm her brother. Right now, I don't think she should know, and you need to respect that because it's my decision." I say curtly.

I know Morgan can hear the disgust in my voice when I speak about other world matters, but he has to understand the secrecy around Rose. After all he wants to keep her as safe as can be. That's part of Morgan's promise, the other is to find the Elite in order to find a safe place to train Rose. This will obviously mean that Rose will leave home, which Morgan already knows is partially why I don't want to tell her the truth.

"It's just that she has already been unknowingly exposed to so much of the other world. There is no way the person she saw at the cemetery is just a guy. He has to be a succubus, demon, enchanter, vampire, or some other hideous thing out of the abyss. He's probably going to try to kill her because you know his appearance can't be coincidental." I say with fear.

"Alex, I promise I will find out what that guy was. I can sense more than one creature in the area, but I can't tell what they are. Someone has cast a spell to hide their exact whereabouts, but I will find out. Until then we have to keep a close eye on her at all times." He says calmly.

Morgan and I hold eye contact for a minute. I know he is doing everything he can. I want him to explain more to me about the other world. I watch as Morgan's eye's flicker across the hall and I turn to see Rose approach us. She looks at us with such innocence I know it's killing Morgan to keep this secret.

"Hey Alex, I'm going to go take care of a few things then I'll pick you up some groceries and I will meet you back at your place." Morgan says casually.

I'm glad Morgan didn't freeze at the sight of Rose, and we really do need groceries. I watch as Morgan lightly touches Rose's arm as he walks by. The secrecy must be killing him on the inside, but he hides it well. His attachment to her has grown, it's obvious he wants to be more than her friend now.

I look back to Rose's face. She's watching Morgan walk down the hall and I can see confusion and ignorance written on her face. She grabs my arm and looks up at me with her adorable green eyes. I know she wants to go home without even asking me, but I can't open my mouth to speak without coming clean. So, I fight back my feelings of guilt and nod at her.

As we set off across the parking lot, I silently wonder to myself if Morgan is right about Rose being better off knowing. But when I help her into the car, she quickly starts dozing away and I know I am making the right choice, or so I hope. I promise to tell her one day but not today. My mind wanders over these thoughts as I drive us home. Home to where we will wait for everything to happen. I only pray that Morgan and I are strong enough to fight off whatever comes after her. I will do anything to ensure she continues to breathe, even if I don't.

Lord Dalibor

Sitting in an over-sized armchair, next to an ornately carved fireplace, in what is clearly a large, much older, dwelling is Lord Dalibor. He sits motionless, other than a small golden trinket that he plays with in his hands.

It's a locket.

Ana's locket. To be specific.

He opens it carefully.

There is no photo inside, but rather a small curl of luxurious reddish-brown hair. Her hair. He stares at it adoringly, looking up with annoyance before the knock on the door.

"Come in." He says with venom. Obviously annoyed with the intrusion.

A gangly, ill looking gentleman in a suit enters the room. Dried blood is on his neck, along with several puncture wounds.

"My lord." The servant says softly, with an Irish accent. "The wraith is here to see you." He adds, with apprehension.

"Send it in." He says indifferently.

A shadowy figure with dark red eyes enters the room. It seems to have no face or body, but clearly Lord Dalibor had been expecting the meeting.

"Lord Dalibor. You summoned me. From the dead, no less." The wraith hisses with curiosity. "This must be important." It adds.

Lord Dalibor clicks the locket closed grudgingly.

"Raising you from the dead is no easy task." Lord Dalibor says smugly.

"So, it is clearly of great importance." He adds.

Lord Dalibor rises from his seat and glides over to the fireplace. He stares into the flames watching them lick at the burning wood.

"How can I repay you?" The wraith asks, respectfully.

Lord Dalibor smirks, raising one corner of his mouth. This is what he had wanted. The creature's servitude. This is the reason that he went through the trouble of raising it from the grave anyway. He erases the smile from his face as he thinks about what he needs from the wraith.

"Simple. I want you to do what you crave!" Lord Dalibor says maliciously. "And I have a particular target in mind." He adds, turning from the fire to face the wraith.

"Who?" It asks, questioningly.

"His name is Alex Parker, a human." Lord Dalibor says, without emotion. "I want his sister, Roselyn Parker, alive." He adds, importantly. "I will leave the how to you. You may do as you please with the brother. But you would be wise to observe them to get at him when he is vulnerable." He also says.

"Such fun this will be." The wraith says cruelly.

Lord Dalibor moves back to the fireplace with inhuman grace.

"It may not be easy." Lord Dalibor says. "There are those who would seek to stop you, and they are near her. I sense them." He adds spitefully.

"Let them try!" It replies menacingly.

"There is small village near her. With ten or so creatures." Lord Dalibor says informatively. "Why don't you get some of the murderous craving out of your system before you handle this delicate task." He adds.

"As you command, my lord." The wraith says, compliantly. "My Lord, if you have found the girl why not go in and take her? Save yourself the trouble." The creature continues.

"There are protection spells on the area, I can't get to her. For now." Lord Dalibor says with frustration. "They are growing weaker, but I am not a patient man. I want her now. Before she disappears." He adds, seriously.

"Of course." It hisses.

"She will be mine!" Lord Dalibor says with enthusiasm. "Go now." He commands.

The wraith leaves quickly. Lord Dalibor holds up the locket in his hand once more. The flames glimmer against it as he rubs his fingertips along the cool surface. He stares at it longingly.

Rose

I remember Alex helping me into the car, but I quickly drift back into sleep. I pray to god I don't have another creepy dream about Lord whatever, he really scares me.

When I open my eyes I'm still in the cemetery, the one with my parents. I know I'm dreaming. I was just in Alex's car and we were leaving the hospital. Obviously, that's where I really am.

I'm already kneeling in front of a grave. I instantly recognize it as my parents even before I read the engraving. *I'm so confused.*

"Why am I here?" I say out loud, but I don't expect an answer from a rock, rather I close my eyes and try to listen to my heart. Your heart always knows the answer.

"You're here because there are things you need to know." A female voice says.

I look up to see who stands before me, their voice is angelic and soft. I can't trust my eyes to tell me the truth.

"Mom?" I ask unsure.

I know it isn't possible, but she seems to be standing right in front of me. Looking at me and smiling with her eyes.

"Yes Rose, it's me!" She says with urgency.

I don't know how, and I shouldn't care. It's my mom and she's here with me.

"How are...?" I start to say but I don't get to finish.

"Rose you must listen closely. We don't have much time before he finds us. He's almost found you. You can't believe Lord Dalibor, he's an evil man." She says with concern.

What? How does she know his name? I guess it makes sense that she would know about that dream because she is my dream too, but I find myself being drawn into her words.

"Why?" I ask not really paying attention.

I just want to hear her voice forever. I didn't remember how beautiful it was.

"Because of Ana, she tried to escape and now he's found her and you." She says quickly.

I want to hear more even if it isn't real, it brought her to me.

"Mom it was just a dream just like this. It's not real and I know you're not real because..." I start to speak but my voice fails.

I can't find the words to explain to my dream mother that she is dead, it just hurts too much.

"I know that I am dead sweetheart, but this is so much more than a dream. This is a message I am sending through our link. But Ana links you to Lord Dalibor as well, so we must be short." She says in a matter of fact tone.

I don't want to be short. I want to sit and talk to my mom forever and figure it out together.

"He can't find you yet, only in sleep so you're safe for now. You need to know that Alex is vulnerable, and he is in danger, he is being targeted. The spell is wearing thin, you must leave home. Very bad things are coming and it's no longer safe. Take your brother and Morgan and go find…" She says in a rush but stops mid-sentence.

She's cut off by an aggressive strike of lightening. Black clouds roll in and the wind becomes terribly strong. A dense fog begins creeping over the ground towards us and shadows reach out of it. My mother turns to me with fear and urgency in her eyes.

"Run Rose, run now!" She yells.

She doesn't have to tell me twice. I am already on my feet and I start running in the opposite direction. I stop in front of the trees and look back. It's disturbing, the fog is wrapped around her knees and I can see the shadows pulling her down into them. I want to go back and help with every fiber of my being, but she told me to run. Dead or alive she is still my mom. I turn to go into the trees towards my house but the woods dissolves around me and I know the dream is ending now.

CHAPTER SIX

Rose

Just like that I'm pulled out of the dream and back to reality. I wake up to the sound of Alex shutting the driver's side door. I look at the clock and it only says three twenty-three. I'm happy when I remember it's only Saturday, which means I have another day to relax before going back to school. I'm not ready to face another year of high school until I pull myself together. Even now high school seems so pointless, it's a jungle. You have to kill or be killed. I'm sure every high school student will agree with me on that.

I've been so busy with my thoughts of high school that I didn't notice that Alex has come around to my door to open it. He helps me bring my stuff up to the house where he continues to drop it in the doorway once we get inside. It is such a typical male thing, I'm pretty sure they naturally invent ways in which to appear helpful without actually exerting themselves. *Men!*

"Sorry it's such a mess in here, I haven't been in here long enough to do anything." Alex says slightly flustered.

I stand behind him clutching my giant teddy bear and wondering why he'd think a little mess will bother me. Trust me when I say a mess is the furthest thing from my mind.

When I get further inside, I realize that it's not just a little mess, it's a disaster. There are dirty clothes and towels all over the place, and dishes sitting on every surface. It doesn't surprise me because he has been at the hospital every day around work waiting for me to wake up. I should say hoping I'd wake up since there had been no guarantee that I would ever wake up. That is a scary thought and it sends a chill up my spine to the wound on my head.

Alex grabs my bags and my giant teddy bear, and he takes off up the stairs. *I'm pretty sure he's just going to dump them on the floor in my room.* He's coming back down when I realize that I'm not ready to go to my room and be alone. I feel an odd shiver at the memories of what happened at the cemetery. I really want to avoid being alone for a while.

"Rose, I'm going to go watch some TV. I'll make some dinner when Morgan gets here with the groceries. Why don't you come watch something with me, maybe we can talk too?" Alex says innocently.

I'm beyond happy that he didn't tell me to go rest in my room. It's almost strange though. He seems to want me in plain view, which takes his over protectiveness to new levels. But I'm alright with it for the time being. There's no doubt in my mind now that he is keeping something from me, and I'm going to find out one way or another. I am a teenage girl after all, I have my ways.

"Sure, what do you want to talk about?" I ask hopefully.

He's not going to tell me what he knows and I'm sure as hell not going to reveal my secrets to him. Trust is a two-way street, and neither of us are on it. *It's his fault.*

"Well when I was driving home, after you passed out. It seemed like you were having a very interesting dream." He says it as a statement rather than a question.

It's true, my dream had involved mom for the first time ever, and then something came for her. Or maybe it came for me and she was simply in the way. I really don't know. Either way she was taken from me again but I'm not sure if I should tell Alex. The last thing I need is for him to think I need therapy.

"What makes you think that?" I ask with mock confusion.

I'm curious to know what it had looked like from his side of my dream. I wonder what my body had been doing in reaction to my dream.

"Well, you were breathing really hard and at one point you were even panting. Your face got all scrunched up like you were upset. Why? What did you dream of?" He asks more forcefully.

I'm glad that I hadn't been talking in my sleep. I don't think I'd be able to talk myself out of it then, which would be an awkward conversation. Then I'd probably have to explain a lot more than I want to. I decide to tell him a little, maybe he'll let something slip and I'll get some clues as to what the hell he knows.

"I saw mom at the graveyard. She was beautiful! She wanted to tell me something, she said you were in danger. She didn't get to finish telling me though because I woke up." I say easily.

There, I think that much information will suffice. It's almost the truth, and it seems to mean something to Alex. I watch his face as he looks thoughtful. He's putting a lot of energy into his brain muscles. I can tell. Plus, he's looking off into space and he hasn't said anything yet.

"Um, hello, Alex, what are you thinking? Does that mean something to you?" I ask impatiently.

He snaps out of his daze and gives me a hard look. His looks soften as he clearly decides to say nothing about it. *Naturally.*

"You sure have some weird dreams kid. It means nothing to me. It must have been a strange, medicine induced dream. Let's watch some TV." Alex says quickly changing the topic.

I guess he thinks he can avoid the conversation with that answer. Normally, I'd go after the truth, but I am just too tired and sore to do much about it. I'll argue with him another day.

"Um, Alex before we go watch TV. I'm just going to call Morgan and see where he got to, I just want to make sure he's ok." I say while Alex melts into the couch.

All I get is a grunt from Alex because he's already closing his eyes, with the remote in hand. That is a good enough answer for me, not that he could stop me from making a phone call.

I walk back to the kitchen when I get a similar feeling of being watched. This time I prepare myself, so I won't pass out again. I look out the doors but I see nothing so I go into the kitchen and through the window I can see a pair of silver eyes looking in at me. I'm positive that whoever it is had been watching me at the pond too, and maybe at the graveyard. The eyes seem to mean me no harm, but I still feel like they are more dangerous than they appear. They look right at me and then vanish. This time I don't panic, I stay calm, well as much as you can when you witness a pair of floating eyes. *Did that really just happen?*

I consider yelling for Alex, but I know if I do, he won't sleep tonight at all. Besides he wouldn't believe me if I do tell him, so what's the point? I have no evidence just my word. I stare out the window for a moment, and when nothing else is around I continue over to the phone. Maybe it's best if I just ignore the weirdness. Just before I get to the phone, it rings.

"Hello." I say questioningly.

I answer the phone timidly, not sure what to expect. I see floating eyes and fog made of shadows. So, I should be ready for anything.

"Rose, I've been so worried about you! Morgan told me what happened. I'll just be getting back from Europe tomorrow night, but I'll pick you up Monday morning. I just had to hear your voice for myself." Hannah says in a panic.

I automatically relax because it's just Hannah. I knew I'd eventually hear from her, and it's not surprising that she knows what has happened. She is my best friend too.

"Hi Hannah, yes I had a little accident." I say as though it's no big deal.

She continues to ask me about what happened, I simply tell her I had got nervous and fell. It isn't a complete lie after all, but I don't want to get into it with my brother in the next room.

After chatting for an hour, she finally says goodbye. I'm about to call Morgan, which had been my reason for going to the phone in the first place. Suddenly, I hear the engine of his truck pulling into the driveway. Everyone seems to have their timing down today. I take a seat at the breakfast bar and wait. Morgan always lets himself in and then he'll come find me. Just as I finish the thought, he comes through the kitchen door with groceries.

"Hey Morgan, I wondered where you were. I was just going to call you." I say.

I wonder if Morgan knows something. He and Alex have been pretty friendly lately. *What am I thinking?* He's my best friend! If Alex did tell him, he would've already told me what he knows, right?

"Sorry Rose, I had to run some errands and get some groceries, obviously. I knew there wasn't much in the way of food here." Morgan says casually.

He holds up his armful of groceries and it makes me notice how hungry I am. I almost jump off my seat to get to the bags. I've been so caught up with everything that's been going on that I have neglected my stomach.

"Wow, and they say the way to a man's heart is through food. You're messing with nature now Rose." He says jokingly.

Morgan has his cocky grin plastered back on his face and it almost seems like everything is back to normal.

"Ha ha, you're hilarious. I'm starving." I say with a little pout.

I can't help giggling at Morgan's ridiculous comment with a matching smile and I think he knows I need to laugh a little.

I help Morgan store the groceries although I consider my stomach to be the best place at the time. But Morgan swears he will make me dinner once they are put away. So, I do my best to speed up the process.

Morgan makes me one of my favorite meals, perogies with bacon and onion. It's probably not the healthiest thing for you but my god, Morgan sure can cook. After we eat and clean up it's about seven o'clock, and we migrate into the now vacant living room to watch some TV. I sit down on the couch and Morgan slips in the movie Grease. It's an older movie, but a classic none the less. Plus, John Travolta in tight pants, who would want to miss that?

"I guess my brother already went to bed, he must be tired." I say.

I feel slightly guilty because I'm the reason he is so tired right now. He's been worried because of me.

"Yes, he is but he knew you'd come back to us, it just wasn't your time. Even if it was your time, he would have fought to get you back. You know that." Morgan says reassuringly.

"Thanks for being there Morgan, it means a lot to Alex and me, but you already know that." I say kindly.

Morgan always has a way of looking at the positive, whether it's me in a coma or Alex being over-protective. Morgan really is a part of our family. I can't explain what it is about him, but he brings me comfort. I just hope he knows how important he is to us. I snuggle up with a blanket and lean against

Morgan's shoulder.

"Rose, no force in this world could have kept me away." He says with honesty and affection.

He holds my gaze slightly longer than usual. When I turn back to the television, I can't help but feel like there was more in his eyes. Something that I never noticed before. But his words replay in my mind.

It's just like him to say something sweet and protective like that. The best part is that I know he means every word of it. Most girls can't say that about a lot of guys. There is something in the way he said it that makes me think he maybe cares for me as more than a friend, but it could be all in my head. *I am very tired.* With the way things are going, I don't really trust my own head. But now that I've started thinking about that, I'm starting to wonder how I truly feel about him. While I sit here snuggled up against him, I'm having conflicting emotions.

It never fails that amongst all the weird ass problems that I have been having, I would have a normal, trivial teenage problem like boys too. I'm getting too sleepy to think about my problems anymore. I feel myself begin to float in to sleep, and thanks to my exhaustion I doubt I'll have any dreams tonight.

"Ahem, Rose? Morgan? It might be time to wake up." Alex says after clearing his throat.

"Mmm…Morgan!" I mumble in my sleep.

My eyes shoot open and I freeze with embarrassment. You know how in the morning you're so out of it that you think your thoughts are silent, but really, you're saying them out loud? Well that just happened to me. I immediately realize there are other conscious people in the room, one sprawled out behind me and one standing in front of me. I look up to see my brother smiling so hard and looking on with sheer joy as I blush profusely. I sit upright and turn to see Morgan grinning proudly, probably at my obvious embarrassment. I stand up so fast I make myself dizzy and I almost end up back on the couch. This is not the type of wakeup call I ever expected or wanted for that matter. I have to think of a reason to escape to regroup my remaining dignity.

"Morning…I…uh…need to go shower." I manage to stutter out.

What do you expect? It's early in the morning so that's as creative as I can get after being woken up like that. I don't doubt they can see right through my plan to "run and hide" from this embarrassing situation, but at the moment, I don't care. I'll deal with them when my facial color returns to normal.

I hurry out of the room and rush up the stairs, determined to put as much distance between myself and the laughter that has broken out in the living room, as humanly possible. Clearly, it brings both my brother and Morgan amusement to see me feeling humiliated and flustered. I'll remember that in the future the next time I have to take their feelings into consideration.

I'm in such a hurry to get away from the guys that I walk right into the disaster zone that has become my bedroom. There are clothes and flowers all over the place. I know this mess has to be my brothers doing but it's exactly what I expected. I knew he was just dumping my stuff on the floor, and it looks like he had gone through everything to pick out a change of clothes to bring to the hospital. And my stupid window is open again. *Holy crap!* I shut my window, grab some clean clothes and head to the bathroom. A nice, hot shower is just what I need to shake the creepy feeling I have.

CHAPTER SEVEN

Alex

Rose was so embarrassed when she woke up on the couch with Morgan. I feel guilty but I'll admit it was amusing. If it had been any other guy, I'd be pissed but Morgan's a good guy. He has his own boundaries and I'm pretty sure Rose is still oblivious to his true feelings. As long as she is, nothing will happen between them. And if something does, I'll deal with it then.

Morgan sits up and looks at me. His smile fades. He knows we have to talk business.

"Morgan, while she's in the shower, I think we should talk." I say unhappily. "Did you find any leads on the Elite?" I ask.

I wish we didn't have to discuss this right now. I would much rather sit around laughing at the way that Rose bolted up the stairs. I know nothing happened, but you can imagine how it looked and how funny her reaction was. Maybe one day that'll be the only thing on my mind.

Morgan's face falls and somehow, I already know the answer. All this waiting is making me anxious. The Elite is our best chance, if he can't find them then Rose is as good as dead. He can't even find a lead on them. Maybe we're too late and they're either holed up hiding somewhere or worse, dead. Either way because of their absence, it's obvious that Morgan is right. There is a war going on and sooner or later we're going to be dragged into it.

"No, I couldn't find my leads anywhere, it's like everyone has disappeared. I'm not really sure what's happening. I'm using some powerful, old magick to get some information. We should have some answers soon." Morgan says confidently.

I want answers. I want to know our next steps. But I also know that the magick Morgan is using will attract others, like a moth to a flame. I figure eventually Rose will notice someone tailing her, or something else strange but I don't have many options. Even if she notices though, I doubt she's going to come to me. I have a feeling that she's being just as honest with me as

I've been with her lately. *I don't blame her.* I'd lie to me too.

"Well, where could everyone be? They don't just disappear, there has to be bodies, news, or some indication of what's happening." I say even though I have low hopes.

"I am doing everything I can, believe me. Wherever they are, magick can't go. Alex, you do realize if everyone's gone then there is no more protection. It may be more dangerous than we anticipated for Rose." Morgan says with worry in his eyes.

Damn! I was hoping to avoid admitting that I should tell Rose everything. I am willing to do many things if it means not having to tell her that I've been hiding a very important secret from her for almost eighteen years. Every time Morgan brings it up, I just shrug it off and eventually he drops it. I hate being pushed but something tells me he isn't going to drop it this time.

"I know. It's probably best if you stay at the house with us for a while Morgan. At least until we figure out our next move." I say moodily.

"Of course, I will." He says.

I know that having Morgan here will help to keep Rose safer, but it doesn't help my feeling of being useless. Morgan's not her brother and yet he has the ability to protect her far better than I can. I can't stop or change anything that my little sister is going through, I feel so powerless.

Maybe she wouldn't be in so much danger if I could protect her but that's not an option. I have to leave her fate in Morgan's hands, and it sucks.

"Alex, I promise to help in any way I can, but I think it's time to tell Rose the truth. No more excuses! As we get closer to Rose's eighteenth birthday her hunters get closer too. She needs to know." Morgan pleads with me.

I know that Morgan is right this time, but I still want to give her the normalcy she deserves. I mean let's face it, her childhood wasn't exactly a walk in the park.

"I think you're right Morgan. Just not tonight, it's too soon after her accident. I just need to give her some time to get herself together. Then I will tell her everything I know, and you can help." I say miserably.

"You're doing the right thing." Morgan says.

"Maybe." I reply negatively.

Morgan knows I'm serious, he can probably see the regret and frustration written all over my face. It's definitely time for her to know what is coming her way. Especially since some of it is already catching up with her. Maybe they've already found her and they're just biding their time. Who knows? I just want her safe. I don't want her to be more traumatized than she already is. I also wish she would just tell me everything that's been happening. Including the things she left out about her mom dream. I know she didn't say everything, because she's just like me. I know I have to be patient but there's so much at stake.

Rose

I stand in front of the bathroom mirror, holding my towel, and glaring at my truly unruly mop of hair when I hear the faintest of whispers. It seems to be coming out of thin air.

"Rose, come with me!" It whispers.

The voice is so eerie and threatening I can't help but panic. Then to make it worse I'm struck with the feeling of a thousand spiders climbing up my legs.

"You will be mine." The voice threatens.

That is all I can take. After everything I've seen and hearing that, my jaw drops and I let out one of those girly, high pitched, glass shattering screams.

Even while I'm screaming, I can hear Alex and Morgan running up the stairs. They come charging through the bathroom door, which only startles me further. Alex grabs me at first sight and, paying my towel no mind, pulls me to him. Morgan stands in front of us looking with wild eyes around the bathroom. Meanwhile all I'm thinking is *I can't believe I'm standing here in a towel, screaming like a baby, because of something no one can see or hear.* I'm also a little stunned at how quickly the guys had reacted to the situation, almost as though they had been expecting something. Morgan turns to me hastily.

"Rose, why did you scream?" Morgan demands.

Morgan's face is drop dead serious. I don't even know what to say to them without them thinking I'm a total nutcase, so I stand there opening and closing my mouth like a fish while I think. *What else can I do?* First, I see inhuman speed, then floating eyes, and now voices that have no mouth. *Oh god!* I truly am flying off my rocker now, even I'm starting to think I'm crazy. *What the hell?* I may as well try telling them.

"I heard a voice." I stammer out.

It's after I say this that I realize I am shaking like a leaf. I carefully pull my arms around myself in a sort of hug, hoping it will help calm my nerves. Morgan rests his hand on my shoulder and gives me an encouraging look.

"What do you mean a voice?" He asks gently.

Alex's grip tightens on my arm as though he is bracing himself, but all I can think is *Wow, a legitimate question.* It's just so not what I was expecting from the laughing duo. I assumed they would look at me like I am some sort of freak show.

"I…I don't know. It was barely a whisper, but it said, "Rose come with me" and "You will be mine." I say as I fight back the sobs. "I'm sorry! I shouldn't have screamed, it just scared me is all." I add in my defense.

No one speaks a word. I see Morgan and Alex exchange a look that seems to speak a thousand words. However, it isn't a "call the psyche ward and get the straight jacket" look. This experience has been weird enough without Morgan giving Alex a knowing nod, and all the while looking sad as shit all of a sudden. I've never seen Morgan look so lost. It just isn't like him. I'm beginning to get the vibe that someone is after me and that the guys are trying to protect me, but I feel silly thinking it all the same. I mean why would anyone be after me? I don't know what to think anymore because a lot of things just aren't adding up and they can't be explained at least not sanely.

Before I know what's going on Alex has snatched up my clothes and is guiding me to my room. I feel extremely awkward, so I clutch the towel tighter to my chest and pray it doesn't drop. I'm embarrassed enough right now.

"Get dressed then come downstairs." Alex orders me.

I find his tone to be mildly alarming, he sounds all military with a "this is how it's going to go" teacher voice. That's all he says before bolting back out of my room and back down the stairs with Morgan on his heels. Morgan doesn't even glance at me when he passes my bedroom. *What the hell is going on here?*

They can't possibly think I'm crazy, or can they? I don't know anything anymore, all I do know is that the world as I know it is becoming a dark, strange and dangerous place.

After I've put on some clothes and roughly towel dried my hair, I head downstairs. I hear my brother and Morgan talking in the kitchen, so I go there. They go dead silent when I walk in and they both give me a strange look. I'm fairly certain that I had been the topic of their conversation. Unfortunately, I'm starting to grow accustomed to the weird looks but all the same, I do a double take to ensure that I am properly dressed. *I am.* I walk over to the breakfast counter and take a seat. Morgan and Alex are standing rather motionless on the other side while I sit. Finally, Alex moves away and makes himself busy pulling drinks out of the fridge. I catch Morgan still watching me and a pained expression passes through his eyes. I hold his gaze with my own and I desperately want to ask him what's going on, but something keeps me silent. His gaze is so intense it feels like he's trying to tell me something without verbalizing it. Morgan stares for one more piercing minute before he turns back to my brother.

"Rose. We believe that you're in shock from the incident. What you think happened couldn't have happened. You need to forget about it." Alex says forcefully.

Morgan gets up and heads for the door looking totally angry. He stops before exiting the kitchen and turns to Alex. Personally, I'm shocked that Morgan would be leaving at a time like this. *How can he?* I'm losing my mind.

Alex shares an understanding look with Morgan, leaving me out of the loop. I hate feeling so left out and clueless. How come they get to have secrets together when Morgan's supposed to be my best friend? I jump off my stool as Morgan heads down the hall and I run after him. I grab his arm and pull him to look at me just as he reaches for the doorknob.

"Really? You're going to bail on me when I'm clearly falling apart?" I say angrily. "You didn't even say goodbye, you're just going to leave." I add through the tears.

My voice shakes when I speak, and I realize I have tears running silently down my cheeks. It's then that I finally allow myself to feel how terrified I really am. Morgan acknowledges how I feel, and he pulls me into a hug. His breath is warm on the top of my head, and his arms feel strong and secure. I don't want him to leave, he makes me feel like everything will be ok. *He's really my rock!*

Alex always seems so unsure of me lately and Morgan kind of balances it out and makes me believe things are going to be alright. His arms are still wrapped around me and if I'm not mistaken, it feels as though he doesn't want to let go either. I breathe in his smell. He smells like a young man mixed with the scent of deodorant. After what must have been a while, he pulls away even though I don't want him to. He looks into my eyes, leans down, and gives me a lingering kiss on the cheek. I feel the heat rise up in my cheeks and I know I am blushing.

"Rose, you'll be fine. I'll be late but I'll see you in school tomorrow." He says.

He gives me a reassuring smile and reluctantly turns and goes out the door. I close the door behind him and lean with my back against it. Just like that Morgan is gone. I still can't believe this. Why would he be leaving me tonight? So much is happening that I don't understand, and he makes me feel better. Now it feels like I'm so alone. Well I still have Alex, but he seems almost more worried than I am. I know in my heart that something is going on and I have a gut-wrenching feeling that it's going to get worse. I don't know what to do.

I go up the stairs and stretch out on my bed. *It's really happening.* I'm going bonkers and now Alex and Morgan both know it. It's the only logical explanation.

I think everything over to myself and a scary and serious thought crosses my mind. I'm going to be locked up in a mental hospital. I don't want to believe it, but I know it's true. If I don't start acting normal, Alex isn't going to have a choice. I know what I have to do. I have to pretend that everything is fine.

Tomorrow I'll go back to school with Hannah, so perhaps a little bit of normalcy will help straighten out the wreck that has become my life. I doubt it but it's worth a try.

I go back downstairs and sit in the living room waiting for Alex. I wipe away my remaining tears while I think. I think of everything that has occurred and I try to piece it together. None of it makes sense though because it's all so strange. I can't logically explain anything in my head. Insanity seems like a fairly realistic expectation now.

The TV is already on, so I flick through the channels in the hopes of finding something to occupy my mind. I come across Family Guy which is one of our favorite shows. This show cracks me up no matter what mood I'm in. Alex is still in the kitchen no doubt trying to avoid his psychotic sister, but it's going to be ok. Soon he won't know that anything is wrong, even if I have to fake it for the rest of my life. I focus on the TV and try to enjoy the show.

Alex

I don't know how I'm going to get any sleep tonight. Rose isn't safe here anymore. I don't need more proof. So why didn't I tell her? I had the perfect opportunity, but I didn't. *Idiot!* I even said I was going to. I'm surprised Morgan didn't blurt it out in anger before he left. *Crap.* Morgan is pissed at me. I understand why. I'm being stupid and selfish letting Rose think she's going crazy. I know I can't keep this secret much longer, it's only a matter of time. *What am I going to do?*

I can hear Rose in the living room. I doubt the show is doing much to distract her, she probably thinks her life is ending. *Poor girl!* I wish I had the courage to tell her even if it doesn't feel like the right time. If Morgan were her brother, she'd already know. She'd probably be better off too.

Shit! I need to talk to him about Rose's dream of mom still. It sounds like more than just a dream. I'm not sure if it's possible but I think it is.

I understand why he needed to leave so bad, but I don't know why he's risking abandoning Rose when it seems like someone is awfully close to getting her. I'm just a person and I love my sister with all my heart but there is only so much I can do to keep her safe. I know what may be after Rose, but I don't have the power to fight them off. I just hope Morgan finds who he's looking for and gets back quickly. He can be mad at me here.

Rose

The rest of the day goes by quickly and quietly. Alex doesn't seem very talkative, not that I mind. I have more than enough on my mind already to hold up a real conversation with someone. With everything that has been happening, I find myself enjoying the peace and quiet.

Alex orders pizza for dinner and as soon as I eat, I go to my room. I change my clothes and get everything ready for school tomorrow before climbing into bed. I drift off to sleep quickly. Maybe tomorrow will be better and all this craziness will end. *Maybe.*

CHAPTER EIGHT

Morgan

I'm driving down the highway farther from Rose and Alex, which makes me nervous, but I have to. I know exactly where I need to go, I'm just not entirely sure what to expect. I need see for myself where the others are or at least know if something has gone horribly wrong.

I think about Rose and Alex and how I've kind of left them unprotected, but by now they should be safely in bed. At least I'm praying they are. I only hope nothing comes for them tonight. Alex knows he has to keep Rose alive at all costs including his own life, but I hate to think he'd be forced to do that. There's really nothing I can do about it now. I can't be everywhere. I've got to focus on the mission at hand.

I'm already driving slightly over the speed limit and I've still got several hours of driving ahead of me. I'm heading for Snake Isle. The island itself is unimportant but within the forest is a hidden portal to a village full of creatures. It lies on the outskirts of the other world and is home to two of my contacts. I have to find out what has become of them before I can make plans with Rose.

If only Rose already knew about all of this, I would have brought her with me. She'd be slightly safer with me than she is at home. I don't have that option though. Alex has told her nothing, and it's not something you can just spring on someone. It'd be hard for anyone who isn't raised to believe, to do just that. Believe. Not to mention hearing that the things kids are afraid of really do exist. For the most part anyway but we know them by different names.

I guess I can always go behind Alex's back and just tell her, but I don't think she'll believe it coming from me. I also can't risk being cut out of her life by her or Alex. She's going to need me more than either of them can comprehend right now. No. I may not agree with Alex's decisions, but I will obey his requests. *For now.*

Several hours later I pull up to a dock positioned on a lake. I see a small motorboat tied to the dock and I think it'll do nicely. It isn't anything special, but I'll make it work. It's four in the morning and fortunately there is no one around to see me. I jump in the boat after tucking my keys in my pocket. I dig around for the spare set of boat keys and find them under one of the seats. It seems like an obvious hiding spot, but the owner probably thinks, who's going to steal a boat? Sometimes humans amuse me. I'll bring the boat back soon and there will be no harm done.

I start the engine and carefully reverse away from the dock. It has been a while since I've driven a boat but it's like riding a bicycle. You never really forget. Once I am in deeper water, I really open the engine up. The breeze is chilly but refreshing. And the mist of water is keeping me alert and awake. If the circumstances were different, I could really enjoy myself.

It only takes about an hour to reach the island and before long I'm pulling the boat onto rock and sand. The sun is beginning to rise now so I want to get out of sight from prying eyes. I immediately walk into the trees knowing where I'm going. I haven't been here in years but it's hard to forget the path. I come into a familiar small clearing and I search on the ground for the symbol. I see the five-star rocks marking out the entrance and I go stand in the center of them. I don't have time to waste if I want to get back to school with Rose, so I quickly begin the incantation.

"Insons insontis cruor per meus vena, dedi continuo pro permission ut penetro!" I say.

The incantation is rough because I haven't performed it in a while. After the words are spoken, I remove a dagger from my coat pocket. I grimace as I pull the blade down across my palm and I watch as the blood dribbles down near my feet. The ground begins to smoke where the blood has seeped in and there is a blinding flash. When my eyes readjust, I am facing a wall of shrubs. I walk to the right as I replace the dagger in my pocket and wrap gauze around my hand to staunch the bleeding.

It isn't the only way to cross into the other world, but it is the quickest. I keep walking until I come across a small opening in the bush. I walk through and the bushes seal behind me.

I find myself looking at a small village with simple wooden cabins. There are no more than twelve homes on either side of the dirt road, and I know this particular village houses no more than fifteen creatures. It's just how I remember it except something is very wrong. Despite it being five in the morning some of the creatures should be outside and there should be noise, but it is deathly silent with not a soul in sight.

I remove the dagger from my pocket and hold it tightly in a fighting stance. I'm prepared for an attack if that may be the case. The village I am in is home to a few vampires, werewolves, and many enchanters. Or at least it used to be although it seems to have been abandoned.

There are several of these villages around the world. They were formed because these creatures formed an alliance, withdrawing from their respective covens. Usually one species of creature doesn't interact in a friendly manner with another. However, these creatures questioned the system and went off on their own. They live in peace with each other while the remaining populations continue to kill one another. Personally, I couldn't live in such close proximity as the vampires. Although the werewolves, really aren't that bad in my opinion. At least that's what I have surmised from experience. Most creatures who oppose their coven's rules are usually hunted and killed but the rest flee to small villages like this one. Even in this day, species aren't supposed to co-habitate.

As I look around it becomes clear that something horrible happened here. There appears to be blood spattered throughout the dirt, indicating a struggle. In my heart I know that many have died. I start towards a cabin whose door is slightly ajar. I slowly push the door open and it creaks. The smell hits me almost immediately, filth, rotting food, and something else. I walk through another doorway and I am face to face with the other stink. Rotting flesh. There is one body and it is decomposed beyond all recognition. I assume it has been sitting here for at least two months. I walk closer as I try to distinguish what it was. I see two elongated incisors and I can only assume it was a vampire. It is a bad omen because if the vampire was killed so was everyone else. Vampires are usually responsible for death, but they aren't easily killed.

I leave the cabin only to stop in the fresh air. Despite how I feel about vampires they deserve a funeral of some kind. I go into the woods and gather branches which I place in the middle of the village in a pile. I drag the corpse out and place it on top. I approach the other homes with caution and do the same. Hours later I have searched every cabin and the body count totals thirteen. That means two creatures have either escaped or were captured. I stand before the pile of branches and bodies and I wish them peace. I use magick to fully ignite the pyre and I watch until there are only ashes left.

I scatter the ashes with an incantation and leave. It's already mid-morning and it's a long drive home. I turn and leave the village feeling depressed and defeated. If my contacts are dead, then basically we are on our own. If they're alive then they'll be tortured for information. It's not a very comforting thought. I hurry towards the bushes.

I want to return to Alex and Rose as soon as possible because the circumstances have changed. Rose could already be found. I'm concerned for their safety even more than I was originally. *Both of them.* If an entire village can be wiped out, then a human and a halfling will be like swatting a fly. I need to speak with Alex and explain a few things. He needs to know more in order to prepare for a fight. He only knows what his parents have told him in letters, which isn't much. I filled in some gaps, but I didn't want to overload him with information that he didn't need to know. The problem is that now he needs to know, and so does Rose.

CHAPTER NINE

Rose

I wake up the next morning to a familiar loud beeping. For a moment I have the horrible thought that I am back at the hospital. Thankfully, this time it is my alarm clock going off, and true to its nature it is the most annoying sound in the world. *Especially in the morning!* I sit up and look around my room and I'm happy to see that my window is closed today. Maybe I'll be able to put all the weird stuff behind me and move on with my otherwise boring life.

I climb lazily out of bed and start getting ready for school. My clock says seven and my body can definitely tell. The house is quiet except for me and I know Alex has already left for work. Hannah will be here any minute to pick me up just like she has for as long as I've known her. I remember the first day we met in grade nine, I was terrified. We had met at orientation and I had been thrilled to make a female friend.

For some reason I always have a hard time making girl-friends. Usually they want nothing to do with me. That's why Morgan was my only friend until Hannah came along and we have remained close friends.

This year is our senior year at Grace Hall Secondary School, and I can't be more excited. It means the world to me to be almost done because unlike most people, I don't particularly enjoy high school. And I sure as hell don't consider it to be the best years of my life. *For me high school is my own personal hell.*

I'm really looking forward to college though where I can be on my own and discover who I want to be. *The sooner the better!*

I think to myself in silence and smile slightly at the thought of seeing Hannah after her return from Europe. She always has amazing stories to share and perhaps she even had a summer romance. I can't wait to hear all about it.

Knock. Knock. Knock.

As I start making mental notes of when and what to tell her, I hear a knock on the door. I don't bother going to answer it because immediately following the knock I hear the familiar creaking of the door opening. With an old house comes the creepy noises but you get used to it. I hear Hannah clear her throat before I hear the familiar sound of her voice.

"Good morning Rose!" She says happily.

"Good morning Hannah!" I reply.

I can't help but smile into the mirror after calling out to her. This is an all too familiar ritual, one that I've missed. I wait patiently brushing my long dark brown hair, knowing from experience that if I stay where I am, Hannah will come up to greet me. Soon enough I hear the footsteps and gentle creaking of the wood floorboards signaling that I will soon have company in the bathroom.

"Rose, every time it's the same thing. I come to the door, I yell for you, and still I end up finding you in front of a mirror." She says jokingly. "You look gorgeous darling. How's your head?" She adds questioningly.

I shake my head and laugh. She always says I look gorgeous even when I just wake up looking like a troll doll. Hannah is accustomed to this ritual too and I think she enjoys it as much as me. We hug "hellos" to each-other and I grab my bag from the floor. I slide the bag over my shoulder and look at Hannah.

"My head is fine. It twinges a bit but its good. Ok, I'm ready to go." I say reassuringly.

Hannah and I head for the door then we go back down the creaky staircase. When we get to the bottom she spins around.

"Rose, I'm really happy to see you. I've been worried about you." She says.

I smile sincerely at her while the worry in her eyes turns into excitement.

"About the e-mail…" She says slowly.

That is the last thing I want to talk about now. I have almost forgotten that I sent her that and now I'm wishing I hadn't. I just want to talk about normal things that don't include floating eyes, voices, or weird dreams. But I am the one who started it.

"Rose here's the thing. I still seriously think you have psychic abilities. It's the only way to explain all the weird shit you've been going through." She says rationally. "I haven't forgotten that you don't believe in that stuff. I'm just saying that it makes sense." She adds with a smile. "I don't want to push because you seem to be doing great now so, whenever you're ready to talk about it, we will. Until then, it's forgotten. Beside we won't be short on topics to discuss, it is our senior year after all." Hannah says with a mischievous grin.

I don't know what to say. I'm so relieved that she isn't demanding to hear more about it. It's as though she knows I want to try and get things back to normal. How do you thank a friend for exceeding your expectations?

"Thanks Hannah!" I say sincerely.

As far as I'm concerned there's nothing that I can say to her to show my gratitude. I'm just so lucky to have a friend like her and I know it.

Hannah doesn't say anything else to me, instead she gives me a sincere warming smile. There is something else behind her smile, a playfulness I've never noticed. I'm definitely curious about what could be making her this upbeat and excited. She turns on her heel and goes out the door and I follow her. We stop on the porch and finally it all makes sense. Hannah lets out a big sigh like she just accomplished the impossible by staying so calm. Sitting in her usual cockeyed parking area is a new car. What else would she be driving but a Lexus 2006 IS. I stare in awe at the sleek vehicle and I can only assume her parents bought it for her. Hannah turns around to face me with a smug grin on her face.

"So, what do you think?" She asks proudly.

"Wow!" I say in surprise.

As if I can say anything else about something so expensive.

"I know right, it's so sexy. It's an early graduation gift from my parents, they gave it to me last week. We're going to look super fabulous riding in this, even more than I did in Europe." She says excitedly.

Hannah and I giggle with excitement as we take off towards the car. We get in and I toss my bag in the back seat and make myself comfortable. Hannah pops in a new CD and smiles over at me.

"Let's make this an entrance we'll never forget!" She says.

"Sounds like a plan." I reply.

I'm glad to see my friend so excited, and I am in a world all my own. All the weirdness seems so far behind me now. All I can think about is the stupid trivial things like boys, dances, boys, parties, boys, grades, and even Morgan. Although I suppose he falls into the boy's category. I start to wonder if he's ok and when he'll be home. I worry about him too.

The car squeals off towards the direction of the school, leaving a trail of smoke behind the new tires.

Twenty minutes later, Grace Hall Secondary School comes into view. The beautiful old brick building standing two stories tall with shrubs and flowers surrounding the perimeter, is a welcoming site to me. I'm filled with pride as we pull into the seniors' parking lot and see all of the students walking towards the front door.

"Rose, just imagine it. This year we run the show. All the girls will want to be us, and all the boys will want to date us." Hannah says giddily.

"Hannah, it's not about the boys remember! This is the year that will define who we become, and what we will do. We apply to University this year, and we have more time to spend with our friends. And don't forget we get to plan all of the events this year." I say.

"Including prom! Oh my god, what if no one asks me? I will be laughed out of the country." Hannah says with dramatic flair.

"Ok, first of all, drama queen much?" I say with a laugh. "Secondly, someone will ask you so don't worry." I say caringly. "And thirdly, having a date is over-rated, you can always be my date. You know I'll probably go alone." I add.

"Yes, but I really want to bring a special guy date, no offense." She says with a longing look. "I guess we have lots to look forward to though." She adds.

I can't help but chuckle at this comment as I roll my eyes and think to myself. I don't want to admit it, but I am hoping I'll have a guy to go with too. I'm also hoping to go far enough away for University, so I'll have to at least live in the dorms. I love Alex but I think that a little independence and space will be good for both of us.

There's so much riding on my last year of high school and I can feel the weight of it on my shoulders. With the weirdness happening I find myself more motivated than ever to achieve my goals. However, finding a boyfriend isn't high on my priority list at the moment.

It's still confusing to me that Hannah is single. She's tall, blond, beautiful, and smart. She really is the whole package and she should have at least one love interest. Then again with her cheerleading and me, her schedule keeps her fairly busy. Not to mention, she does hold very high standards.

"Rose, I know that look. Stop over thinking things." Hannah jokes.

"I am not over thinking things and even if I am. I do not have a look." I say with a smile.

I know it's a lie. I do have a look. Morgan reminds me all the time. He especially enjoys telling me he can see smoke coming out of my ears. He always makes me laugh, or at least he used to but not so much lately. He hasn't really smiled much either.

Hannah immediately laughs at me but regains focus when she catches sight of some empty spots. She quickly drives towards one of the empty spots. She puts her foot down on the gas pedal a little harder than necessary, but I don't blame her, we've been weaving through the lot for the last ten minutes. We're hoping to grab some breakfast before we have to go to class. As Hannah pulls into the middle spot, I see two nice cars speeding towards the spots on either side of us. One car is a Mercedes-Benz, the other a Cadillac. Both cars look to be newer years and look overly expensive. The windows are tinted so dark, you can't even make out if someone is inside. I doubt the degree of tinting is legal.

"Well I hope they don't think they are always parking beside us. They make my new car look like shit. Even if there are hot boys inside." Hannah says to me.

Hannah opens her door and jumps out. I watch her give one of her cutest smiles and matching waves to whoever is in the Caddy. I start to get out, but I pause because I realize the person driving the black Mercedes has already begun opening their door. As they step out into the daylight, I'm shocked at how utterly beautiful the guy is. He looks like a freaking model. He has jet black hair that's carefully sculpted, which he obviously takes the time to style. Not to mention he has to be at least six feet tall. His clothes are clearly designer brands and the boy wears them well, they fit him like a glove. I look at his face and see that he has piercing gray eyes, which are looking right at me. I suddenly become aware that I am staring, and I quickly try to look away, but I'm not fast enough to go unnoticed, so I look back. *Oh my god!*

He stands there completely relaxed looking in the window at me for too long. The eye contact makes me feel uneasy and I'm sure he notices but if anything, he seems to thrive on it. He gives me a slight smile and reaches out to my door handle. He pulls the door open with such ease and grace that I am hypnotized. He's still smiling at me when the cool breeze dances across my face. I know I must be blushing because of the warmth in my cheeks but I hope it isn't noticeable. I step out of the car and have to look up to see into his face and those beautiful gray eyes.

"Thank you..." I say nervously.

My voice comes out as just more than a whisper and I am instantly embarrassed.

"My name is Caleb, and you are?" He says calmly.

Caleb's voice sounds the adverse of mine. He sounds confident and sure of himself, which is the way I'd die to feel. His voice doesn't waver and his presence commands attention.

"Rose." I say.

I answer quickly while I suffer from a multitude of emotions, embarrassment, attraction, excitement, envy and every other emotion caused by hormones. Simultaneously, I'm still trying to give Caleb my attention.

"Well Rose, it was a pleasure meeting you. I am sure I'll be seeing you around quite a bit." He says with a knowing grin.

After he speaks there is a shimmer in his eyes. It gives him a mischievous appearance and his knowing smile adds to it.

All too quickly Caleb turns and heads towards the other car giving Hannah a half nod as he passes. I haven't even noticed until now that the occupants of the other car have gotten out and are waiting patiently at the trunk, no doubt for Caleb. There are two of them and believe me they are just as attractive, but they don't share Caleb's dazzling gray eyes. They are dressed just as fashionable as Caleb, but it is obvious by their physical appearances that they are not closely related. One of the boys has short blond curls while the other boy has brown hockey hair. They all appear to be roughly the same height, give or take an inch.

They look over at me for a brief moment before turning towards the door of the school. Caleb glances back as he starts walking and I swear to god he winks at me. Now maybe I'm dreaming but I'm adequately convinced that it actually happened. The three of them fall into step with one another while I stand transfixed on them. Finally, I shake my head and return to my body. Hannah looks at me with an ecstatic smile as she walks around the car to me. I reach into the back of Hannah's car and pull out my backpack, slipping the strap over my shoulder. Hannah seems to be in a trance of sorts, but she snaps out of it when I shut the car door. I give her an expectant look and I'm not disappointed.

"Ok. Those guys were amazingly good looking. I know who's going to be taking me to prom. The hot one with the brown shaggy hair." Hannah says confidently. "The super sexy black-haired guy seems to have his eyes on you. Yay I'm so excited." She says.

Hannah does a little jump to show her enthusiasm, but it only makes me giggle at her.

"Hannah you always find someone to be amazingly good looking." I say.

We both laugh as we head up the parking lot to the doors. It doesn't seem likely that a guy like Caleb would be interested in me, but the thought makes me delighted all the same. I don't understand why but he made me feel slightly flustered and short of breath. After all he is just a guy, usually it's Hannah who gets all discombobulated by the male species but not me. Instead Hannah is abnormally quiet, and I find it exceptionally strange. Other than her outburst about her soon to be prom date, she hasn't said a word about the new arrivals. I begin to wonder what could possibly be occupying Hannah's mind so successfully. I become jealous when I envision her daydreaming about Caleb even though it's completely ludicrous for me to feel that way. I dismiss the idea from my mind and laugh nervously at my behaviour. It's completely irrational for me to feel so envious of my friend when she would help me in an instant.

I need to regain my focus on classes and University. It won't do me any good to be so easily distracted by a guy.

CHAPTER TEN

Rose

Hannah and I reach the front doors and go in, then, we automatically head down the hallway that will take us to the Oasis. It's a small area of the school that has been decorated as a coffee house of sorts. It has squishy armchairs, and dim lighting. It's pretty awesome actually. It has a cafeteria and ample seating where we can get a snack before classes. We sit our bags on the chairs and head for the café. There's no line yet since most people barely make it to school on time, let alone early.

"What would you like? Breakfast is on me today!" Hannah says happily.

I consider my options and in-the-end, French toast wins. Hannah gets the same and then pays for the food, grabbing two chocolate milks before we walk back to our seats. We sit across from each other and make ourselves comfortable. I start to wonder when Hannah is going to bring up the guys again. And this time, I am kind of counting on her predictability, because I want to talk about Caleb. As her best friend I know that it is only a matter of time, unless there is something more important to focus on.

"Ok." Hannah says with unease. "It's time to discuss the elephant in the room. And no, I am not referring to the devilishly handsome guys we just met even though we are going to." She adds with longing. "It's time to look at our schedules Rose. We can't put it off any longer." She says in defeat.

Finally, I understand the reason for Hannah's silence. She's worried about our class tables. In our fourth year here, we have been informed that because there are so many students, there will be different schedules. The school's population has grown so much that they had to alter the lunches and class times in order to accommodate the growing population.

"Ok Hannah. Do you want me to go first?" I ask kindly.

"Yes!" She replies.

I have a gut feeling that the schedules aren't going to make either of us happy. I don't want to be the one to say so though, Hannah is so hopeful that it'll work out. I reluctantly pull out my schedule and try to prepare myself for what I know will be a huge let down.

"Alright, first period I have algebra, second period I have chemistry, third period I have history, fourth period I have study hall, then I have lunch, fifth period I have French and sixth period I have Spanish. What does yours look like?" I ask nervously.

"Awe Rose, we only have one class together. First period I have algebra, second period I have biology, third period I have physics, fourth period I have law, then lunch, fifth period I have chemistry and sixth period I have history. Man this sucks! We only have one class together and lunch. This is so unfair." Hannah whines.

I hate to tell her, but I knew we'd have different schedules. After all, considering this is our senior and final year, come next year she'll be pre-med at some very prestigious university. And I will be at a less expensive university for I don't even know what yet.

"Well, at least you have other friends. I'm going to be sitting alone." I say with genuine sadness.

We both know this is true, but she gives me a sympathetic half-smile. Even though, I don't mind being alone so much. Neither of us dare discuss the fact that we're going to end up at different schools next year.

"I guess…Alright well, we should go to home room and then I'll have to meet up with you at lunch. After school I'll have to find you after sixth period, so I'll probably have to text you." Hannah says grumpily.

"Sounds good!" I say pretending to be enthusiastic.

I try to hide my disappointment. Truthfully, we've never been in different classes. We always took turns during semesters deciding which classes we would take together, so we would cover both of our interests. It goes without saying that neither of us will need to be told to keep our cell phones turned on. We'll likely text each other during classes.

We pick up our bags and head back down the hallway. This is the first time we won't have every class together and I'm nervous but excited at the same time. We won't be able to sit together and mindlessly gossip throughout the lessons while the teachers drone on anymore. On the other hand, maybe this distance will be a good thing. I can actually focus on my grades this year without making Hannah feel ignored.

As we continue down the hall we turn and go up the staircase. Turning when we are on the second floor, we can see the rest of our friends. Or rather they're Hannah's friends. They're waiting outside the algebra room for her as expected.

The group consists of a few cheerleaders and some of the school jocks. I notice that May is standing hand in hand with Eric, which is normal. They have been a couple since grade nine. Clearly, the summer hasn't changed that. Nathan and Kyle are standing there smiling in Hannah's direction, while

Ashley and Camilla stand there looking less than patient.

Hannah and I had a good laugh at their expense when summer started because they had both taken the time to ask her out. The boys had been angry with each other until they realized they had both been rejected. Hannah just wasn't interested in either of them. Of course, Ashley and Camilla are still mad and uber jealous of Hannah. They were hoping to be dating Kyle and Nathan, but it didn't happen even after Hannah said no. They will still be civil with us though, if only because of Hannah's social status.

As we start filing into the room, I notice someone I haven't seen before. He has dirty blond hair and brown eyes. He's sporting a just rolled out of bed hairstyle. He's a good-looking guy and he looks friendly to boot.

I walk down the row carefully, so I don't trip, and take the desk next to him. Hannah drops into the seat next to me and her entourage shoo people out of the way so that they can take the seats next to their queen bee. Hannah turns back to her followers after giving me a smile, they are clearly immersed in talks of cheerleading practices and other things I likely have no interest in. *Surprise, surprise!*

I turn back to the new kid and smile when he looks up. I recognize an opportunity to have another friend to speak to who will want to talk to me, rather than people who tolerate me but don't actually like me. He smiles back at me and I find it's an encouraging act.

"Hey. I'm Rose. You must be new here?" I say amicably.

"Yeah, my name is Tyler. I just moved here from New York. My parents get shipped around a lot for business, and this time they decided to leave me one of their houses so I can stay at one school for a year." Tyler says.

"That's got to be hard. Hopefully you enjoy it here." I say politely.

Tyler comes off as a very laid-back individual. He has a calming tone to his voice. He seems like a non-judgmental person which makes me feel more comfortable.

"Well Rose, it's a pleasure to meet you! I met Kyle, Eric and Nathan at football camp over the summer. I met May and everyone else last week, but I heard a lot about you and Hannah, so I couldn't wait to meet you. According to them you and Hannah are like sisters, the inseparable kind." Tyler says.

My hopes for a new friend drop slightly when he says he was at football camp. Unfortunately, that means he is a jock, which means he'll eventually ignore me just like the others. That is once he learns that I am a big nobody. Still I'm hopeful. He already knows a bit about me from the others and he is still talking to me. That's a good sign. Maybe he won't be like the other popular kids.

I stifle a small giggle because part of what he said is true. Hannah and I are like sisters, practically inseparable. We met in the first class, on the first day of grade nine, and we instantly became best friends. We tell each other everything. What we want, how we feel, and what we are worried about. We have very few secrets from one another. Well at least as far as she knows. This sudden realization sends a stab of guilt into my belly. I fully intend on telling Hannah more of my crazy news, but does it make me an awful friend for not already telling her?

I go quiet after our small introductions, too much guilt. Thinking about all the weirdness has a way of making me not want to carry on a conversation with anyone. He doesn't seem to notice the change in my attitude though. He goes about taking out a notebook and a pencil, obviously ready to get class started. I look to my left just as Hannah is about to ask me something, but she stops and rolls her eyes as the teacher clears his throat. Everyone is quiet and directs their attention to the front of the room. Nobody wants to let the teacher know that they are going to be a pain in the ass just yet. First impressions are the most important after all.

After an hour of the math teacher droning on and on about basic fractions and decimals, this first class comes to an end. Finally, everyone is free to go. It is a very welcome feeling. I already know my basic math, so today's lesson wasn't exactly captivating. As much as I had tried to, I couldn't keep focus on the lesson. My mind kept wandering to the silver eyes I saw at the graveyard. They were magnetic and intoxicating. When that's not on my mind, Caleb's eyes are. It's only been an hour and already this guy is taking over my mind. It frustrates me to think this guy is having this effect on me. I decide that it's probably best if I try to forget about this morning altogether.

Hannah follows me out of our homeroom but we both stop in the hallway. Hannah turns to me and gives me one of the saddest looks I've ever seen on my beautiful friends' face.

"Hannah it's only a few hours and then I will see you at lunch." I say reassuringly.

"I know. Just for the record though, This. Sucks." She says angrily.

Hannah heads down the opposite hall and I watch her groupies following behind her. She's heading off to biology and I get to go to chemistry. *Lucky me!* I head off on my own, stumbling through the crowd.

When I arrive at the class, I notice that most of the seats are full. After I sit at an empty desk, I glance around me and see Tyler sitting at the back of the room with Eric. May is obviously not in this class, which explains why Eric is sitting with Tyler. Both boys see me looking their way and they give me a smile. Well Tyler smiles, Eric cringes. I'm not surprised, if Hannah's not by my side the popular group pretends that I don't exist. At least in this class I'll have some alone time, and Tyler's friendly face.

The lesson begins almost immediately. We are just being introduced to the periodic table of elements, which makes for an easy first class. The teacher is rambling about the element iron and its properties. The classroom door opens and my heart stops.

In walks Caleb, designer jeans and all. I will always remember that Fe is iron because that is the last thing I heard before seeing Caleb's stunning gray eyes. The white t-shirt he wears cuts across his arms in just the right way showing off his muscles and I doubt I'm the only girl to notice. He looks at me and begins walking in my direction, his gaze is more intense than ever. I look down at the table sure that he'll walk past me but as soon as I look up Caleb stops beside the desk and smiles at me.

"Mind if I sit here?" Caleb asks with a charming smile.

"Uh…no…of course not!" I stutter in reply.

I am a bit flustered and slightly caught off guard as he sits down next to me. There are two seats away from me and yet he chooses to sit with me. I have mixed feelings about this, but it is mostly joy.

I can feel the heat rising in my face already. I'm sure everyone is going to notice me blushing profusely but fortunately it is at that moment that the teacher turns off the lights and puts up an overhead. The overhead is supposed to demonstrate the first layer of elements and how they're composed. Of course, all I can think about is how close Caleb is to me. I risk sneaking a glance at him and to my disappointment he is focused on the lesson. I find myself bothered by the fact that I want him to be looking at me. So, my thoughts of his eyes are now replaced with the reasons for my own actions. On the one hand it's nice to have something different to think about, but on the other hand it's embarrassing that I am so infatuated with a guy that I don't even know.

I definitely have to talk to someone about this. It requires discretion as well as secrecy, but because of the topic Morgan is out since that would just be awkward. I don't think I'll be able to get Hannah alone until we go home, so this conversation is going to have to wait.

I look back over to the clock once the teacher turns the lights back on. I am completely at a loss when I realize it has only been twenty minutes. I still have thirty minutes of class left to endure the agony of sitting beside this gorgeous boy. It is even worse when the teacher announces that the student that we are sitting with is our lab partner for the semester. With time left for class the teacher gives us an assignment to do. It involves writing a three-hundred-word paper on the element of our choice. My thoughts immediately drift to iron for obvious reasons. However, he suggests silver and insists that it will be better. So, I go along with it, wanting to make as little eye contact as possible. I set to work on the report but have to stop when I remember I know absolutely nothing about silver, other than it's pretty.

"Rose, we can finish this after school! I'll go to the library and borrow a book on silver, and meet you at you house if you want? Or I can drive you since your friend drove?" He says confidently.

Again, the heat starts rising in my face, I don't know what to say to him. I feel like I am being asked out on my first date all over again, even though technically I've never really been on a date.

Before I'm able to stop myself, I am making plans to meet him at his car after sixth period. I see him smile to himself in what I can only guess is triumph of making me blush or getting permission to drive me home. I honestly can't tell. It is so hard to read his eyes for some reason, as if some invisible wall stands between me and the answers I so badly desire. As I look into his eyes, I swear I can see a flash making them have a silver glow, only for a second. It reminds me of the boy in the cemetery, but I quickly swat the idea away. It's probably just the light reflecting in his eyes. There is just something so familiar about his eyes and I find it hard to look away.

"Great I'll meet you after school!" He says with another flash of his pearly whites.

After that, we silently read our textbooks while the rest of class goes by. I don't think I actually learned anything in class, but I am trying. There are just too many things on my mind that take precedence over school. *Mostly Caleb.* My thoughts are interrupted by the grave-yard memories that come flickering back. It causes a dull throb in the back of my head. I bring my hand up and give my wound a gentle rub. The twinge of pain subsides but the area is still sensitive. I do my best to forget the creepy memories and try to focus on my next class.

CHAPTER ELEVEN

Rose

The next of my classes are uneventful. It turns out that Tyler is in my history class as well, so we sit together. He's the only one I know in the class and it seems he is in the same position.

The history teacher isn't exactly interesting. It appears that his preferred method of teaching is sitting on the edge of his desk, reading out of the textbook. Let's not forget that he reads in a very monotonous tone as well. He doesn't even make an attempt to get anyone involved in his topic. Most of the students are happily chatting quietly amongst each other.

At first, I try to pay attention and I would at least sit quietly for the entire class, but then Tyler flashes me a grin and strikes up a conversation with me. I won't lie, it's surprising in a pleasing way that he still wants to associate with someone of my social status, and it just proves that there are decent people out there.

"So Rose, I hope I'm not overstepping my boundaries, but the others say you're not really much of a joiner. I'm not trying to offend you! I just figure since we're both stuck in this horrendously boring class, we may as well get to know each other." Tyler says honestly.

I'm not offended in the least. In fact, he's definitely trying to say I'm an outcast in a nicer way than I would have. To be perfectly honest, the fact that he wants to get to know me despite what he's probably heard really speaks to his character. I guess jocks aren't all the same.

"No offense taken. And no, I'm more of a do my time at school and go home, kind of girl." I say quietly.

"That's understandable. I don't mean to pry but why don't you join cheerleading with Hannah? That would probably be fun, and you'd seem like a joiner." He says suggestively.

This is one of the first times anyone has asked me why I am the way I am. Most people just shrug me off and ignore me when they discover that I don't fit in the same mold as them. I'm not even really sure how to answer his question.

"I'm honestly not sure. I guess I just don't think I'm the cheerleading type. It's just not who I am." I say thoughtfully.

"Tell me Rose. Who are you?" He asks with curiosity.

I feel a small warmth start in my cheeks. I'm a bit flustered because I'm not used to having to talk about myself so much. No one has ever wanted to know who I am. Tyler's still looking right at me waiting for my answer, but how do you answer that question? To be honest, I don't know who I am. I just know deep down that I'm meant to be special, that there is more to me than even I know yet.

"Honestly Tyler, I haven't really figured out who I am. I'm just trying to survive high school." I reply honestly.

"Aren't we all?" He says with a chuckle.

He turns back towards the teacher to briefly pay attention. I'm feeling a bit shy because it turns out that even though he's a jock, he's just trying to get through high school too. It makes me wonder if maybe everyone feels the same way. Maybe everyone isn't so different. Perhaps people put up a front so that they'll feel as though they belong. It's a nice thought but I know for a fact that some people, like Hannah, know exactly how to navigate their way through high school. They don't have to just get by.

I look back over at Tyler and at the same time he looks over at me. We share a silent and slightly awkward smile before turning away. I don't feel the same way looking at him as I do looking at Caleb. It's just comforting to know that there is one other person who isn't completely consumed by their high school persona. It even makes me feel more normal, which makes me question who Tyler really is, rather than what I assume. I can definitely see Tyler and me becoming good friends though.

I'm not left to my thoughts much longer. Before I know it the bell rings and everyone else shoots up out of their seats. I don't blame them, I haven't even been listening, but I know the lesson had likely been boring. I look over to see that even Tyler has bolted, I'm the last one heading out the door.

I walk out into the hallway alone and I'm only vaguely aware of all the people. I'm still clumsily trying to shove stuff into my bag. I grab my cell phone while I'm thinking about it and check to see if Hannah has text me. She has! It's a simple message. It says. "I'm bored, find me in the oasis at lunch." I always love how direct and to the point she is, considering she's a girl. I smile to myself while I shove my phone back into my messenger bag. I still have my head down when I turn the corner. I should know better than to look down while walking. I'm so short people tend to not see me coming.

Wham! I hit something solid and start falling backwards. I feel a strong pair of hands grab me at both shoulders before I hit the ground. I'm more than a little embarrassed that I walked right into someone, even more so when I realize that someone has to help steady me upright on my feet.

I keep my gaze down and wait for them to quickly walk around me and say a smart-ass remark. To my surprise it doesn't happen.

"Are you alright?" They ask.

It's definitely not what I expect to hear, and I look up to see blond curly hair and blue eyes. Now I'm beyond embarrassed because my hero is none other than one of Caleb's friends. What I feel now resembles shame to be accurate. Caleb's friend is looking at me with a concerned expression, so I finally remember my words.

"Um...o-of course. Sorry! It was my fault. I wasn't watching where I was going." I stutter.

I really just can't believe my luck. I mean seriously. Can I make a bigger ass of myself? I stand still and think to myself about how I am probably flushing a complete tomato red. Not to mention I'm concerned that he thinks I'm a complete moron.

"Hey, it happens. It isn't your fault. What class are you headed for?" He asks kindly.

"West wing for study hall." I say shyly.

"Perfect. I'll walk you there and warn you of any future obstacles." He says with a smile.

I smile weakly. Awesome, I get to spend the next hour of class living down my clumsiness. His joking nature about our little incident is encouraging though, at least he seems to have a sense of humor and he's not an ass. I had assumed he would be one because of his perfect appearance. I guess today isn't my day for making assumptions about people. I was wrong about Tyler too.

"Sure, thanks." I say happily.

I'll admit that I am still a bit embarrassed and secretly I'm hoping this won't get back to Caleb. I don't want to deal with him thinking I'm a completely uncoordinated dork.

We walk towards the west wing side by side. I glance over at his face and he looks at me with a small smile. His smile makes me feel the remotest amount of unease. It just seems like the type of smile you give someone when you know a big secret about them. We continue in silence all the way to the classroom. When we enter the room, there is only one table left.

Study hall consists of a series of circular desks surrounded by six chairs each. It appears that chairs have been moved from the empty table though leaving only two. We both head for the empty chairs and sit down. I remove my bag and pull out a notebook and a pencil. I'm not sure what I'm going to work on, but I'll think of something.

"So, how does study hall work here?" Xander asks me.

"Well basically, you can do whatever you want for the hour. A teacher pops in every ten minutes or so to make sure we are all behaving, but that's pretty much it." I reply.

"Really, that's pretty sweet." He says.

It occurs to me that every other school might do their study halls differently. Although, I sort of suspect that he's just trying to make friendly conversation. It's good to know that our hallway collision hasn't scared him into not speaking to me.

"I'm Xander by the way." He says introducing himself.

I reach out courageously and he takes my hand in an introduction.

"Rose. I remember seeing you this morning with Caleb." I say before I begin to flush.

I shake his hand timidly. I'm already uncomfortable with the amount of eye contact I've had today. I'm almost to the point of feeling jumpy and anxious, which I'm hoping will pass before I meet up with Caleb after school. I've got this sensation in the pit of my stomach that makes me think Xander is going to become a large and familiar part of my life. Not in the boyfriend kind of way but in the friend that I can trust sort of way. I don't really like the thought of having so many close friends. It will make me feel vulnerable and readable, but Hannah would remind me that's not a bad thing. I think the first day of school has my nerves slightly rattled and that's all, nothing more. *So I hope!*

I realize that even though there has been a substantial amount of silence between Xander and me, at no point is it one of those awkward moments. In fact, I find that just his company is enjoyable without being verbal. I don't know why, and I don't have the time to consider the answer either.

"So Rose, what do you normally spend study hall doing?" Xander asks in a friendly tone.

"Well, when I'm not immersed in a conversation with someone, which I'm usually not. I find this is a good time to organize my thoughts and occasionally my homework." I say.

I smile at him as I say the last part because I don't think I've ever finished my homework in study hall. I certainly have no intention of explaining to him that my current thoughts involve his super sexy friend. That would just be awkward and weird. There is a look in his eyes though that assures me that if I want to talk about anything, I can with him. Maybe he'll even believe that I'm not crazy, though I begin to doubt my sanity more every day. That's not a risk I'm willing to take today.

I watch Xander shift uneasily in his seat, but he is still angled towards me in an attempt to engage me in conversation it seems. I shift my body towards him to demonstrate that he has my full attention. *I do know my manners!*

"So, Caleb tells me that you two have a report to write after school." He says.

"Yes, we do. It's for chemistry, he chose silver." I ramble nervously.

I don't know why I'm boring this poor guy with all the details. It just kind of came out. *God!* He probably already knows anyway. It's a reflex action of mine to keep talking when I'm nervous. I end up rambling a lot. He looks at me for a long hard minute and then excuses himself.

I'd say he's strange but compared to me he seems normal. I watch as he leaves the room, and I glance over at his books. On the very top sits a small book in a brown leather binding. It looks old and worn but at the same time it looks familiar. I feel almost like I've seen it before, but I can't for the life of me remember where. I run my fingers over the cover and am mesmerized by the feel of the cool leather against my skin. There's no writing on the cover, just indents that form a symbol that I'm sure I have seen somewhere. I can't figure out what the symbol is though. My hand is about halfway across the cover again when a warm hand comes down on my wrist. It's Xander. He came back in the room and I didn't even notice because I was too busy being rude and nosy. My behavior is inappropriate, and I know it despite the fact that I was trying to decipher the symbol. He keeps his hand firmly on my wrist without hurting me as he takes his seat. He slowly releases my wrist which I reflexively pull back.

"I'm so sorry Xander, it just looks so interesting." I say through my embarrassment.

I apologize sincerely to him and automatically my face tilts to the ground. I'm embarrassed with my behavior but almost uncontrollably interested in why he reacted the way he did. It's almost as though he has something to hide! However, it's usually not like me to snoop through other people's belongings.

"It's alright. No harm done, it's just a book." He says easily.

Although he says it's not a big deal, I can see him watching me out of the corner of his eye. He seems as fascinated with this situation as I am. Unlike my uncomfortable chemistry class with Caleb, my study hall incident flies by. Before I know it, class is over and I'm almost sad to say goodbye to Xander. As the bell rings, I half expect him to take off running from me, but he doesn't. Instead he waits patiently while I collect my belongings before we leave.

We set off down the hall towards the oasis together. It's lunch time which means I can finally sit down with Hannah. I'm hoping she's not being swarmed by her followers when I find her. She usually herds them away at lunch and makes it our special time instead. Xander continues to walk with me as I consider my reunion with my bestie. It dawns on me that perhaps he has no one to sit with at lunch and I don't want to be inconsiderate.

"Xander, I'm meeting Hannah in the oasis, you're welcome to join us." I say politely.

"Well, I've got to meet up with Caleb and Jason, but I'll see what they're up to and maybe we'll meet you there." He says with a smile.

"Sure." I say.

I'm a little astonished that I had the nerve to invite him. I only hope he doesn't think I'm trying to use him to get closer to Caleb because that isn't my intention. I will be perfectly happy if Xander comes alone. Though seeing Caleb again will also make me happy.

I assume Jason is the other guy who had been with Caleb this morning, it's the process of elimination. Either way it seems like Hannah and I might end up with some company.

I walk down yet another hall and venture through the double doors. I pause briefly and look around. I catch a glimpse of Hannah sitting alone at a large table in the middle of the room. It's fairly crowded in the oasis for lunch, but I slowly and carefully make my way to her table. I sit down across from her and give an exaggerated sigh. I slip my bag off my shoulder and let it drop to the floor. I'm ecstatic to see she's already got some fries waiting for me, I wasn't looking forward to waiting in line. She smiles at me as I scarf down my fries.

"God Rose, it took you long enough. I was starting to think you were going to stand me up." She says jokingly.

"Hannah, I would never do that!" I say.

I speak through my mouthful of fries which makes us both giggle. I am surprisingly very hungry, but I know the way I am eating isn't very attractive. I start nibbling at my food just in case someone is watching. Hannah immediately bombards me with ramblings of hot guys and complaints about homework. I am listening intently when she stops speaking abruptly. Interested in what has caused her sudden silence, I look around to see Caleb crossing the cafeteria with his gaze set on us. He is flanked of course by his two equally attractive guy friends. They stop beside our table and show us warm smiles.

"I've been told that you lovely ladies invited us to lunch." Caleb says charmingly.

Caleb's voice sounds so smooth and confident that it almost seems pointless to reply with an answer. Before I can make any welcoming gesture though, Hannah beats me to it. She gestures to the empty seats at our table and the excitement is obvious on her face. Caleb's sits on my right while Xander sits on my left, and Jason sits next to Hannah which seems to make them both content.

"Thank you for the invite ladies!" Caleb says.

Although his "thank you" is implied to both of us, he doesn't take his eyes off of me. It makes me nervous and excited at the same time. Xander likely told him it was me who invited them to lunch.

"No problem." I say.

I try my best to sound unimpressed and alluring but it probably didn't come out the way I wanted it to. I blush a little under the heat of his gaze, Hannah is looking at me with a satisfied smirk. I finally realize that despite all of our friendliness and conversation, its good manners to introduce everyone.

"So, I don't know if everyone has met, but I'm Rose and this is Hannah." I say.

"It seems your manners are better than mine Rose. I'm Caleb, that's Xander and that's Jason. I didn't mean to be rude." Caleb says apologetically.

He points to each of the guys as he says their names and it confirms what I thought. Hannah immediately goes back into a private conversation. If I didn't know any better, I'd say there is something between Hannah and Jason. Their facial expressions say it all. Xander is silently observing everyone and Caleb engages me in conversation.

It turns out that Hannah has physics with these guys while I have history. I definitely got the sour end of that deal. From my own observations, it seems like the guys haven't spoken to Hannah though until now. So, I feel better in a selfish, guilty kind of way. I also think that with the way the guys are talking to us, makes it seem like they're under the impression that we'll be hanging out on a regular basis. Not that I mind, but the idea of seeing Caleb frequently makes me feel flustered and winded. Perhaps being around him more will help me get over these feelings. I can see myself being happy in our little group, it's different but awesome. I really feel like I belong, and I didn't think I'd ever have this.

CHAPTER TWELVE

Rose

The bell rings throughout the school, signaling the end of lunch. Slowly and reluctantly we all rise from our seats, our gathering is officially over. The oasis quickly begins to empty as students hurry off to their classes. Xander looks over to me with an expectant look before speaking.

"I'm guessing you have French next?" Xander says.

"Well actually I do!" I say surprised. "How did you know?" I ask.

"Lucky guess, so do I!" He says, pleased with himself.

Of course, I don't believe it was purely a lucky guess on his part but at the moment, there are no better solutions. It seems to me that someone may have taken a peek at my class schedule at some point. Either way I'm enjoying Xander's company more than I would have expected. I even find his silence calming.

Xander leads the way and I follow closely behind him, which seems odd to me considering he is the new student. Just as we reach the double doors leading to the hallway Caleb sneaks up behind us.

"Don't forget Rose, meet me at my car after school." Caleb says while flashing me a heart melting smile.

I nod at him to acknowledge that I will remember. Caleb speaks in such a serious tone and gives a careful glance at Xander. I only somewhat see the exchange in my peripheral's because I take the opportunity to smile a "goodbye" to Hannah as she departs. Although everything is a bit strange, Xander and I head towards French class.

He looks over at me, gives me a slight smile and continues walking. It almost makes me think that Xander is actually trying to communicate with me through a smile. I'm positive that I am simply reading too much into his silence. The idea of non-verbal communication is as impossible and as far-fetched as Hannah saying I'm psychic.

Xander is completely silent until we arrive at the classroom door, which

71

is well out of hearing distance from anyone.

"Ladies first!" He says.

Xander gestures me through to pick the seats, and I oblige him.

"Thank you!" I say, blushing.

We sit together at the back of the room, but we don't speak during the teachers' ramblings. I can still feel him watching me out of the corner of his eye. Strangely it doesn't bother me this time though, although it does arouse my curiosity. It just seems like Xander's normal behavior.

French class is a blur and quickly comes to an end, we've hardly had any real time to whisper to each other. The French teacher was very observant and wanted all questions spoken in French. Needless to say, I am more than happy that class is over.

As I pick up my books, I discover that we have Spanish together next, as well as Caleb and Jason. I'm psyched to finally have a class with all of the guys. Plus, this means that I don't have to walk awkwardly to Caleb's car after school. We head back down the crowded hallway, side by side.

When we enter the Spanish room, I notice Caleb and Jason are already sitting at two tables. They are saving seats for us and it's kind of flattering. I automatically take the seat next to Caleb, who doesn't seem surprised by my actions. I watch Xander take his seat next to Jason before I turn to my own desk partner. Caleb smiles at me and I nervously return the gesture.

"So Xander mentioned that the two of you had an interesting study hall?" Caleb says.

Caleb lifts an eyebrow at me as he talks and I instantly blush. I am once again embarrassed for my rude behaviour earlier today.

"Oh no, he told you. I don't know what happened. My manners just totally went out the window." I say guiltily.

"Don't worry, you didn't offend him or anything. You simply caught him off guard. That book is like a journal to him, and he didn't think you'd take interest in it if it was sitting there. He blames himself." Caleb says apologetically.

"I didn't mean for him to feel bad. I am just overly curious for my own good. It's something I've got to work on." I say with a nervous giggle.

"Not to worry. He's over it. Oh, by the way, I hope it's alright, but I explained to Hannah that I'll be driving you home today." He says confidently.

I do my best to give a smile but all I keep thinking about is that damn book now. What could possibly be in there that is such a secret?

I'm grateful that I don't need to tell Hannah that I'm getting a ride home with Caleb. I don't know, there is something eerie about the way these guys seem to have everything planned out to the second. Or maybe it's finally happening. I'm becoming my brother, distrustful and paranoid. Whatever the reason, it does feel strange knowing I'm going to ride with some guy I barely know. I'm beginning to wonder if I'm making a very wise choice. Oh well, I'll deal.

The teacher quickly comes in and immediately starts speaking in Spanish. Everyone falls silent and listens closely, not that it matters. I along with most of the class have no clue what she just said. The teacher stops speaking in Spanish long enough to explain that we'll be starting with the Latin American version of Spanish. I can't help but notice that Caleb, Xander, and Jason seem completely at ease listening to the other language. It also becomes uncomfortably clear that the guys are not only familiar with the language but fluent. I'm pleasantly surprised and I realize that I have once again judged the guys based on their physical appearance. I'm the last person that should make superficial judgments, stereotypes are almost always wrong.

While I contemplate my thoughts, the teacher puts up an overhead with different Latin symbols. I immediately recognize one symbol and I almost choke on my tongue. It's the same symbol that is on the cover of Xander's journal. I'll never forget the star symbol with seven points. *Never!* Under the symbol it says "veneficus navitas typicus" which isn't English, obviously. It doesn't state what it means in English, and the teacher isn't translating it for us. I know what this means. I'm going to have to translate it myself at some point. I can't very well ask the teacher about it with the guys in the class. I quickly scribble down the Latin scripture and stash it in my pocket so I can research it later.

About halfway through the class I start thinking about what Caleb said, and it occurs to me that there is no way he could have known about the study hall incident. At least I didn't see any cell phones going off, and I had only been separated from Xander for less than five minutes. *Weird!*

I find myself slightly concerned. What have I gotten myself into with these guys? I don't understand how these guys can possibly communicate so efficiently in secrecy. This mystery truly bothers me but the longer I dwell on it, the less it makes sense. I give up finally, just in time for the bell to ring. Caleb waits beside me and when I leave the room, he's at my side and Xander and Jason are behind us. We all make our way through the halls towards the parking lot. I can't help but notice that the other students leave a wide berth for the guys, no one even comes close to shouldering them. Even popularity doesn't earn the teen royalty this kind of respect, the guys automatically receive it.

It's different that the four of us walk in utter silence and I don't even feel the need to be verbal. We're all content just being in each other's presence, speaking isn't needed. However, right now I have so many questions that it's hard to enjoy the quiet. When we approach the vehicles Xander and Jason split off and climb into their Cadillac without more than a wave. Caleb moves ahead of me and stands with the passenger door of the Mercedes held open. I nervously climb in and while he gently closes the door I hesitantly buckle up. *There's no turning back now!*

Caleb smoothly climbs into the driver's seat and it's as though he was made for this car. He backs up and we start to leave. I see Hannah walking towards her car, and she smiles and waves excitedly at me. The windows are so tinted though that waving back seems pointless. With that we are speeding towards my house, as I direct him at turns.

A strange feeling falls over me as we race closer to my home. It's not foreboding but it's almost like a warning. I remember that Alex will still be at work and we will be totally isolated, my anxiety mounts. Suddenly, we're pulling into the driveway and he parks in front of my creepy, old house. I know then for certain that things are about to change drastically, I can feel it. I feel compelled to tell Caleb everything and accept him into my life. My desire for Alex's understanding has never even been this strong.

Before I know it, he is out of the car and at my door in the blink of an eye. *Well this is it!*

CHAPTER THIRTEEN

Rose

The passenger door gently swings open and Caleb stands there with an incredibly brilliant smile. He stretches out his hand to help me from my seat and I take it gladly. His skin is smooth, warm and his touch seems to tingle on my skin. As my hand slides along his so easily he grips my hand gently but firmly. He practically lifts me out of the seat and then all I can think about is how strong he is. I feel like a delicate little princess the way he's acting with me and it's kind of nice.

We walk up to the porch and he follows me up the steps. Just as I reach for the door, I feel his hand on my foreman and he spins me to face him. I spin so fast that I get a bit wobbly and he uses both hands to brace me. I notice how hard my heart is pounding while his hands rest on my arms and I hope he doesn't notice. The way he looks at me makes me feel like he already knows me. As I look directly into his eyes, I swear I see a silver flame flicker through his eyes, but it can't be possible. I am reminded, once again, of the cemetery boy but that couldn't have been real. I keep looking into his eyes but all I can see is their usual gray beauty.

"Rose, I have a confession to make. I finished our report during my free period." Caleb says guiltily.

I'd be lying to say I wasn't confused because if he's already written our report then I don't know why he bothered to drive me home. He must have ulterior motives. I just need to find out what they are. Even before I speak, I know it's going to come out sounding childlike and afraid.

"Oh…um…I guess I should say thank you!" I stutter. "So, if you already wrote the report, why did you bring me home?" I ask nervously.

I don't know if I really want to hear his answer because secretly, I want him to want to hang out with me. Unfortunately, there's always a chance he will tell me that he didn't want to be an ass and break our plans.

"Well, to be honest I figured since we're going to be lab partners, we should get better acquainted. I hope that's alright?" He says smoothly.

Ok so I'm doing my best to not jump up and down in front of him because I think that would make me seem a bit eager. I'm slightly caught off guard though because it sounds as though he's a bit shy when it comes to personal matters. A guy like him constantly exudes confidence and he seems almost vulnerable at the moment.

"Sure!" I say, trying to keep my voice calm and casual.

That's all I can come up with to say. I can't think of anything else that will make me seem mysterious and alluring. What do you say when the most incredibly gorgeous and charming guy asks to hang out with you, all the while still holding your arm?

I feel the heat begin to rush to my cheeks, I've been blushing an awful lot today. The heat is starting to feel normal but just when I think I'll have to turn away, like a prince he saves me.

He releases my hand and I take the opportunity to lead him inside. The way I see it, I have two hours to get to know this guy before Alex gets home and ruins the party. God only knows how Alex will react when he sees him. Not only that but Morgan could come in at any second, he's already late.

Caleb follows me into the living room while looking around appreciatively. I try to remember that since I'm the host I should at least try to act like it, even though it's kind of new to me.

"Um Caleb, can I get you anything to drink?" I ask lamely.

"Sure...I'll take a coke if you have one!" He says automatically.

"Absolutely, I'll just be a minute. Make yourself at home!" I say.

I turn and go back out towards the kitchen. I have no idea what I am doing! The only guy who ever comes to visit me is Morgan, and he walks around like he owns the place. *Oh god...Morgan. What am I doing?*

Morgan and I are supposed to be just friends but after the whole couch incident it feels like things are different. I may not be a genius, but we seemed to be getting closer. I mean we fell asleep cuddling on the couch together. What will happen with us now? I can't imagine that he will want Caleb around. The thing is Morgan and me, it's well...complicated. We're best friends and despite what I have been feeling for him, I don't know if I am prepared to risk our friendship over it. Hell, can I really know that Morgan is interested in me? *It's so confusing.*

Plus, there is just something that draws me to Caleb. I can't help it! When I look in his eyes it feels like everything makes sense for a change, like he's been a part of my life longer than I can remember. I know how strange this sounds but I feel like my life is meant to be something else and Caleb is the way for me to find it. I've never really believed in fate but maybe it's real.

I try to pull myself together. Right now is a really bad time for me to fall apart. I realize I have been staring into an open fridge because I was so deep in thought. A few minutes have actually gone by, so I grab two cokes, and head back to my guest.

"Hey there you are! I was beginning to think someone had taken you." Caleb says jokingly.

Although I'm sure Caleb didn't actually mean it seriously, I had a flash back to the voice I'd heard in the bathroom. He doesn't know how accurate his playful, harmless joke could be.

"Sorry about that! I had to find them. My brother likes to hide them on me." I say nervously as I hand him a can.

Maybe it's a completely lame excuse but hopefully he'll buy it. I don't want him to know that I was actually standing around frozen in thought because well…That will make me seem a bit unstable. It's just not normal. And more than anything right now, I just want to be normal.

"No problem. I'm quite comfortable. I put in a movie for us to watch." He says.

"Oh ok." I say as I take a seat.

I focus on the television to see which movie he has put on. It's the Covenant. It just happens to be my favourite movie, so I can't help but smile. Immediately I am impressed with his taste in movies. More important than our movie is our seating situation though. I have sat down near him but not close enough to say, "I'll do anything you want." Somehow every few minutes he manages to get an inch closer to me without being obvious.

Halfway through the movie we are side by side with our legs touching. He has his one arm stretched out on the back of the couch behind me, and his other around his drink. He appears to be totally comfortable and at ease. *I'm the exact opposite!* I've never been this close to someone like him. It makes my heart race and I feel very girly. I love the fact that we're smiling at the same parts and more so when we glance at each other. When he smiles his eyes light up and he shows off his perfectly straight and white teeth. *It's incredibly attractive!*

Near the end of the movie I start to relax, then I tense up again because I hear a terrifying noise. The sound of Alex's '67 Camaro is coming up the driveway.

He's home early and unless he's blind, he can see the black Mercedes in the driveway. I freeze up because I know if I move away from Caleb, he will think I am a complete dork. If Alex finds us sitting so close, he will kill us both. *Crap!* What a predicament! I hear the front door slam shut and in walks Alex. He follows the sound into the living room and stands in the entrance staring at us. I'm so nervous I feel like I'm going to pass out, but Caleb is calm, like this happens to him every day. I certainly hope he isn't that experienced with girls.

"Alex, you're home early!" I say in a timid voice.

You can hear the fear in my voice, and it just makes me sound guilty.

"Yeah I am. Who are you?" Alex asks curtly.

Alex doesn't hesitate in switching his attention to the male intruder. I can tell that he isn't impressed about my surprise company. There is really nothing I can do about it now though. I just hope Caleb can handle being in the spotlight.

Caleb smoothly gets up and walks around the couch to shake hands with Alex, all the while flashing an innocent grin. He's either very clever or very stupid to be so bold. He is voluntarily putting himself in front of my crazy, over-protective brother.

"Hi, I'm Caleb. I assume you're Rose's brother Alex. It's a pleasure to meet you!" Caleb says casually.

I'm astonished with the way Caleb carries himself, like he knows he doesn't owe anyone anything. He just seems so sure and comfortable with his actions.

"Ok! What are you guys doing?" Alex asks suspiciously.

I know that Alex still doesn't trust Caleb, but he briefly glances at me for an answer.

"Well, we were just watching a movie." I say shakily.

I answer him but I'm hoping he will return his gaze to Caleb. I still think it's possible that Alex will get physical with Caleb. Instead they stand there staring at each other for several seconds. Finally, Alex caves and breaks the silence.

"Well Caleb, will you be joining us for dinner?" Alex asks resentfully.

I can't believe it. I thought for sure Alex was going to ask him to leave but instead he invites him to dinner. *Weird!* Not that I mind but it's just strange. I will never understand male behaviour.

"I'd be honoured to stay. Thank you for the invitation!" Caleb says charmingly.

The next thing I know Caleb is back sitting really close to me again and Alex has walked off to shower and make dinner. I don't understand what just happened between them. It seemed like some sort of idiotic male domination, bonding thing or something. I guess I may as well enjoy it while it lasts. Caleb and I finish watching our movie.

Somewhere into an episode of Family Guy Alex yells out that dinner is ready. Both Caleb and I get up and head to the kitchen. Something tells me this is going to be one of the most awkward meals of my life. I just hope I can handle this.

I sit down at the side of the table and Caleb chooses to sit directly across from Alex. It reminds me of watching the discovery channel. You know the show where two male animals compete for dominance and neither wants to back down. However, the show always results in blood being spilt and I hope that doesn't happen here.

I hear Alex clear his throat and I know what's coming, the dreadful interrogation. I don't think I can watch Caleb go through this, so I get lost in my own thoughts. It's the only other option that will allow me to keep my sanity. Besides Caleb seems to know what he's doing. He will be better off without me paying attention.

Later, I am definitely going to have strong words with Alex and his rude behaviour. He has no right to treat my guests this way. Male or female! I mean it's not like he's the boss of me, even though he is my legal guardian.

Alex

"So, Caleb, you attend Grace Hall with Rose?" I ask.

I don't know this Caleb character, but I already don't like him or his expensive car. Not to mention I really don't like his interest in my little sister. I don't know if it's because I am her big brother or if deep down, I know he might mean her harm. Either way I have to find out more. To be honest I would have pegged the guy to be my age if not older, but definitely not a high school student.

"Yes, I do. In fact, my housemates do too. We transferred here from the states." He says.

"Oh really. From where?" I ask nosily.

"A small private school in Salem!" He replies.

As soon as Caleb says where he's from, my worst fears are confirmed. I know it can't be a coincidence because not many people come out of Salem. *At least not humans!* I notice too late that I am staring at him with my mouth slightly open. Caleb absolutely noticed. Judging from the look in his eyes, my reaction has merely confirmed his suspicions. I see him glance briefly at Rose, who isn't paying any attention to the conversation. I'd fight him right now if he hadn't of looked at her. But in his eyes, I see understanding and compassion. Is it possible he's not a threat to her? Perhaps this is one giant coincidence, but I doubt it!

"Alex...Forgive me but it looks like you have concerns about Salem?" He questions me.

I can't let on to this Caleb guy about Rose any more than I already have. Despite what I think I saw in his eyes. He could be after her. I can't just accuse him of it though, so I am going to have to tread carefully.

"No. Well...Other than the fact that it seems like quite a long transfer for boys your age. I have heard about the unsolved murders and missing people. Salem appears to have several issues right now." I say calmly.

"I see. We have been emancipated you could say, for a long time now. As for the mysterious crimes, you can understand why we left!" He states it as a matter of fact.

I don't care what he says because I don't trust him one bit. The fact that he's here with friends and no parents is unsettling. Not to mention it's too convenient for them. There is something wrong with the way he looks answering all of my questions. He either has something he's trying to hide, or he figures he can handle us if we discover something that he would rather keep secret. I wish Morgan were here because he'd know immediately if this Caleb is just a hormonal teenager or if he's something more.

Morgan will have to look into it later.

Rose

When I finally tune back into dinner, I notice that it's strangely quiet. The guys make eye contact occasionally but that's about it. I almost wish I had been listening to their conversation, maybe then I'd know what's going on. It's like a sinking ship though, you can't bear to watch when there's nothing you can do but you can't look away. That is the story of my life, one embarrassing disaster after another with no way to avoid it.

Dinner ends thankfully and Alex starts cleaning up. I catch him watching us at the table though and I'm considering asking Caleb to a different room.

"Rose, thank you for dinner but I should be going." Caleb says sweetly.

Well, so much for my other room idea. I'm a bit disappointed but he did hold out against my brother's third degree, so that's a good sign. He probably just has things to do. *Hopefully!*

"Oh, of course! I'll walk you out." I say politely.

I can feel Alex's eyes on us as we leave the kitchen, but he doesn't say anything to embarrass me, thank god!

When we walk to the front door, he opens it and gestures for me to step out with him. So, I do! As soon as we are alone on the porch with the door closed for privacy, Caleb turns and looks at me with those captivating gray eyes of his.

"I had a really good time Rose. I hope we can do it again!" He says.

His words seem truly sincere but it's hard to believe. I mean Alex gave him the third degree and I barely said two words during dinner. Then again, what reason would he have for lying?

"I'm glad, so did I!" I say.

I'm still contemplating our evening in my head when I feel his hand grab mine. He brings my hand up to his lips and places a very delicate kiss on the backside. He even bows slightly, it's totally a fairy tale moment. His touch leaves a tingling sensation once again and warmth where his lips were. Naturally I blush, again. *Surprise, surprise!* He smiles at me with his eyes which seem to sparkle in the sunset.

"I'll be seeing you soon I hope!" He says seriously.

He gives me a smile and releases my hand. I know he can tell that he has me flustered and he seems to be enjoying it. He heads down the steps to his car and all I can do is watch. I give him a goofy smile as he pulls out of the driveway, but I still just stand there. It's as though my brain is taking a vacation. It's been such an exciting night that I'm sad to see it end. Caleb seems so complex and interesting and let's face it, he's fun to look at! I realize that is a shallow thought but there is nothing wrong with finding someone physically appealing. I mean shit! Most teenage romances are based solely on attraction.

I finally come back to reality to see that Caleb is gone and I'm actually really cold right now. I know I should probably go in, but I don't want to. I'm not ready for Caleb to be gone, it feels like we never really had any alone time. It's strange but I feel a very strong connection to him and it's hard to ignore. *Oh well.* My time is up, and I have to go back inside and face the warden, which is my older brother. I will definitely be seeing Caleb again.

CHAPTER FOURTEEN

Rose

The second I reach out for the door handle my beautiful evening is shattered. I barely get to grab the handle before it swings open from the inside. It appears that Alex was spying the whole time and now he's standing staring at me with aggravation.

"What?" I say slightly annoyed.

I try to face him with as much attitude as I can, even though on the inside I'm still smiling. I figure playing stupid is my best course of action.

"What do you mean what? You're letting a guy you've known for one day, touch you!" Alex says angrily.

I can tell that Alex is definitely pissed off, but I also detect a hint of embarrassment. More than likely it's because we're arguing about a guy touching me and this is new to both of us.

"Oh my god Alex! All he did was kiss the back of my hand. It's not like we were feeling each other up. Besides, it's not like you weren't my age before you slept with someone anyway. I mean is it that awful to think that someone is attracted to me. I'm not a little kid anymore." I say defensively.

I'm not faking the attitude now. It really enrages me when he thinks he can raise me anyway he wants. I'm his sister not his child and he needs to accept that he can't protect me from life. Besides I feel the need to defend Caleb's character because he was nothing but a gentleman tonight.

"Well what about Morgan? How's he going to feel about this? He's going to think you were leading him on until something better came up. That kind of makes you a tease!" He says.

"Whoa! First of all, Morgan and I are friends and we're not together. So I haven't done anything wrong. Secondly, my romantic life is not going to revolve around the guy you choose, ok? I get that you and Morgan have become really good friends, but you haven't even stopped to consider my feelings. I'm not going to be with someone just because you approve of them. And thirdly, my love life really is none of your business, so back off!" I scream at him.

Alex stands there staring at me after my rant. I have never yelled at him like this before, and he seems just as shocked as I am. I don't wait for his retaliation though. I storm off up the stairs and slam my bedroom door behind me. I hope he gets the message to leave me alone the rest of the night.

I sit on the end of my bed and stare out the window. My problem is that I like Morgan, a lot. He's been my best friend since we were kids. I'm pretty sure he spends more time at our house than he does his own. Morgan means a lot to me but then there's this new guy, Caleb. There is just something about him. I don't think I believe in the whole destiny thing but when he's with me it just feels right somehow. I have a huge desire to know him if nothing else.

I know I'm going to have to wait and see what happens with both guys, after all, it's not like I am committed to either of them yet. I just hope I haven't been leading either of them on, I don't need to dig myself a hole because dating is already so complicated.

There is nothing I can do about it now. I may as well let the issue go for now and get some sleep. I change into a tank top and shorts and climb into bed. I snuggle into my pillows and I know I am going to dream of Caleb and Morgan tonight. I can't wait to tell Hannah about Caleb though. I end up just rolling around in the bed because I am too wound up to sleep.

I'm on the verge of sleep but I don't want to keep my eyes closed. I was listening when Alex had rooted around and got ready for bed. I look over at my clock and it says eleven fifteen, which means that Alex went to bed almost two hours ago. Yet I still find myself restless and unable to let the dreams wash over me.

As I continue to lie in bed, I hear this strange "tap, tap" sound coming from my window. I turn on my lamp to go check it out. When I get to the window, I open it so I can peer out. I know it seems a bit risky given the past events, but I just can't contain my curiosity. When I lean out and look down my eyes adjust to the dark and I see a familiar face.

"Caleb, what are you doing here?" I say surprised.

I glance in the driveway and see the sheen off his black Mercedes sitting silently. I am shocked and anxious at the same time. Truth be told I can't stop thinking about him, and I am thrilled that he is standing below my window smiling up at me. I smile a big smile back at him as my body trembles slightly from nervousness.

"I was in the neighborhood and thought I'd come for a visit. Can I come up?" He asks.

He's so polite for asking and of course I want him to, but I don't know if it can be done. At least, not without Alex waking up.

"I don't know if I can sneak you in, Alex might wake up if I come downstairs." I say sadly.

I'm trying to keep my voice down as it is, but I want him to know I want him to come up. I'm sure he can hear the disappointment in my voice.

"If you want me to come up, I can climb up but you're going to have to move back." He says confidently.

"Ok. If you think you can get up here." I say with a disbelieving tone.

I love that he's so determined to get up here with me, but I don't know how he is going to do it. I back up anyway and go to my dresser mirror. I figure I have time to make sure I look alright before he gets up here.

I'm checking my tank top and shorts when I hear a small shuffle behind me. I turn around and Caleb is already climbing through the window smiling at me. He looks completely unfazed by the climb and for some reason that troubles me. It doesn't seem right.

"Who are you?" I say with curiosity and amusement.

I asked him in a playful way but now that he is walking towards me, I would like an answer.

"I thought we already covered introductions." He says smoothly.

He raises one eyebrow and gives me a mischievous smile. He stops mere feet from me and grabs my hand. My heart starts to race in anticipation of the tingle as he brings my hand to his lips. He places a delicate kiss on my hand and even when he lets go the tingle still lingers. I feel the warmth rise from my chest and plant itself on my cheeks. How can I not blush though? I feel like Juliet in "Romeo and Juliet", a classic love story that every girl wants to be a part of.

"I told you I'd be seeing you soon!" He says smugly.

He says it as though he's daring me to contradict him. I watch as he walks over and stretches out on my bed. He tucks his arms behind his head, and he looks entirely at home. Instantly I become scared. After all, I don't know what he expects from me but hopefully it's not what most boys want. I stand there holding my arms looking like a frightened child."

"You can come sit with me Rose, it's alright. I won't bite…yet!" He says jokingly.

He smiles hard to himself as if he alone knows a funny secret. I realize that if worst comes to worst, I can always scream for Alex. I slowly move to sit next to him, and he remains sprawled out without a sign of concern.

"So Caleb, what are you doing here?" I ask calmly.

I'm not trying to be rude. I just have to ask. I don't buy the whole in the neighborhood bit.

"Honestly? I couldn't stop thinking about you and I had to see you!" He says sincerely.

He blushes a very small amount and it occurs to me that this boy is completely into me. I am flattered and surprised because I am totally infatuated with this boy too. He even makes me feel attractive in my pajamas.

"Forgive me Rose, I don't mean to come on too strong. I'm just impulsive and I couldn't wait to see you tomorrow!" He says sweetly.

I'm charmed that he has such strong feelings for me, but it also alarms me because we have known each other for less than a day. Then again, I haven't been able to stop thinking about Caleb either. And secretly I'm ecstatic that he has taken the risk to come see me.

"That's really sweet Caleb. To be honest I've been thinking about you too." I say shyly.

I feel flustered. Nervous and excited at the same time. But I take a seat next to him on my bed. I give a shy smile and find myself quickly looking away from his beautiful gray eyes. He's watching me closely, trying to read my every move. I'm still not sure where exactly this chat is going but he isn't acting like he wants in my pants. So, I figure I am safe.

"So why are you still up? You don't look like you've been sleeping well?" He asks.

I don't really know how much I can tell him, but I figure "what the hell?" I need to tell someone before I go crazy.

"Well at the risk of sounding like a lunatic, I suppose telling you won't hurt." I say timidly.

Caleb props his head up on one arm and gives me his utmost attention. It's almost hard to speak with the weight of his gaze on me in such concentration.

"Truth is Caleb, I haven't been sleeping well. I have had a lot of weird things happening to me in the last two weeks." I say cautiously.

I absolutely refuse to go too in depth with my story.

"I hope you don't mind me asking but what kind of weird things?" He asks.

He appears to be genuinely interested in my problems rather than freaked out, but I don't really know how mentally stable Caleb is either. After all, he did climb in my window.

"Ok well, I've been hearing threatening voices, and I thought I saw someone at the cemetery before I fell down, but what I think I saw isn't humanly possible. I think I might be losing my mind." I say, feeling depressed.

I can't believe I'm telling him all of this. I haven't even told Morgan or Alex. Here is this drop-dead gorgeous guy in my room, and I'll be lucky if I haven't just scared him away.

"Rose, I doubt you're losing your mind. Perhaps the things that you can't believe have actually happened. What if what you've seen is real?" He asks curiously.

"It's nice that you don't think I'm crazy Caleb, but you haven't heard or seen what I have. Everything is just too inconceivable to be true." I say bluntly.

I like that he is on my side, but I really think everything is too absurd to have taken place. I want so badly to believe that I'm not going batty, but it seems like the only logical reason. It's as though he can read my mind and is trying to comfort me.

"You know Rose, sometimes things occur that can't be explained by logic or reason but that doesn't mean it's not real." He says thoughtfully.

I merely smile and give a small nod. I hadn't planned on him sticking around, I thought he'd have already cleared my window after hearing everything. We're both silent for a minute lost in our own thoughts.

"Rose, can I ask you something?" He says.

"Well you just did. But go ahead." I say smartly.

I can't help but smile at my own witty comment. Though it doesn't seem to have phased the seriousness of Caleb's attitude other than him having a small smile. I have become exceedingly comfortable talking to him.

"Do you believe in fate?" He asks.

I'm considerably caught off guard by his question, but I give serious consideration to my response.

"I guess I do to a certain extent, but it's also kind of a scary concept that our lives are beyond our control. I guess it can also be encouraging to be part of a greater plan than our own. Why do you ask? Do you?" I ask shyly.

"Absolutely, I think it's satisfying to know that you will be included in life no matter who you are." He says without hesitation.

I think about this for a long time, and finally he asks me some brainless questions about my family and friends. I don't get around to asking him because we moved around, and now I am lying on his chest trying not to make it a big deal. I begin to feel myself drift into sleep as the pauses between his questions become longer. I don't remember much except being in a dream. It includes the pond that I cherish so much, and strangely enough the eyes I had seen in the tree line turned out to be Caleb. It's nonsense of course.

I assume he is taking over my conscious and subconscious mind, and speculate it is nothing more than that. I think he would have told me if he'd been watching me. With that thought implanted in my brain, I drift off into a deep sleep where I don't dream anymore. Even in sleep I'm aware of the warm body beside me. He's so still, almost as though he isn't breathing. I feel the heat radiating from him and I smile in my sleep. I feel like I can handle anything that comes my way, as long as Caleb is with me.

CHAPTER FIFTEEN

Rose

I wake up with the sun shining through the window. I sit up in bed and look beside me. Caleb has obviously snuck back out the window sometime after I fell asleep. There's also no sign that Alex is aware of my late-night visitor. In fact, I wouldn't even know Caleb had actually been here if it wasn't for the fact that my window was open, letting in the morning cold. I walk over to close the window and I look out, there's not a single cloud in sight. This can only mean it's going to be a great day. *How could it not be?* I am undoubtedly going to see Caleb again and just the thought of him makes me smile.

I go to my mirror and am thrilled to see how compliant my hair is being so all I do is brush it out. I go to the bathroom and brush my teeth then I go back to my room to pick out an outfit that hopefully really turns heads. After half an hour of looking I decide on a pair of dark denim slim fit jeans with a dark purple dressy shirt and my favorite leather jacket. The jacket was a gift for my sixteenth birthday from Alex. It holds more sentimental value to me than any other piece of clothing. It helps that it also looks amazing. I put on my shoes and go back to the bathroom to apply my makeup. I don't often bother with makeup, but I want to look my best for a certain someone. I'm pretty sure I spent most of the night with Caleb, assuming it wasn't all in my head. My hand still remembers the tingle of his touch and kiss, so I know it was real.

I hear my phone buzz from my bedroom and I run back to my room to get it. I look at it and I have two missed texts. The first is from Hannah saying she is going to be late for school, but she doesn't say why. I find it odd but I'm sure she has a good reason. The second is from Morgan saying good morning and that he will pick me up for school because he got Hannah's text too. I guess he's back in town.

Crap! This has to be some sick twisted joke. Either that or god is punishing me for my misdemeanour last night. Morgan is coming to pick me up and I look amazing, but the shitty thing is that I look great for another guy. I wasn't expecting this problem, and to be honest I haven't really thought about what I am going to tell him in the first place. As much as I have been denying it to Alex, there is something developing between me and Morgan.

Well, there's not really anything I can do about it now! I sigh in resignation and grab my messenger pack as I head down the stairs. I drop my bag at the door and go into the kitchen to waste time. On the counter is twenty dollars and a note from Alex. It says "I'm sorry, here's some lunch money. Love Alex." The note is scribbled out like he was in a hurry and he probably was.

I can't smile, I'm still so angry with him but the money is a nice gesture. I pocket the money and hear Morgan's truck coming up the laneway. I hurry back to the door, grab my bag and go out on to the porch. Just as I shut the door, Morgan is getting out of his truck smiling at me. I can't help but smile back, after all its Morgan my best friend, and he looks really good today. He runs up to me and pulls me into a hug. Then he takes my bag and runs it back to the truck. I end up meeting him at the passenger door where we just smile at each other. His smile is bright and gives me a warm-glowy feeling. That's the moment it hits me. I realize then that I have real, more than friends, feelings for him.

"Morgan thanks for picking me up this morning. I hope it wasn't too much trouble. I would have taken the bus if I'd known earlier that Hannah was going to be late." I say guiltily.

"Rose, you know I'd be anywhere for you! It's no trouble at all." He says easily.

He says it with such sincerity it makes me feel guilty for thinking about Caleb. Thinking about Caleb is already hard to do because Morgan really is such an amazing guy. Doesn't it figure that I'd be interested in no guys one minute and two guys the next minute? *Hormones suck!* Just as I'm thinking about this, I come back to reality just in time to realize that Morgan is holding the passenger door open for me.

"Thanks." I say quickly.

I shyly take his offered hand as he helps me into the truck. His hand is warm and familiar, and I feel safe. That's how Morgan makes me feel, safe! However, right now at this point in my life I feel like I need to take a risk. I'm so beyond confused! I don't know what I want or who.

He lets go of my hand and shuts the door, then he quickly comes around and climbs into the driver's seat. He starts the engine and I buckle up. Morgan doesn't, but I am always cautious. Taking a risk is sounding better and better.

We speed away towards the school and in no time at all we're pulling into the parking lot. I haven't spoken the whole way here. Morgan goes to the senior's parking lot and pulls in where there are several empty spots. I quickly look around and start to relax when I see that the Mercedes and the Cadillac aren't here yet. I look over and not surprisingly Morgan is looking back at me with a strange expression.

"Rose are you ok? You didn't say a word all the way here." Morgan asks, confused.

He seems so concerned about me, but really, I have just been holding my breath praying that Caleb and his friends weren't here. I can't exactly tell Morgan that though.

"Yeah, um I'm fine. I just don't want to be late." I say lamely.

"Alright well, do you want me to walk you to class?" He asks kindly.

He's being so sweet, and it sucks because all I want to do is get the hell out of the truck.

"No, I'll be fine." I say quickly.

"Ok well I won't make my classes today, but if Hannah doesn't show, I'll meet you after school then." He says.

I'm being a total bitch, I know. I should just be up front with Morgan and Caleb and see who is still interested in me. I'm not stupid though, neither of them will want me then, and I'm really enjoying the attention for once. I have to do or say something though because Morgan is probably hurt. I'm definitely coming off kind of cold.

"Thanks for everything Morgan." I say softly.

I lean over and give him a kiss on the cheek to make him understand how much he means to me. Out of the corner of my eye I see the black Mercedes and the silver Cadillac pull in. I give Morgan a quick smile, say "bye" and stumble out of the truck with my bag.

Caleb and Xander get out of their cars and smile at me as I approach them. But Jason appears to be missing too. I don't know how much Caleb shared with the guys about last night, but they don't seem like the types to tease and taunt. I'll be mortified if they do but they all seem like gentlemen, so I doubt they stand around gossiping about me. Caleb waves me over to his side and I reluctantly listen.

As I walk over to them, I hear Morgan turn off the truck and open and close the door. I know he is following me, and I don't predict this will end well. One protective, jealous, possible boyfriend meets my other possible love interest. Nothing about that sounds comforting or encouraging.

I get over to Caleb and I see him look over my shoulder. His smile fades until it looks like he's ready to kick someone's ass. I never thought I'd see him sneer at someone, but it's happening now. Again, I see a flash of silver in Caleb's eyes, but it's gone as quickly as it came. I turn to see Morgan walking right up to both of us.

"Rose, why'd you get out of the truck so fast? Is everything ok?" Morgan asks.

Although Morgan is directing his question at me, he doesn't look away from Caleb. And the look in his eyes is intense.

"Yeah, no I'm fine. I'm just going to head in. Um, Morgan this is Caleb, and that's Xander. We have a few classes together, so we met yesterday." I say uncomfortably.

I'm hoping to deflate the tension from this situation before fists start flying. Morgan already has his fists balled up. Although, Caleb looks calmer.

I can also see Xander watching the conversation intently. I can see him whispering occasionally to Caleb, but it doesn't break his focus on Morgan. I don't want to imagine the kind of damage Caleb could do to Morgan, and I hope I don't have to find out.

"Ok, well I have to go run some errands so like I said, I'm ditching my classes, but find my truck after school." Morgan says dominantly.

If the talking had ended there, everything probably would have been fine. You know what they say though, boys will be boys! *Whatever that means.* Morgan is clearly trying to demonstrate his male dominance or whatever hell his excuse is for being childish.

"Actually, Morgan is it? I was going to bring Rose home this afternoon just like yesterday." Caleb says casually.

"Caleb, I really don't think Rose's brother would appreciate that!" Morgan says.

"Alex didn't seem to mind when he invited me to dinner last night!" Caleb says smugly.

Morgan and Caleb both take a step towards each other, but I stay firmly in between them. This is not going well at all, so much for the idea of us all hanging out. Xander looks only slightly concerned with the current situation though because he looks fairly relaxed a couple feet behind Caleb.

"Well, that won't be happening tonight Caleb!" Morgan says rudely.

"Sure. Why don't we let Rose choose her own ride, after all she's a big girl!" Caleb says easily.

I try to ignore the fact that they're talking about me like I'm not standing right here. In my opinion Caleb is the only one acting like an adult but Morgan is letting his childishness get the best of him.

"Why don't I just call Alex and see what he thinks?" Morgan says threateningly.

I snap out of my daze really quickly, and all of my pent-up anger comes bubbling to the surface. *Who the hell does he think he is?* It's just like saying "I'm going to tell dad!" I'm positive that public humiliation is the worst feeling ever.

"Excuse me? Morgan, what the hell is wrong with you? Don't you dare call my brother. I can ride with whomever I choose. Thanks!" I say angrily.

"Rose, I'm just trying to look out for you." Morgan says with a pained expression.

"Well stop! One crazy ass brother is enough, and you're supposed to be my friend. I'm going to ride home with Caleb and Alex will just have to deal with it." I say firmly. "Oh, and I'd appreciate it if you're not there waiting for me!" I add just to hurt Morgan.

Morgan is crushed, I can see it in his eyes, but he left me no choice. If I don't start standing up to them, they'll keep bossing me around and it'll get worse.

"Fine! Do what you want. Caleb…Not a scratch on her, got it?" Morgan says threateningly.

Morgan stomps back to his truck, clearly sulking! I know my tone of voice was hurtful, but I just can't believe he'd sink to those levels. As far as I'm concerned, he got exactly what he deserved and probably what he needed.

I'm not quite sure why he assumes Caleb will let me get hurt but Morgan's comment doesn't seem to have bothered him at all. He's just standing there looking gorgeous and maybe a bit smug. He obviously feels victorious, although I don't get why. I'm incredibly embarrassed about the spectacle that just went down but there's nothing I can do about it. I finally turn to apologize to Caleb, but I have no idea where to start.

"Caleb, I'm so sorry! Morgan's not normally that overprotective." I say apologetically.

"Rose, it's ok. I get it. He's your best friend so he cares about you, and his feelings for you are probably strong. I know he's just trying to protect you and I don't blame him, you're an amazing girl." He says understandingly. "Oh, and you look beautiful today!" He adds making me blush.

"Oh…Thank you!" I say happily.

I don't care how Morgan is feeling right now. I'm too entranced with the attraction I feel for Caleb and the fact that he said I look beautiful. Let's not forget that he thinks I'm amazing. I swear, I must be blushing a shade of scarlet, and it just seems to make him happier. I don't doubt Xander can see it too.

Caleb, Xander, and I leave the parking lot and head for the front door. No one says a word about what just happened, and I'm thankful for that. Once we enter the front hall it's a zoo as usual, students rushing around everywhere taking care of their business. The guys all say goodbye to me, and we go our separate ways. I catch Caleb looking back at me and he winks before rounding a corner, so I head off to class with butterflies in my stomach. Tyler catches up with me in the hall and walks to homeroom with me.

"Hey Rose! No Hannah today?" He asks.

"No, she's running late!" I say.

Answering Tyler's question really makes me wish that Hannah was here.

For once I have some female drama to discuss and she won't be around to hear it. After the morning I've had I don't know how I'm going to get through the day without her and some girl time.

"Hello…Rose…Um we're here. Are you ok?" Tyler asks nervously.

"Oh, yeah. Sorry! I just have a lot on my mind." I say distractedly.

"It happens! As long as you're good?" He says.

"Yup!" I say.

I follow Tyler into the room, and I realize everyone is already here minus Hannah. Tyler immediately goes to sit with the teen royalty, and he gestures at the empty desk next to him. I smile and politely shake my head to say no. Sitting with them will only be more depressing because Hannah's not here. I choose to sit alone near the front of the room. To be honest I don't want to talk to anyone right now. It's not that I don't appreciate Tyler's offer of friendship but more that I just need some time to reflect. So, I sit alone in seclusion and yet no one seems to care or notice.

I'm relieved when the bell rings signalling my freedom and I make sure I'm the first one out of the class. I hurry off to chemistry class hoping that seeing Caleb will put me in a better mood and end my torture. *I know it will.*

CHAPTER SIXTEEN

Rose

When I get to class, I sit in my usual seat and save the seat next to me for Caleb, not that anyone else tries to sit with me. Before I know it the bell rings and Caleb's nowhere in sight. He's late. I hope he'll be here soon and that his absence doesn't have anything to do with the awkward situation with Morgan this morning. If Morgan has chased him away then I might die of humiliation, or I might kill him. *I haven't decided yet.*

Class moves by at painfully slow pace and I hope that every noise I hear outside the door is Caleb. It never is and the waiting is pure torture.

Finally, the bell rings and the sound is wonderful. I don't waste anytime leaving, I didn't know that chemistry would be so unbearable without Caleb, but it was. *I wonder why he didn't come.* The question bothers me as I walk in the direction of history class.

As I turn the last corner to class, I do something I should have learned not to do. I walk while looking at the damn floor again. I just don't like making eye contact with everyone, especially people I don't know. Only occasionally do I end up walking into people, like yesterday when I walked into Xander. It did break the ice for our introductions though.

I keep walking with my head down when I feel a hand close on my upper arm. It's a warm hand with a firm grip, unfortunately that doesn't rule many people out. I can feel the heat radiating through my leather jacket. Immediately I assume its Caleb, then I panic because I realize it could be Morgan. When I look up, I am disappointed but surprised to see blond hair and blue eyes in front of me. Xander.

He stands there semi smiling and looking me right in the eyes. He lets go of my arm quickly when he notices he has my attention and he looks a bit stressed.

"Sorry to grab you like that Rose, but you weren't looking up and I need to talk to you." Xander says apologetically.

"Oh, it's ok! I wouldn't have seen you if you hadn't grabbed my arm.

Does this talk have anything to do with Caleb missing chemistry class?" I ask.

"Well yes. Caleb had to leave, something came up, but he should be back in time to drive you home." He says casually.

I don't know if his departure is because of Morgan or not but I'm glad Xander came to tell me about it. I'm trying not to show how upset I am that Caleb won't be in class but it's really hard.

"I understand!...Actually...Xander do you want to leave? I really don't want to be here!" I say.

"We shouldn't!" Xander says nervously.

"Please Xander? I'm leaving anyway but I wouldn't mind your company!" I say.

"Alright! If you insist on leaving, I'll take you." He says uneasily.

I didn't put a whole lot of thought into it, but he almost seems reluctant to leave with me. Maybe it has something to do with Caleb not being here or knowing what's going on. I don't care, it doesn't matter as long as I don't have to stay in the hell hole anymore. They call it school, but I call it prison. *I just need to escape.*

"Great, let's go!" I say happily.

Right away we turn around and head back towards the front entrance. When we open the doors the fresh air hits me and I instantly feel slightly better. It's turning into a beautiful day, it's even sunny and it feels good on my skin. I can feel the stolen energy being returned to my body and it makes me want to smile. I even catch Xander grinning on the way to his car. We walk through the lot arriving at the silver Cadillac after only a few minutes. He opens my door and even holds out his hand to help me in. These guys must have attended a class on etiquette because it's definitely not what I'd expect from three emancipated teenage boys. *I mean really.*

Once I'm in the car I realize that I'm doing it again. I'm getting in a car with a guy I barely know. I don't know his last name, if he's a good driver or even if he has his license. You'd be surprised with how common illegally driving is here. It's another risk and it excites me. It makes me feel like I'm taking back control of my life, and I'm no longer just someone's puppet.

The thought sends a rush through me to my brain, and I'm thrilled. Xander obviously notices the change in my attitude, or at least he must have when he climbed in. *How could he not?* I'm grinning from ear to ear like a small child at Christmas.

Xander looks over at me and smiles. He turns the engine over, and we speed away from the school. We're going dangerously fast but he's shifting gears so smoothly that it's hard to tell when we accelerate.

"So, where to Rose?" Xander asks curiously.

I'm so caught up in the moment that I completely forgot that we don't actually have a destination picked out. I haven't really given it much thought either.

"Anywhere but home!" I say quickly.

"As you wish!" He says.

I don't know where we're going and to be honest, I don't care either. I've never felt more-free, or in tune with myself than I do now. This is how I imagine I would feel if my parents were still alive, I'd be sincerely happy. Everything seems so perfect and I know exactly where I want to go now. *Duh!*

"Xander, can we go to my favorite place in the whole world?" I ask pleadingly.

"Of course! Just tell me where." Xander replies happily.

I've never brought anyone to the pond before, it's always been my little paradise. I didn't want to share it with Morgan, Alex or even Hannah. It's been mine and mine alone, but it feels right sharing it with Xander. I don't think he and I are all that different and when we get to know each other we will see that we have more in common than we think.

In fact, I've met four new people this year, and so far, it feels like we all come from the same world. It's nice to feel a sense of belonging instead of feeling like an outcast. It's a refreshing change of pace for me. I wonder if they all feel the same way. At least they have friends and can fit in with everyone else. *I just can't!*

I start telling Xander about the pond while I give him directions. He doesn't ask me why I want to go there, instead he just goes with it.

We pull up across the road from the woods and he puts the car in park. I already explained that we'll have to walk a short-ways. It doesn't seem to bother him. He helps me out of the car and hooks his arm through mine to help me navigate the woodsy path. It's a kind gesture even though I could tumble my way down the path in the dark, and I have before. That's how frequently I come here.

We only walk for about fifteen minutes when we come into the clearing where the pond is. I glance over to take in Xander's expression and he looks impressed.

"Wow!" Xander says in surprise.

"I know. I've been here hundreds of times, but it still takes my breath away!" I say.

In the daylight the water sparkles, and you can see right to the bottom. The trees that line the clearing appear as though they are dancing in the breeze. The grass around the pond is a brilliant green, and there are butterflies flying around the flowers. To make it even more like a fairy tale you can hear birds singing in the trees around us. It truly is magical and I'm glad I am sharing it with someone.

"Xander let's go swimming!" I say spontaneously.

"Right now? We don't have towels or dry clothes, we'll likely freeze."

He says sensibly.

"I don't care!" I reply.

I kick off my shoes and throw down my leather jacket before I cannon ball into the water. He was right, the water is chilly, but I don't care. I want to be spontaneous and have fun for once. I resurface just in time to see Xander dive in. He copied me and removed his shoes, coat, and because he's a guy even his shirt. I'm glad that he joined me because it just might be what we both need.

Xander surfaces next to me and we both smile. I wade into the shallow water and climb on the rock bluff that juts out over the water. I dive in letting a small scream escape my lips before the splash. I pull Xander down by the leg before rising to the surface laughing.

We goof around in the pond for hours and when we finally get out, I wish I had some dry clothes to put on. Xander offers me his dry shirt and coat but I decline. Getting wet was my idea and it doesn't seem right making him freeze. I sit down on a rock and ring out my clothes and hair the best I can. The breeze has become cold and it's not helping my situation.

Xander starts building a circle with the small rocks and places twigs, dead leaves, and dried grass in the center. I watch him pull a lighter out of his pocket which I think is odd but convenient. I don't know why he carries a lighter since I haven't seen him smoking. Then again maybe he does. *Who knows?* He starts a fire between us, and it helps to dry my soaked outfit and warm me. For a few minutes we sit silently enjoying the glow of the fire in the fading sunlight.

"So, why'd you want to leave school so badly?" Xander asks.

"Just one of those days where life feels so complicated that you need to get away." I say.

"Does this complicated life have anything to do with what happened this morning between Caleb and Morgan?" Xander asks knowingly.

"Well, to be perfectly honest…Yes! Just between you and me, I'm torn. Caleb seems like an amazing guy and I'm drawn to him, but Morgan and I go way back, and we have history." I say sadly.

"Ok, so you like Morgan?" He asks.

"I do like Morgan…I think. But being with him feels forced. It's what Morgan and Alex expect. I'm tired of doing what they want, and I want to make my own choices. Caleb makes me feel different, and I like it. There's just something there. I like him too. I guess I'm confused, I don't know who I want, you know? I also don't want to lose my best friend. It' complicated!" I say.

After my agonizing truth I feel so frustrated that I begin to cry. It's not a giant mess, just a few stress tears. Xander leans over and hugs me which comes as a complete shock to me and I slowly hug him back. Most guys run in the opposite direction when a girl starts to tear up but Xander doesn't even seem uncomfortable. He takes his time letting go.

"Everything will be ok Rose! You'll see. These things have a way of working themselves out. Don't forget, you have friends and family here for you. That includes me!" He says.

"Thank you! I know you're right but lately it feels like my friends and family are hiding things from me, mostly Morgan and Alex. It just feels like a lot of stuff is being thrown at me and it's overwhelming." I say with a sigh.

I look down at the fire because I'm a bit embarrassed about my emotional outburst. Xander doesn't say anything, instead he reaches over and gives my hand a small squeeze. It's such a small gesture but it brings me comfort.

"Rose, I wish we could talk longer but it's getting late and it looks like a nasty storm is coming." Xander says.

"I understand." I say.

I look up into the sky to see that it's gray and black. I don't know when the weather took such a bad turn, but it doesn't matter now. The clouds look threatening and the wind has picked up. I go over and put my shoes and jacket on while Xander does the same. We put some dirt on the fire before we head back down the path arm in arm.

The storm seems to have us both on edge and I try my best to walk down the narrow path. It's hard though when the wind is whipping wet hair into my face. As we come out of the woods, sheer panic hits me at the sight of my brothers Camaro.

"Oh shit!" I blurt out.

"Are you in trouble?" Xander asks calmly.

"Well, I'm guessing Morgan has been a little snitch, so yes, definitely. You better go, I'll see you at school tomorrow. Assuming Alex doesn't murder me!" I say jokingly.

I try for a laugh, but it comes out shaky and nervous. I give Xander a little push in the direction of his car and I watch as he reluctantly walks away.

I start towards the Camaro, knowing that I'm going to be grounded for life. Xander almost looked like he wanted to come over and take the blame for me, but it would have made things worse. Besides I don't want to put my new friend in the line of fire.

Once I get close enough to my brother, I can see the sour expression on his face. I consider making a run for it, but I have to go home eventually. I notice that Morgan is in the backseat which means Alex will know everything. I open the passenger door and climb in as Xander takes off past us. I'm careful not to make eye contact with Alex or Morgan until I know how I am going to handle this situation. I stay quiet as I buckle up and neither of them say anything to me as we head home.

CHAPTER SEVENTEEN

Caleb

I hear the front door open and close from where I'm sitting in the living area, I already know its Xander. *Finally!* I watch as Jason leaves the room to greet him. I'm angry that he left the school with Rose, but I know he is trying to be a friend to her.

The moment he left the school with her, he told me. He saw an opportunity to get her to open up and he took it. I would have done the same thing.

After a minute or two Jason comes back into the room with Xander following behind him. Xander looks mildly distressed but he didn't say there was a problem.

"Xander, how did it go?" I ask curiously.

"Well that depends." Xander says carefully.

"On what?" I ask.

Jason and Xander make their way to the couch across from me and they sit. Meanwhile I'm tensing for bad news.

"It depends on whether or not you have a plan B." Xander says.

I let out a groan. If Xander is even mentioning making a new plan, things must be pretty bad. Jason knows it too.

"What's our situation?" Jason asks calmly.

"Well she has no idea about anything. I mean none!" Xander says.

"How is that possible?" Jason asks in surprise.

"Alex and Morgan!" I say with annoyance.

Her brother and her friend are proving to be a bigger obstacle than we anticipated. I knew Alex was looking at me strangely during dinner and asking some pointed questions. And this explains it. Rose has no idea, but he knows everything.

"The older brother?" Xander asks curiously.

"That would be him." I say.

"You think he knows and he's not telling her." Jason questions.

"There's no doubt in my mind that he knows. Alex may be human, but Morgan isn't. They think they're protecting her. I just don't understand why. He's coming for her no matter what." I say thoughtfully.

"Well, this changes things." Jason says.

"It does." Xander agrees.

I stare into the fire and watch as the flames lick at the brick surrounding it. I never even considered needing a plan B so we're going to have to start from scratch. I thought this would be easy. We get in, we get the girl, and we get out. I didn't think we'd have to be the ones to tell her the truth.

"Alright. This sucks. But there's no other way. We have to tell her." Xander says.

"We can't just tell her. She hardly knows us. She'll assume we're crazy." Jason says.

"Well what do you suggest? We can't sit around and wait for Alex to tell her." Xander says reasonably. "We don't have that kind of time." He adds.

"You're both right." I chime in putting a stop their argument.

I turn away from the flames and look at the guys. They're watching me and waiting. They're waiting for me to tell them about our plan B.

"We have to wait, get closer to her, all of us. When she trusts us more, then we make our move." I say strategically.

"Ok." Xander says.

"It could work." Jason says positively.

"It has to work." I say seriously.

Xander and Jason nod somberly. They know exactly what I'm getting at. If we found her, it's only a matter of time before everyone does. We all fall into a thoughtful silence. There's a lot at stake here.

"Well...Um...I could get closer to her best friend?" Jason asks timidly.

"I bet you could." Xander says. "Hannah's a very pretty girl." He adds with a smirk.

Jason glares at Xander as if to tell him to shut up. He was with her last night, which is why they both missed school. I smile to myself. I see no harm in having a little fun while we're here. Besides getting to know Hannah might actually be helpful.

"I think that that is actually not a bad idea Jason." I say. "I mean if you don't mind of course." I add.

Jason smiles at me. It's been a long time since Jason has had any interest in a girl. The fact that she happens to be Rose's best friend is a coincidence.

"I'll call her now." Jason says happily.

Xander and I watch him leave as he dials Hannah's number. I can hear him talking to her in the hallway and after a few minutes, the talking stops. Jason comes back in with a grin on his face and it's pretty obvious what just happened.

"Hey, um Hannah asked me to come hang out…" Jason says. "Is that cool?" He asks.

"Sure." I say. "The sooner the better!" I add.

"Ok, see you later." Jason says.

Xander and I watch Jason leave. We both know that there's something between him and Hannah. I say good for him. He deserves it. Besides his absence means I can get some more information on Rose without feeling like I'm under scrutiny.

"So, do you think Rose has any idea?" I ask.

"Not really. I mean she said that she thinks Alex and Morgan are keeping things from her, but I don't think she really knows." Xander says.

"Morgan! He's going to be a pain in the ass." I say tiredly.

I don't know why I didn't see it before. I've been watching her for weeks now and I've seen them together. If Morgan is one of us, that would explain why Alex knows so much. If Morgan is like us, he's going to be difficult to handle, especially being one of Rose's best friends.

"I'm sure that she will give you her trust." He says.

"I hope so. Unfortunately, it complicates things even more." I say. "That'll make two." I add.

Xander looks at me with concern. He knows who I'm talking about but it's weird. Why would his kind be out here?

"So, Tyler is…For sure?" Xander asks.

"Yes. He's definitely a werewolf." I say confidently. "My guess is that Rose has no idea about the company she's keeping." I add seriously.

"Well that goes for us as well." Xander says guiltily.

"I know." I say with a sigh. "I wish we could tell her, but we can't. Not yet." I add helplessly.

Xander nods at me. Neither of us feel very good about hiding what we are from her but for now it's what's best. I look back at the fire and watch the flames dying down. The embers glow a bright red and my guilt starts to consume me.

Xander shifts in his seat uneasily and I turn back to him. He still looks distressed and then I realize he knows more than he's said.

"What is it?" I ask sternly.

"Rose. She said something to me, and it might be nothing, but it could be something." Xander says carefully. "She mentioned being overwhelmed with the things that are happening to her. It leads me to believe that she's experiencing things that she won't understand." He adds.

I think about it for a moment and he's right. She mentioned something to me too. It sounds like there are multiple things and I'm not responsible for all of it.

"You're right. We don't have much time left." I say. "We're going to have to act soon." I add seriously.

Alex

I can't believe the nerve of this girl. After everything I've done for her and still do for her. I even let that Caleb boy stay for dinner yesterday. Now today she's accepting money from me and then ditching school and disappearing with another boy that I haven't even met. He could be dangerous, or worse he could be the one that Morgan warned me about. I somehow doubt that if she knew everything, she'd be any more cautious either. She'd just be more angst ridden and disobedient because I've been keeping everything from her for so long.

To make matters worse, Morgan has cautioned me about this Caleb guy and his friends. He thinks they aren't who they say they are, but he can't tell me exactly what we're dealing with yet. What am I supposed to do? Ban her from seeing them? *Yeah right!* Then she will find a way to see them without me knowing. *I can't win!*

When I finish thinking everything through, we pull into the driveway. I barely get to put the car in park before she jumps out and slams the passenger door. I have to let Morgan out on my side because she's so anxious to get away from us. I know that Morgan is someone I can trust, he's respectful of me and her. Right now, she probably knows that Morgan has informed me of everything that went down today, so she's not going to be happy with him. I know how much Morgan hates having to ruin her fun, he just wants her safe. *So do I!*

"Rose, wait in the kitchen. We need to talk!" I say.

She stomps up the porch steps and slams the front door without verbally answering. I don't expect anything less from her. Hell, I was worse at her age, but she doesn't need to know that. Besides our situations are completely different, no one was hunting me!

"Alex. Don't worry. I think she heard you!" Morgan says jokingly.

Morgan stifles a laugh as we head for the door. Leave it to him to make a joke that my sister won't even look at me, let alone talk to me. I know he's just trying to hide that fact that he's scared she'll never speak to him again, but I know she will. We walk up to the door and go in. We go directly to the kitchen and Rose is sitting there, arms crossed, giving us both the death stare as we sit down.

I already regret my decision to hide things from her. Now I have to keep lying to keep my original lie a secret. I just hope she knows that I love her, despite how this conversation goes.

CHAPTER EIGHTEEN

Rose

I know exactly what Alex is thinking right now. He's going to act like he's our father, tell me I'm a spoiled, snotty, stupid child, and try to ground me for life. I say try because like hell I'm going to listen. I refuse to let my brother ground me. I dare him to try though because I've had enough. I can't live like this anymore and if that means I have to leave, so be it! I don't think I'm being over dramatic either, I believe my attitude is long overdue.

I watch as Morgan sits down across from me and Alex stands at the head of the table. He's conveniently placed himself between me and the door. *Let the yelling commence.*

"Rose, what were you thinking? Did you wake up this morning and think hey I wonder what the stupidest thing is that I can do to annoy my brother?" Alex asks sarcastically.

"Yes Alex! As matter of fact I live to be yelled at by you." I say just as sarcastically.

I think the sarcasm is a good addition. Its very rebellious teenaged angst meets an I don't give a shit attitude. *I'm definitely feeling it.*

"What you did is completely stupid and reckless! You're acting like a…like a…" He starts.

"Like what Alex? A teenager?" I say interrupting him. "God forbid that I can't be as perfect as you. I didn't ask you to skip your teenage years and be my father. That was your own damn choice." I add angrily.

"Yeah and I can see now that it was the wrong one." He says hurtfully.

This argument is escalating to a level of nasty that I didn't think we were capable of.

"Guys come on…" Morgan says.

Even Morgan can see that it's getting out of hand and I hear him trying to deflate the situation but I'm too heated to care. I can be just as hurtful as he can.

"You and me both! This is why Candace broke up with you. You're psychotic! Instead of going out and partying with her like a normal guy. You followed me around or obsessed about what I was doing. She loved you and she wanted to be with you, but you wanted her to be my mother. Finally, she couldn't handle it anymore. That's why she left. You drove her away! That's why you'll always be alone." I scream back at him.

Oh my god! Now that I've said it, I wish more than anything that I could take it back. Candace was the love of his life and he lost her because he always put me before himself or her. I had no right to throw that in his face. He loved her so much and when she left him six months ago, he was a mess. Hell, he's still not dating anyone or even hooking up for that matter. Losing her destroyed him and I can't believe I could hurt him this way. I feel awful and Morgan is standing now with his mouth open in shock. I know I went too far.

"Rose, you're an ungrateful little bitch!" Alex says coldly.

"Whoa now!" Morgan interrupts.

I watch Morgan speak and move towards Alex to get his attention but he's staring at me like I'm the worst thing that's ever happened to him.

"Screw you Alex!" I yell as I stomp towards him.

Smack. I stand there with my eyes wide and my hand on my cheek.

"Shit!" Morgan says.

I hear Morgan swear but like me he's frozen to the spot. I'm still in shock that Alex back handed me across the face. My cheek feels like it's on fire and I can feel the tears welling involuntarily. *I don't know what to do.* I'm stuck between being angry, upset, and shocked.

"I hate you Alex. I wish you weren't my brother!" I sob.

I race out of the kitchen and up the stairs as the tears start pouring out. I slam my bedroom door shut behind me and collapse onto my bed, while my body convulses in sobs. I can't believe everything I said to him and I really can't believe he slapped me. Alex has never been physically violent with me. I mean I know he used to get in a lot of fights at school, but I always assumed he'd never hit a girl, especially his own sister. He doesn't seem to realize that I'm only seventeen and I need to be able to act like it sometimes. With him it's all or nothing though and being a teenager is unforgivable.

As I cry into my pillow, I hear an exchange of words downstairs. I know its Alex and Morgan. They've clearly come out of their shock and it sounds like they're arguing about something now. I hear the front door on the house creak and slam shut and I know someone has left. Then I hear the Camaro start up and I can't help my curiosity. I go over to the window with my tear streaked face and watch my brother's car go down the driveway. I know Morgan is still here though, he wouldn't leave me after what just happened. Seconds later I hear a knock on my door, so I wipe my cheeks and go answer it.

"Hey Rose, can we talk?" Morgan says pleadingly.

"Well that depends. Are you going to tell me I'm stupid and make me feel bad?" I say defensively.

I know I'm being rude, and he just wants to check on me, but I still have some left-over anger. I'm still so angry with him. But I open the door anyway.

"No of course not. I want to make sure you're alright and apologize for my own stupid behaviour! What I did was wrong. Treating you like a child and telling your brother. I'm supposed to be here for you, and I haven't been. I am so sorry! I really messed up." He says.

I walk over and sit on the edge of my bed. It's hard to make eye contact with him after he just watched me get the crap slapped out of me. I want to be mean and sarcastic because it's easier than being vulnerable with someone, but I know I don't need to. Not with Morgan.

"Yes, you did mess up." I say rudely. "But thank you for apologizing." I add.

Morgan must be feeling brave because he walks over to the bed and sits beside me.

"I know you're perfectly capable of making your own choices, but I worry about you. You have no idea how special you are or how much you mean to me." Morgan says honestly.

"I don't know if I'm as special as you think I am." I say averting my eyes.

This conversation sounds a lot like a confession now. In the corner of my eye I notice Morgan turns to me on the bed. He brings his hand to my chin. He gently tilts my head up, so I have to look him in the eyes, and he doesn't let go. He stares into my eyes with his baby blues and it's comforting.

"You are. Trust me!" He says.

He says it easily as if he doesn't feel our friendship changing but I know he does. I can feel it too and it makes me nervous. He uses his free hand to brush back my hair and peer at my reddened cheek. I see his features turn into a frown, and I can only assume he's upset that Alex hit me. He lets his hands fall to his lap but still looks into my eyes.

"I'm sorry he hit you. I know it doesn't change things and it doesn't justify his actions, but he's disgusted with himself." Morgan says.

"I know." I say.

I do understand. I kind of bitch slapped him with the whole Candace thing, metaphorically speaking. I'll never forget that he lashed out at me physically, but I know I'll forgive him one day when the feelings aren't so fresh.

"So, where did Alex go?" I ask changing the topic.

I watch as a look of concern crosses Morgan's face before he answers. I know I'm probably not going to like the answer.

"The bar. He's probably going to get tanked! He's going to crash at my place tonight because he feels so guilty that he doesn't want you to have to be around him. He knows that what he did is wrong and now he's trying to deal with it. He's always been a scrapper, but he swore he would never hit you or any other girl for that matter." Morgan says.

I hate that my brother is going to get drunk over this but he's stubborn and nothing I say will make him come home tonight. Not until he thinks he's learned his lesson.

"I didn't mean what I said about hating him. He's my brother and I will always love him." I say sadly.

"He knows. He just hates himself right now for a lot of things." He says.

It upsets me even more to know that Alex is sad and alone right now. I should be there for him but I'm the reason for all this mess. A few stray tears start trailing down my cheeks again and Morgan puts his arm around my waist and squeezes me in a hug. It's very comforting and I'm reminded of the strong bond we have that enforces that he'll always be there for me.

I look up into his face with tears still falling down my cheeks and he takes his finger and wipes away the tears. For the first time I think I understand how much he cares about me. I can see it in the way he looks at me.

I'm still looking into his eyes when he closes them and leans in to kiss me. I don't know how I feel so I let it happen. His lips are warm and soft, and I can feel his arms wrapping around me. He has a gentle grip on my lower back, but he holds me tightly against him. I kiss him back before I pull away.

"I'm sorry Morgan but I can't do this right now." I say with new tears.

His head drops and he takes a deep breath. I fidget nervously.

"No, I'm sorry. I shouldn't have done this, not now." Morgan says sadly.

He gets to his feet and starts back towards the door. A few feet from it he stops, turns back to me, and nervously runs his hand through his hair.

"I'm not trying to pressure you Rose. I just need you to know that I'm crazy about you. I have been for a while." Morgan confesses.

"I'm flattered Morgan, but I don't know how I feel." I say.

"Caleb." Morgan says calmly.

He says it as a statement rather than a question which is good since I don't know what to say. It's not entirely because of Caleb but he won't understand if I try to explain it, so I say nothing.

"I'll be downstairs on the couch if you need me." Morgan says sadly.

"Ok." I say weakly.

For a minute he just stands there while silent tears of frustration spill out. Then as the awkward silence stretches, he leaves.

I lay down on my bed and close my eyes. I don't know if I'll be able to sleep right now, it isn't even completely dark outside, but I let the exhaustion take hold.

CHAPTER NINETEEN

Rose

I wake up from a dead sleep and my eyes scan the room looking for the reason why. There doesn't seem to be one except that my window is slightly open. I turn on the lamp and crawl across my bed to the window. I can't see anything except darkness and shadows, so I close the window.

I feel strange and unsettled almost like there are more important things I should be doing instead of sleeping. I sit on the edge of my bed and think. *What could be bothering me?* Besides the obvious absence of my brother and our vicious argument, I have no idea. Then again there's Morgan and the kiss. Maybe that's what it is.

Either way I don't think I could sleep right now. I get up and go to my desk. I sit down and fire up my laptop. *If I'm not going to sleep, I may as well do some research.* I never did get around to checking out that symbol on Xander's journal.

I load up the Google search engine and type in "veneficus navitas typicus", it's all a bit confusing but it shows the seven-pointed star again. It takes me about an hour to sort through the mumbo jumbo, and I finally figure out that it means "a being of magical power" or something close to that. That doesn't really explain much so I keep digging.

After flipping through several translator sites, I find it to mean "Magick Energy Symbol". I don't really understand, and I end up finding a really old website that contains some stuff from a similar book. The pages have been scanned in so it's hard to decipher the writing. I only get pieces and fragments but it says "strange creatures of unknown existence......wielding different powers............appear human in form............few weaknesses..........different world/realm............transformation process unknown............spoken titles in Croatian language............mystic spells......deadly skills............speed inhuman............krvi nestasko......utvara......thought extinct."

That is all I can understand but it's not enough to make sense of. It does sound strangely familiar like I've read this before, but I don't remember. Talk about déjà vu. Everything is so unclear, but I'll be damned if I'm going to sit back and do nothing. I'm going to figure this out if it makes me crazy. But maybe tomorrow because I'm tired so I'm going to go back to bed, and I'll pick up where I left off as soon as I can.

I turn off my computer and close it after several hours, and then I crawl back into bed. I find myself wishing Caleb was here with me but then my thoughts travel to Morgan. I fall asleep thinking of them both.

I wake up in the morning to Morgan standing in my doorway. To be honest it's kind of creepy. I can only imagine how I look. I certainly don't feel well.

"Good morning Rose, you're running a bit late so you better step on it?" Morgan says.

I glance at the clock to see what he means. It's a quarter to eight. I'm almost an hour behind schedule. I'm definitely going to be late for school.

"Shit. Ok I'm getting ready. Did Hannah call?" I ask.

"No but your phone went off a couple times. It sounded like a text. If she's still playing hooky, I'll drive you." Morgan says with a smirk.

I give him a smart ass look as I head for the bathroom and of course I can't resist giving him a hard time for his past misdeeds.

"Are you going to behave like a grown up today?" I ask sarcastically.

"Yes, I will play nice. I'll even drop you off with Caleb and them out front, as long as you meet up with me for lunch." Morgan says in an effort to compromise.

He says Caleb's name as though it leaves a bitter taste but at least he is trying to be civil. I know Caleb will do the same.

"Ok, but only if I can bring whoever I want to lunch with us." I say.

"Fine." He says reluctantly.

I listen as Morgan walks out the door and goes downstairs. I check my phone while I brush my teeth. Morgan was right. I have two text messages; one from Hannah and one from an unknown number.

I read the unknown number text first: Hey. I'm going to pick you up for school today. I'll see you soon. Caleb.

Oh my god! Caleb's picking me up. *Oh my god!* I can't believe it. I start hyperventilating a little as I scroll to Hannah's text. It says: Ok so I would come pick you up, but it turns out that Caleb really wants to. I said he could as long as I can pick up Jason because carpooling is better for our environment. Ha ha. Anyway, I'll see you in Algebra. We so have to talk. Hannah. P.S. I gave Caleb your number.

I spit out my toothpaste, do my hair, and get changed in record time. I grab my bag and meet Morgan in the hall downstairs.

"So is Hannah coming?" Morgan asks.

"Not exactly." I say guiltily.

Morgan looks at me questioningly just as a car horn honks from the driveway. He doesn't try to hide his feelings of disgust as he opens the door.

Caleb leans against the hood of his car with a dazzling smile aimed at me. I can't help but smile back and I feel a blush creeping into my cheeks.

I suddenly realize that Morgan is standing there watching me, and I try to compose myself. I only blush harder.

"Thanks anyway Morgan, I'll see you at lunch." I say kindly.

He gives me a small smile and nods. *I'm lucky I got that.* I head towards Caleb and his black Mercedes.

"Hey!" I say happily.

"Hey." Caleb replies.

He follows me to the passenger door and opens it for me. *What a gentleman.* When he climbs in, I look over at him just as he looks back.

"So, Morgan's going to join us for lunch." I blurt out.

I watch his face carefully but if he's having any negative thoughts, he hides it well.

"Ok. So, lunch is going to be entertaining." He says with a grin.

"Caleb, promise me you'll be on your best behaviour?" I ask nervously.

"Ok, but only because it means so much to you Rose and I want you to be happy." He says sweetly.

The car takes off towards the school and when we get there, we're only ten minutes late. Caleb walks me to Algebra. I shuffle in and take my seat next to Hannah. We don't have an opportunity to talk with the teacher droning on and on but it's not surprising. We'll have to have a girl's night sometime.

Lunch comes and we all meet up at the oasis even Tyler. You can feel the tension between everyone and I'm regretting my group lunch decision now. No one is really talking except for me and Tyler, the others are dead silent. They are so busy staring each other down that they're not even hearing what I say, and if they are then they're too uncomfortable to acknowledge it. *Talk about awkward.*

After all my classes, Caleb drives me home. Coincidentally enough, Morgan pulls in when Caleb gives me a kiss on the hand to say goodbye. *Figures!* He smiles his stunning smile at me, and I try not to be to happy about the tingle on my hand. He shuts the passenger door for me, and I say "goodbye". I walk to the porch and see Morgan and Caleb staring each other down for a minute, but then they move on. Morgan smiles as he joins me on the porch, and we head inside. My brother should be home soon, and he'll be glad to see Morgan over and no one else.

CHAPTER TWENTY

Rose

The next couple days fly by in a haze and before I know it, it's Saturday. I sit on the edge of my bed after lunch and enjoy the quiet. I can hear the television in the living room downstairs reminding me that Alex is here, not that it matters. He's avoiding me. *Who knows why?*

Caleb has been occupying most of my time lately and when he isn't, Morgan is. I haven't had time to obsess over the weird crap I researched, let alone talk to Hannah about my strange love triangle. But it's Saturday and she's coming over for some much-needed girl time.

I head downstairs to wait. Hannah should be here any minute. I walk into the living room to find Alex slumped on the couch, only sort of watching the show.

"Hey." I say as I take a seat next to him.

"Hey." He says curtly.

We both sit silently and stare at the T.V. There's so much that I want to say to him, but I don't know how. If I tell him that I know he's hiding something from me, we'll just end up in a big fight. But he's a guy. If I don't say anything neither will he. *Men!*

After several awkward moments in complete silence I give up. I can't confront him without proof so I may as well stop trying. I get up from the couch and head for the door. I'm going to go outside to wait for Hannah.

"Rose?" Alex blurts out as he turns to look at me.

"Yeah." I say in surprise.

"I know I don't say it much or even show it but…I love you." He says uncomfortably.

"I know. I love you too." I reply with a smile.

I step out onto the porch and take a deep breath. The cool air feels refreshing. I swing my legs over the railing and perch on the edge as the wood creaks under my weight.

I meant what I said, I do love Alex. He's my brother. Sure, we fight but I'll always love him because we're family. We both just want to protect each other even if that means arguing. The more I think about this, the more I want to come clean and confess everything to Alex. Not to mention the warning I got in my strange mom dream. I mean, what kind of danger could Alex be in?

I shrug off my concerns just as Hannah pulls up in the driveway. She gets out of the car smiling from ear to ear. No doubt Jason has something to do with it.

"Hey." I say carefully climbing off the railing.

"Hey." Hannah says with a big smile.

"My room?" I ask anxiously.

"Absolutely!" Hannah chimes as we head inside.

We speedily go upstairs, and Hannah hastily shuts my door behind us. I take a seat on my bed and Hannah does the same.

"You're in a good mood." I say observationally.

"Yes I am." Hannah says giddily. "I can't help it. I'm in love!" She says.

"Does Jason know?" I ask jokingly.

"Of course. We're soulmates." She adds with a squeal.

I watch as Hannah gets ready to tell me everything.

"Jason was at my place before I came over and he's so amazing. My parents absolutely love him, and I adore him. He so kind and sweet, he opens doors for me and pulls out my chair. I swear to god Rose, it's like he's from another time." Hannah says quickly as she falls back onto the bed and stares dreamily at the ceiling.

"Well he definitely sounds like a catch." I say happily.

"Oh Rose, he is. When he kisses me it's like the ground falls and I'm floating in the air. I've never felt like that before." Hannah says sincerely. "He's the man I'm going to marry one day." She adds with confidence.

I watch Hannah's face light up with the memory of Jason. I've never seen her get so consumed by one guy, she's so happy. *I envy her.*

"I'm so happy for you." I say smiling at Hannah.

She sits up and focuses her attention on me. Her smile disappears and in a split second she looks serious.

"What?" I ask nervously.

"You know Caleb is crushing on you hard-core, right?" She asks, the smile returning to her lips.

I blush profusely. "I know he likes me." I say shyly. "So does Morgan. He kissed me the other night." I add.

"What? Why am I just finding out about this now?" Hannah says with mock anger.

"We haven't been alone in a while." I say innocently.

"It totally makes sense now." Hannah says.

"What does?" I ask curiously.

"Jason asked me about Morgan and you. At the time it seemed strange

110

but now it's obvious that Caleb wants the dirt on you two." Hannah says.

"Oh. Well what did you tell him?" I ask.

"Just that you guys have been friends since before you could talk and Morgan has always been there for you." Hannah says honestly. "I also said that there have never been any romantic feelings between the two of you, because I didn't realize that there were." She adds.

"Oh." I say only semi-relieved.

"You don't have the same feelings Morgan has, do you?" She asks curiously. "I mean, did you like when he kissed you?" She adds.

"I don't know." I say truthfully. "Maybe I did a little. But I can't get Caleb out of my mind either." I add feeling embarrassed.

"Oh Rose, what are you going to do? You have two guys pining for your affection." Hannah says jokingly. "The horror!" She adds.

"Thanks Hannah." I say tossing a pillow lightly at her head. "I'm glad my love life amuses you." I add with a sigh.

"This doesn't have to be a bad thing." Hannah says.

"How do you figure?" I ask.

"Morgan likes you and so does Caleb." She says as a matter of fact. "So, why not let it play out. Let them do what they got to do." She adds.

"But doesn't that seem a bit manipulative?" I ask uncomfortably.

"No way!" Hannah says defensively. "You're not leading them on. You're just going to see where things go, you know, keeping your options open." She says.

"Options are good." I say with a smile.

"Yeah they are." Hannah says slyly. "But just for the record, I'm rooting for Caleb. He is Jason's close friend." She adds.

We both fall into a fit of giggles. It's crazy that we're both being pursued by guys at the same time. I definitely didn't expect it.

"So..." Hannah asks expectantly as our giggles subside. "Is Morgan a good kisser?" She adds bluntly.

"I guess..." I say unsure of how to answer.

"Oh god, you guess." Hannah says bursting into a new fit of giggles.

"Well I don't know. I have nothing to compare it to." I say.

Hannah stops laughing and looks at me intensely.

"You mean Caleb hasn't even tried..." Hannah says surprised. "What's he waiting for?" She adds.

"I guess he likes to take things slow. Or maybe he's really not that into me." I say.

"Huh. We'll see about that." Hannah says defiantly as she pulls out her phone.

She hits the speed dial before I can say anything, and I watch in confusion.

"Hey, Jason. What are you guys up to tonight?" Hannah asks. "Rose and I want to hang out with you guys." She adds before I can stop her. "Great. We'll see you soon." She says confidently and hangs up.

Oh my god.

"Hannah, my brother won't let them come over here." I say in panic.

"Relax Rose. They're not coming over here." She says calmly.

"Oh." I say disappointedly.

"We're going over there." She says happily.

"What?" I ask in disbelief.

Hannah gets up and drags me off the bed. I stumble behind her down the stairs and towards the front door.

"Hey." Alex says from the couch.

We backtrack to the living room where my brother sits staring at the T.V.

"Where are you guys going?" Alex asks without really caring.

We are so busted. What was I thinking? I should have known that we'd never get away with this. I'm a horrible liar.

"Um....We...Um..." I stutter.

"What Rose is trying to say Alex is that we're going out for dinner, a movie, and maybe some ice cream afterwards." Hannah says smoothly.

"Ok well stay together and be safe." Alex says, without looking at us.

"We will." Hannah says pulling me towards the front door.

I hold my breath until we're both climbing into her car. That seemed way to easy. He hasn't been the same since we fought. I half expect Alex to come rushing out, demanding to chaperone us. I breath easier as the car speeds away from my house but only for a minute. Fear of my brother finding us out is quickly replaced by fear of being in Caleb's house without any parents. *Holy crap.*

"I can't believe we just got away with lying to Alex!" I say excitedly.

"Confidence is all you need for an effective lie." Hannah says.

"So, do you know where the guys live?" I ask curiously.

"No." Hannah says flatly. "But we're going to follow Jason. He's at the store so watch for the silver caddy." She adds anxiously.

We start driving down the main street of our small community when the silver caddy pulls in front of us. Even if it wasn't the only one in town, we'd know it was him by the darker than dark tinted windows.

"Well, here we go." Hannah says giddily.

Yes, here we go. I think nervously to myself.

CHAPTER TWENTY-ONE

Rose

I should be excited about sneaking off to Caleb's but the farther we drive the more I feel like I'm going to have a stroke. My hearts pounding, my hands are shaking, and I'm starting to sweat. I'm not sure if it's nerves or if I'm having a panic attack but Hannah is blissfully unaware. What would she think if I asked her to turn around? Not that I'm going to. I wouldn't be able to live with myself if I blew off this opportunity.

"I think we're almost there, Rose." Hannah says happily.

I look ahead to see Jason applying his brakes and turning off the main road into a heavily treed driveway. *Great, it's totally secluded.*

"This is going to be so much fun!" Hannah squeals.

"Yeah." I lie through my teeth.

I'm not saying it won't be fun but having a heart attack is definitely not fun and right now that's how I feel. *Pull yourself together.* I tell myself as I try to slow my breathing.

"Rose, come on." Hannah says excitedly bringing me back to reality.

I realize that we're here. The car is parked, and Hannah is hanging impatiently out of her door waiting for me. Jason's waiting near the steps for the both of us. I follow Hannah towards the house, but I don't really take the time to appreciate the architecture. I'm too busy trying to hold it together. *I can do this.* I keep telling myself, but it doesn't do much.

"Hannah, Rose, welcome!" Jason says kindly when we reach the steps.

"Thanks." Hannah says sharing an intimate look with him.

All I do is give a shaky smile as we follow up the steps and in the door.

I hardly take notice of how clean the house appears as we follow Jason into what appears to be the living room. There's an old leather seating set situated around an antique coffee table but there doesn't seem to be a TV. The room is spotless. It's definitely not what you'd expect from three teen age boys.

"I'm just going to go put these away." Jason says lifting the bag of groceries in his hand. "Make yourselves comfortable." He adds before heading through an adjoining doorway.

"Oh, we will." Hannah says mischievously as she sits on the sofa.

I watch as Hannah leans her head back and closes her eyes. It's obvious that she already feels right at home.

I walk over to the far wall where an old bookcase sits covered in a small veil of dust. I run my fingers across the bindings of the old books and take notice of how aged they all look. The titles are faded and hard to read. I'm about to pick one up when I hear the door swing open.

"Look who I found?" Jason says as Caleb appears behind him.

"I'm glad you guys could make it." Caleb says without breaking eye contact with me.

Caleb's face is unreadable, but his eyes say something else. They take my breath away because they're filled with emotion, happy and excited emotions.

"Thank you for the invitation." I say feeling surprisingly calm.

Caleb continues to watch me with intensity from the doorway while Jason moves back to Hannah. I'm forced to look away as heat begins creeping into my cheeks and instead, I watch Hannah and Jason. It's interesting to see the way they interact.

Hannah gracefully leans over the back of the couch as Jason closes the gap between them. He stops mere inches from her and his eyes lock onto her face.

"So, what would you guys like to do?" Jason asks speaking to all of us but keeping his focus on Hannah.

"Not to be rude but I think Rose and Caleb can entertain themselves." Hannah says looking to me for agreement. "And you can entertain me. Maybe show me your room." She adds.

Maybe it's just me but at that moment Jason seems to blush. He's still smiling at her, but he's clearly caught off guard by her openness. *Strange!*

"I'd be happy to." Jason says stretching out his hand.

Hannah slides off the edge of the couch and takes his hand in hers. They leave the room hand in hand without looking back. Honestly, they're adorable together. It's so clear that they're crazy about one another. I'm happy for them.

I turn my attention back to Caleb and not surprisingly he's already focused on me. I'm starting to get used to his eyes always being on me.

"They seem happy." Caleb says observationally.

"I think they are." I answer truthfully. "Are you?" I ask automatically.

I'm shocked with my own question. I don't know where it came from or why I asked it. It just sort-of came spilling out.

"I suppose I am in general." Caleb answers, watching me carefully.

"Are you happy?" He asks bluntly.

"Um…" I pause not knowing the answer. "I guess." I say weakly.

"That doesn't sound very convincing Rose." Caleb says moving towards me.

"It's complicated." I say uncomfortably.

Caleb keeps coming towards me until he's close enough to reach the books. He reaches out and gently touches the books before looking back to me. He's so close that I can feel the heat coming off him, and I can smell a sweet scent.

"They're family histories, authors and poets that our families knew generations back." Caleb says about the books.

"Oh." I say surprised. "That's a lot of history." I add jokingly to hide my interest.

"You have no idea." Caleb says in his serious tone.

Caleb smiles at me and gestures towards the couch. I quickly lead the way to the couch well aware, that he's very close behind me. I take a seat and Caleb sits down beside me. The silence begins to stretch.

"So…" I say nervously. "How do you like Grace Hall?" I ask lamely.

School. That's my big conversation topic. I'm so hopelessly lame.

"It's…Different." Caleb says. "There are certain people who make it worthwhile." He adds.

He smiles at me, his eyes burning a hole in my face while my cheeks go red. It doesn't take Hannah to tell me that he's flirting with me. *Yay!*

"Well I'm glad you feel that way." I say trying to play it cool.

"How about you?" Caleb asks, one eyebrow raised.

"What about me?" I ask shyly.

"Do you like school?" He asks curiously.

I think about it for a moment. I mean no, I don't like school but it's definitely more bearable with him. But I wouldn't complain if things were a bit more normal. It also wouldn't hurt if my brother weren't hiding things from me. But if everything was great, I feel like maybe there'd be no place for Caleb or his friends. Something about them fits so perfectly into my life right now. I can't exactly say all of this to him though.

"Schools fine. It wouldn't hurt for some things to change but the people in my life are pretty awesome." I say blushing slightly.

"What things would you change?" Caleb asks curiously.

"Oh…Just things." I say trying to avoid the answer. "I don't want to bore you with the details." I add politely.

"Rose, nothing you ever say could bore me." Caleb says honestly.

I look into his eyes and I see a flicker, something so strange and familiar at the same time. In that moment I have a distinct feeling of déjà vu, like we've had this conversation before. Maybe it means that I can tell him everything and finally open-up to someone. *But it's a risk I'm just not willing to take.*

"It doesn't even matter." I say shrugging off my disappointment.

I would have liked to have told him, to have him understand without thinking I'm crazy. Honestly though, who would? Even I think I'm crazy.

"Alright. Well if you decide you want to talk about it. I'm always here." Caleb says sincerely. "I'm going to go order some pizza. Is that ok?" He asks.

"Yes, that sounds good." I say.

"Ok." He says as he gets up.

"Um Caleb…" I say nervously.

"Yes Rose." He says turning back to me.

"Thanks." I say simply.

"Of course." He says sweetly before leaving the room.

It's comforting just to know that he's here for me just like Xander said he was. Which reminds me, where is Xander? I haven't seen him. Hopefully he's not avoiding our "double date." I'd feel awful if he was.

Caleb walks back through the door and sits with me again.

"Pizza will be here in thirty minutes." Caleb says.

"Cool." I reply. "So, where's Xander?" I ask.

"He's visiting a friend. He'll be back tomorrow." Caleb says.

The way Caleb said it makes me think it was somewhat rehearsed. Maybe he's hiding out and they're only saying that he's out of town. *No.* I doubt these guys would do something like that. They know they don't have too.

"Well I hope he has fun." I say considerately. "Maybe he can hangout next time." I add.

"I'm sure he'd like that." Caleb says.

The silence takes over again, but I don't feel the need to talk. Just being with Caleb is interesting. It feels relaxed, normal even. I think he feels the same way. We sit there in quiet contemplation together but before I know it there's a knock at the door.

Knock. Knock. Knock.

"That'll be the pizza." Caleb says heading for the front door.

He comes back in carrying the pizza box and sits it down on the coffee table. Jason and Hannah come from the hallway looking flustered but presentable. Just in time. *What are the odds?*

"Hey. How'd you know the food was here?" I ask a bit confused.

"Oh. Uh. Lucky guess." Jason says with a glance at Caleb.

Hannah rushes to the seat beside me, tosses the pizza box open and starts eating. Jason and Caleb automatically sit across from us. The rest of us grab our own slices and we all start chowing down.

We have an enthusiastic conversation about the best and worst teachers at Grace Hall and have several good laughs. By the time things start to calm down, the pizza is gone, and Hannah has managed to sit on Jason's lap.

"Thanks for the pizza Caleb." I say gratefully.

"Yeah. Thanks." Hannah says fully focused on Jason.

"No problem." Caleb says.

Within seconds, Hannah and Jason are lip locked and going at it like they forgot all about us. Caleb gets up from his seat smirking and shakes his head. He looks at me while I fight to stifle my laughter and gestures for me to follow him.

We leave the other two to enjoy their steamy make out session. Caleb leads me out into the hall and to a curved, cement staircase leading into the basement. It's pitch-dark and Caleb stops on the second step and turns back to me.

"Don't be afraid." Caleb says, reaching out for my hand. "You can trust me." He adds.

I take his hand without a second thought and let him guide me to the floor. We walk down a dark hallway and Caleb flicks on a light in a room on the side. I follow him in and quickly realize we're in his bedroom.

There's a king size bed sitting at one end of the room, with a dresser and flat-screen TV directly across from it. There's also a desk and a bookshelf with several precariously piled books teetering on the edges. It's nothing like what I expected.

The bed has a canopy made of a dark red fabric. It sits up higher than most on an ornately carved wooden frame. It's covered in silk sheets, a matching comforter, and lots of fluffy pillows, even the dresser matches the bed frame.

"This is your room?" I ask quietly.

"Yes." Caleb says, watching me with an amused expression. "Why? What's wrong?" He asks worried.

"No nothing, it's just...Well it's cleaner than I expected." I say with a smirk.

Caleb laughs as he walks to his dresser. He's still smiling when he turns back to me with the remote in hand.

He walks back over to me and hands me the remote. I reach for it without being able to take my eyes off his. He just looks so happy right now. His eyes are practically screaming it. I grip the remote blindly and I quickly realize that his hand is partially under mine.

It's different than the other times I've held his hand. There's something about the moment that feels incredible. I don't know how to explain it, but it feels like we're connecting. *Lame, I know.*

"Sorry." I say holding his gaze but releasing his hand.

"Don't be." He says quietly. "Here." He adds giving me the remote again.

I grasp the end of it and shuffle to the bed. I stop at the edge, hesitating for a moment before I climb up and flick on the TV. Caleb slips a movie in and joins me. Unlike me, he's completely unfazed by our proximity or location and he leans back into the pillows. The title plays.

"Bram Stokers Dracula?" I ask surprised.

"Have you seen it?" Caleb asks.

"Of course, I have." I reply. "It's a classic, but the book is better. The books are always better." I add.

"Agreed." Caleb says happily.

"What do you think of Dracula?" Caleb asks suddenly, about an hour into the movie.

"Well that depends on my mood." I say with a laugh. "On the one hand, I feel bad for him. He wants to be in love, but he can't have it the way he is. On the other hand, he's a killer so maybe he shouldn't have love." I explain.

"You can't really believe that. Everyone deserves a chance at love." Caleb says.

"Maybe...I really wouldn't know." I admit shyly.

"One day you will." Caleb says confidently.

"I hope so." I say honestly.

I wonder what makes him so sure that I'll experience love. I want to believe that I will but it's hard to think that somewhere in the mess that is my life, love is waiting for me.

"What if you're just not destined to have a normal life, including love?" I say sleepily.

"Normalcy is all about how you see things." Caleb says kindly. "No matter how messed up your life is, love always finds a way." He adds reassuringly.

I lean back on the pillows with Caleb's comforting words playing in my mind. I feel very relaxed and several hours later when Hannah comes to the room to get me, it's clear that neither of us want to leave. But there's Alex, so we need to.

All the way home and until we pass out, we gossip about the guys. It almost seems perfect but the more we talk about them, the more something feels slightly off. I just can't put my finger on it.

CHAPTER TWENTY-TWO

Rose

Weeks have gone by now and nothing exciting has happened. It's the same old, same old. School is as thrilling as ever. *If sitting in prison is your idea of thrilling.* The only highlight is dividing my time between Morgan and Caleb. Morgan is still playful with me and seems to take full advantage of any situation where we have physical contact, but he hasn't tried to kiss me again. Caleb is the same as usual. The occasional kiss on my hand, or intense, longing gaze. He has had opportunities to make a move. I mean, most of the time he brings me home. But for whatever reason he hasn't tried anything, even when he visits me at night. But at least I don't have to hide anything from Alex.

Though, I don't even know if he would care now. He's been distant, quiet, uninterested and uninvolved in my life. *Not like himself at all.*

On a happier note, Hannah and Jason seem to be officially together. They've become even more "lovey dovey" with each passing day. Despite my mixed-up love life. I'm happy for both of them, but at the same time I'm jealous. I want what they have, or at least something similar.

With it being October now, attention has turned towards the Winter dance in a couple months. No one has asked me yet. And by that, I mean Morgan or Caleb. I don't know if either will. I don't know what I would say if they both did. *Yet, it would make me feel special.* I probably won't be going though.

So now here I am again. Thursday evening and I'm sitting on the couch with Morgan waiting for Alex to come home. He's late tonight but only by an hour or so. No need to worry like he used to do on a regular basis. Besides it's not like we're mindlessly waiting. We're kind of goofing around too. Every now and then Morgan will give me a soft elbow to the ribs, and we'll end up in a fake wrestling match. It's fun.

Mid wrestle I hear the Camaro and I watch as Alex comes through the door. We haven't really spoken since he told me he loved me. Things are still a bit awkward since the fight. A lot of things were said that aren't easy to take back. Neither of us have forgotten yet.

"Hey." I say affectionately to Alex.

Alex turns to look at me but says nothing and keeps walking. *Something's wrong.* He wouldn't ignore me like that and the way he looked at me was creepy.

I turn to Morgan with a look of confusion on my face. He seems equally confused but there's something else too, concern maybe. He looks concerned for some reason.

Morgan gets up and heads for the kitchen. I follow only steps behind him. I want to know what's going on.

We watch Alex pull out a TV dinner and toss it into the microwave. He sets the timer and then looks at us, but he still doesn't speak. I don't know what is going on, this isn't like him at all. The look in Alex's eyes is murderous. I swear it's as though he's disgusted by the very site of us for some reason. I have no idea what to say to him or make of his attitude.

"Hey! Alex, is everything ok?" Morgan asks cautiously.

I'm glad he's here because I don't know what to do. I just know that something isn't right, and I want Alex to be himself so we can forgive and forget.

"Yeah, I'm fine!" Alex says curtly.

His voice is cold and sharp. He's acting and talking like a robot and it's worrisome. When the microwave beeps, he looks at us with an utterly bored expression before he turns his attention on his food. He sits at the table, ignoring the fact that we're standing there, and starts eating. Morgan and I can do nothing but stare. He finally decides to acknowledge that we're watching, and he looks up at us.

"What the hell do you guys want? I'm eating!" Alex says through gritted teeth.

Alex has never spoken to us like this before. Morgan seems just as perplexed as I am at the moment.

"Alex man, this isn't like you. What's wrong? You're freaking us out!" Morgan says timidly.

It's then that I see a flicker of darkness in Alex's eyes. It resembles a flame but its unnatural looking and sends fear flooding through me. It's like a switch has clicked in his brain and he just doesn't care anymore. I feel like he's changed somehow, and he frightens me.

"You guys want to know what my problem is? Fine! It's the two of you." Alex says with a smile. "Rose, you're such a brat, I hate that I have to call you my sister and I wish you weren't born. And Morgan, let's not forget about you. You act like my friend just to get closer to Rose, well screw you.

You have a home, why don't you stay there!" He says angrily.

I know the tears are coming before they do but soon after I'm balling at the hurtful things he said. Morgan is clearly caught between feeling incredibly angry and being very concerned. I watch feeling frightened as Alex throws his dinner across the room and storms out of the house. He spins his tires so fast that his tires fling gravel back at the house. I run upstairs and for the second time in weeks, I cry into my pillow. *This is all my fault.* He hates me now. I have pushed him away and this is what I deserve. I never thought I could do anything to make him hate me though. I'm blubbering, face down in my pillow and I can hear Morgan in the kitchen, likely cleaning up the mess.

I sit up on my bed and pull my knees to my chest. A few minutes later Morgan walks in, crosses the room swiftly, and throws his arms around me. I rest my head on his shoulder with my nose in his neck and I keep crying, like a lost little girl.

"I am so sorry Rose!" Morgan says sincerely.

"For what? You didn't do anything. I made him hate me!" I say sadly.

"No, you didn't, this isn't your fault. Something isn't right. That isn't Alex." Morgan says.

"Morgan, what are you talking about? That is Alex only he hates me now!" I sob.

I don't understand what Morgan could possibly mean when he says it's not Alex. I'm pretty sure that he is my brother, unless I'm in some alternate universe. Morgan doesn't even bother to explain or elaborate in his comment, he just shakes his head and holds me tighter.

I look up into his blue eyes and see the sparkle hiding in the sadness. His arms are still wrapped around me. There is something in his eyes that I usually don't see. Fear. *He's afraid of something.*

His grip around my body tightens and he keeps looking into my eyes. He leans in again and presses his lips against mine. His kiss is gentle and sweet. I kiss him back lightly, still unsure of my own feelings. He pulls away reluctantly and lets his arms drop.

"I'm sorry. I've wanted to do that for a while." He says with a smile.

I let out a nervous chuckle. I smile back at him and feel the heat creeping into my cheeks.

"It's ok." I say honestly.

The problem isn't knowing if I like, Morgan or Caleb. It's figuring out who I want to be with. *I like them both and it's killing me.*

"Rose, I need to go tonight. Keep your cell phone close, lock your door, and if anything happens, call me!" Morgan says seriously, rising from the bed.

"Wait. Seriously. You're leaving?" I ask shocked. "Is this because of me?" I add sadly.

"No. Of course not." He says sweetly. "I don't want to confuse you and I don't expect a choice. I just wanted to kiss you. And I want to stay but I have to take care of something." He says anxiously.

"Ok." I say with resignation.

I have no clue what Morgan is expecting will happen, nor do I know what he needs to go do. It's comforting that he thinks he is going to handle things though, whatever the situation may be. I don't have the slightest clue about what to do or where to start. Everything feels so out of control, and like my life is in ruins.

Morgan gives me a kiss on my forehead and leaves. I hear his truck take off in a hurry and I'm left alone in my house. I cross my room and shut and lock my door just like Morgan asked me to. I may not understand why he asked me to do this, but he wouldn't have if he didn't have a reason. *I just wish I knew what it is.* I still have the occasional tear fall while I go stroll over to my bed and lay down. I just want this Alex thing to be an awful nightmare that I can wake up from.

When I wake up its pitch dark and I know something woke me. I look at my alarm clock and see that it's only one in the morning. I roll onto my back and I'm about to try going back to sleep, when something feels off. I'm groggy but I know that I am being watched. I catch a figure in my limited vision. I suck in a gasp and flip on my lamp. I breathe out when I realize that it is just Caleb.

"Oh my god Caleb. You scared the shit out of me!" I say through deep breaths.

"I'm sorry Rose. I came in the window, but I didn't want to wake you." He says.

He walks around the bed and sits beside me. He is wearing a black V-neck shirt and dark blue jeans. His hair is perfect as usual, and he looks amazing.

"So, what are you doing here?" I ask surprised. *It has been a while.*

"Well, this may sound strange, but I had a weird feeling and I had to see you." He says.

"Really?" I ask confused.

I find it hard to believe that a feeling is what brought Caleb to my room, but he knows he doesn't have to lie to me to come in my window, he's done it before.

"I know it's weird." He chuckles. "It's hard to explain." He adds truthfully.

"That's ok it's been a weird night." I say with a sigh.

"Rose you don't need to explain anything to me." Caleb says knowingly. "I just saw that Morgan's truck wasn't here, so I figured I'd come stay with you, if that's ok of course?" He asks.

"Actually, I'll feel a lot better if you do, but if Alex sees your car…" I start to say.

I stop mid-thought because I'm not sure Alex would care anymore but I certainly don't want to set him off again.

"No worries! I parked down the road, so he'll never know." Caleb says reassuringly.

I do feel a lot better with someone here, especially Caleb. He makes me feel warm and tingly and we've never even kissed. I'm sure if Caleb and I start making a habit of his sleep overs, then that will eventually change, but there's too much on my mind to be thinking of that. Anyway, where's Morgan? What's he doing?

Caleb takes a place next to me on the bed, but he stays on top of the blankets while I am under. I roll over to turn off my lamp and I stay on my side facing my clock. I feel Caleb's hand go over my hips and rest on my belly. Just when I start to think that I know what I want, an intimate moment like this change's things. I push my back against his chest, and I can feel his breathe on my neck. I feel so close to him right now. I'm beginning to see a pattern forming with me snuggling with guys. I'd be concerned but it's harmless, at least I think it is. I can't really focus on this right now. I have more important things on my mind.

"Thank you, Caleb!" I say quietly as I drift off in his arms.

I wake up suddenly again even though I know I just fell back to sleep not long ago. I open my eyes but instead of seeing Caleb and my room, I'm looking at trees. I'm wearing the exact same thing I fell asleep in, but I know this is a dream. I'm back at the cemetery, standing in front of my parent's graves. *I remember this well.* I turn around to look at the tree line in the distance. I see the familiar shape of the curious figure again. All too quickly they're coming at me in a blur and they stop right in front of me. I don't think I feel like I'm going to pass out this time, but my eyes are still closed. It seemed like a good idea at the time, and now I'm afraid to open them.

"Rose, do you remember this?" The voice asks.

I recognize the voice and I'm so surprised I start to fall backwards again. I clench my eyes tight and wait for the pain that will soon be unleashed on the back of my head. Instead I feel two solid hands grab me by the shoulders, hauling me back upright. I open my eyes and there's Caleb smiling at me. He let's go but watches me carefully to make sure I don't fall. If this wasn't just a weird dream, I would begin to think that the boy at the cemetery had been Caleb all along. Obviously though, it's not possible and this has to be a dream. Though, I'm beginning to have my doubts about reality.

"Caleb? What are you doing here? Am I dreaming?" I ask nervously.

"I need to talk to you. It's important!" Caleb says urgently.

"Ok." I say with confusion.

"Rose, do you trust me?" He asks seriously.

"That's a silly question." I say. "I let you sleep in my bed." I add.

"I need to hear you say it!" He says forcefully.

"Well I probably shouldn't but I do Caleb, for some unknown reason I trust you!" I say with mild amusement.

Clearly, I'm dreaming so it's alright if I say all the things I could never admit in real life. Besides it might be kind of fun to see where my mind takes me if I play along.

"Good." He says more calmly.

"You never answered my question. Am I dreaming?" I ask again.

"Yes and no! You're dreaming but you're not controlling the dream. I apologize but I had to hijack your mind." Caleb says apologetically.

"Sure." I say not really paying attention.

Ok I want to play along, really I do but it's hard not to laugh at myself. Not to mention it's really confusing because I don't know where this stuff is coming from. Some dark, twisted part of my brain obviously.

"Rose, I need you to believe me, at least a little." Caleb says pleadingly.

"Uh, ok…I'll tell you what. If you lose the shirt, I'll give you the benefit of the doubt and keep an open mind. Deal?" I say bravely.

Caleb's cheeks turn pink and for a moment he seems shocked into silence. I won't lie but I panic for a minute because if I actually told him to lose the shirt I would die. I calm down and remind myself that it is just a dream. In fact, my dream Caleb is trying to hide a smile right now from my proposal.

"Rose! You're not taking me seriously." Caleb says frustratedly.

"Oh gosh! Ok I believe you…Happy?" I say giving in to myself.

He doesn't look happy at all. Apparently, my dream version of him is even more brooding than in reality. It's too bad because this could be fun.

"Ok try and stay with me Rose. Your still safe in bed next to me, but your mind is in the dream realm with mine. The how is not important right now!" Caleb says impatiently.

"Ok. So, I'm still cuddled up with you in my bed but part of me is here too? That's what you're saying." I say.

His face flashes an angry look with my obvious disbelief.

"Rose, that is the truth. Why are you making this so difficult?" He asks.

"The truth. Ha." I say angrily. "I wish people would tell me the truth." I add.

His facial expressions go from defiant to defeat in seconds and I know his reply will suck. But what does dream Caleb know anyway? *Absolutely nothing.*

"I am trying too." Caleb says steadily.

"Sure, you are! Just like Alex and Morgan." I say stubbornly.

"Rose please! We don't have time." He begs.

"Ok." I say acknowledging his pleading tone.

I resign to play along with my subconscious, only because I don't want to upset dream Caleb. I just have to say that I have a surprising lack of control over my dream.

"Thank you! Do you remember what happened here? Before you woke up in the hospital?" Caleb asks thoughtfully.

"I think so…But…Hey! The real you wouldn't know anything about that." I say. "Not unless you were…" I start.

"There? It was me." Caleb says calmly. "The person who scared you was me and for that I am sorry. I thought you already knew. If I'd have known, I would have done things differently or at least caught you, but you surprised me." He says sadly.

I shake my head in disbelief, this is so confusing. There is something in his eyes that makes me want to believe him but it's so farfetched, and I have too many questions.

"Uh uh…no! It was a figment of my imagination and nothing more. Come on Caleb, do I look stupid to you?" I say defensively.

"No, you look smart. So put the pieces together." Caleb says.

"Look if what you're saying is true, that would mean you have inhuman speed and god knows what else. So, what are you? An alien? You have to understand how crazy this all sounds." I say.

"You probably won't believe me." Caleb says hopelessly.

This Caleb sounds so sad and lost. I almost want to hug him, but wouldn't that be like hugging myself?

"Try me." I say patiently.

"Ok…You need to know that there are some things out there that can't be explained logically. There are creatures that exist not because of science but because of another world. A world that I, Xander, Jason, a few others and…you belong to. We're all a part of this world in different ways." He says slowly.

"Ok so exactly which planet are these…creatures from?" I ask.

"We're not from a different planet Rose, we exist in your world. Our realm is never far." Caleb explains.

"Okay and what are these creatures? What are you specifically?"

"We have many names but some you'll know. There's the carbonjak/enchanter, the muški melez and ženski melez, or half breeds, the utvara, krvi nestasko and…" Caleb pauses. "And there's the krvi čudovište, the vampire." He says sadly. "I'm a vampire Rose but we're not as evil as people believe, at least not all of us. You need to know and believe these things because you're being hunted, and I want to help you. You're part of our world!" He pleads with me.

I've got to be kidding myself right. I mean just because I am having one hell of a messed-up dream where someone spits a foreign language at me, doesn't make it real. It feels real though and the scary thing is that some of it makes sense.

"Caleb, I'm sorry but I can't believe it. You're insane, or rather I'm insane because it's my dream. I mean it's not even that convincing because if you're some unknown creature, shouldn't you look different. I mean for god sakes! You look like a male model and your body screams sex appeal. The only thing that is inhuman about you is how sweet, sexy and chivalrous you are, and how badly I want to kiss you every time I see you." I admit.

I start pacing in frustration with everything my mind has created.

"You really feel that way about me?" Caleb asks ignoring my disbelief.

"It doesn't matter how I feel about you, you'll never know because this is a dream." I say frustrated.

Caleb takes a step towards me and gestures with his arms in a plea for me to believe him.

"You're so innocent and ignorant Rose. I wish you could stay that way. I truly do. You must be so happy in your life full of the mundane, where you feel you belong." Caleb says.

I stop pacing and stare at him in amazement. I briefly forget that he's not real.

"You're messing with me, right? I have never felt like I belong. I have always felt like an outcast. I can't believe I'm telling myself these things I already know. I wish you were right and that there was more to my life. I would love to feel like I belong. Do you have any idea what it's like to feel like you will never belong anywhere and know that everyone else is content with their own stupid, little lives? I want to believe you, I do, but I don't." I say as tears start.

"I think I do know how you feel." Caleb says.

"How could you possibly know how I feel?" I say.

"Because, I'm a monster by nature, my instinct is to kill. Yet I refuse to do these things. Even among my own kind I'm an oddity. I am one of the only vampires to befriend an enchanter and a half breed. Some co-exist but they aren't friends. I am one of the few vampires who can still feel things. I'm an outcast too." Caleb says.

"I'm so sorry Caleb! I'm sorry that the only way I can have you in my dreams is to make you sad and so messed up." I cry.

"Please Rose? You're intelligent. Look into what I've said and piece it together. Don't forget there's a reason Alex doesn't want you out of his sight." Caleb says.

"Ok then. I'm going to go walk around until I wake up now so you can go away." I say.

"Just remember, when you need me come find me my little Rose." He says sweetly.

Caleb disappears and I'm left standing alone in the graveyard. I'm thinking that I shouldn't go to bed so emotionally messed-up from now on. I'd like to avoid any more of these weird ass dreams, hot guy or not.

When my alarm wakes me up in the morning, I automatically look next to me. Caleb is no longer next to me in bed. I turn off my alarm clock as I sit up. That's when I notice that Caleb is sitting in my desk chair, watching me. I blush slightly at the thought of me snoring or drooling but it quickly fades. I look outside the window and it's a gray depressing day. I watch the tree outside my window, sway in the wind and then I look back to Caleb. He's watching me with a concerned, pained expression. It scares me a bit and I move towards Caleb to talk.

"Caleb, what's wrong?" I ask trying to forget my dream.

"About two hours ago, I think your brother was standing outside your door." Caleb says.

"Oh! Did he say anything? The door is locked so he wouldn't be able to come in." I say.

"No, he didn't say anything. He just stood there for like twenty minutes. He didn't even turn the doorknob. Does he do that often?" Caleb asks concerned.

"No! Well not that I'm aware of but he's been different recently. Very recently. It started yesterday, he came home and he just kind of snapped." I recall.

I look off into the distance and try to fight back the feeling of tears.

"Oh…ok. Well, I'm going to take off because Morgan will likely want to take you to school today. So, I'll see you there!" Caleb says.

"Alright." I say puzzled.

He walks over, unlocks the door, and leaves. No smile, no kiss on the hand, nothing! I hope I haven't done anything offensive, like say Morgan's name in my sleep. I guess I still like Caleb, but he has a tendency of showing interest one minute and showing no interest the next. He's so difficult to read sometimes.

I take a quick shower and get dressed. I grab my phone and bag and head down the stairs. I hear Morgan pull in, so I head out to meet him. He smiles at me as I walk up to him, but it isn't a heartfelt smile. He walks me to the passenger side, opens the door and helps me in. He is quickly in the driver's seat taking us to the school.

I can't help but notice that everyone is acting strangely. Everyone seems less talkative and just more robotic, if that makes any sense. Me? Well, whenever I'm in the house I feel drained, like it's sucking out my life force. *Weird.*

The days are starting to blur together, and we all fall into a kind of rhythm together. It's very strange. Morgan always drives me to school, but he doesn't always attend classes himself. I get dropped off with Caleb, Xander and Jason in the morning and we usually meet up for lunch. Sometimes we all eat lunch together, including Morgan and Tyler and sometimes it's a different combination of the guys and Hannah. Either way I'm never alone. I've become better friends with everyone, especially Jason because when he is alone with you, he can talk your ear off. I even spend some one on one time with Tyler and he turns out to be pretty cool.

Caleb always drives me home after school now, and I seldom go out. I've become quite a hermit unfortunately. Alex is coming home less and less and when he does, he's almost always drunk. He never eats with me anymore and he's developing dark circles around his eyes. Caleb and Morgan have noticed this as well, and they usually steer clear of him. If the very look in his eyes didn't frighten me so badly, then I'd confront him about his health. I'm still waiting for the real Alex to show himself though.

Morgan and Caleb take turns sleeping over but they both keep a distance from me romantically. They both seem really preoccupied mentally with other matters. I feel too drained to talk to either of them about anything. If you look in a dictionary, catastrophe would be the definition of my life.

CHAPTER TWENTY-THREE

Rose

It's Friday in December. We have one more week of school before Christmas break. And I have every intention of making things better during the holidays. Especially with Alex, but also with Morgan and Caleb. I am finally going to make a choice. Things are finally going to change.

"Will I see you at the dance tonight?" I ask Caleb curiously as we pull into my driveway.

I'm not hinting for him to ask me, but I'm just wondering if he's going. I have been having strange thoughts about my dream of him. That in some miraculous way, it wasn't just a dream. I have decided to find out once and for all. I have translated a question for him in Croatian. I figure I'll ask him and if he answers then he knows the language and it was not a dream. If he looks at me like I am crazy, then I'm losing my mind.

Hannah and I are going to get ready at my house, and then Jason is going to take us. Hannah only agreed to this because she felt bad when neither Morgan nor Caleb asked me to go. *Like I said, everyone has been a robot.*

"I'll be making an appearance." He says with a smile. "Save me a dance." He adds irresistibly.

He gets out of the car, comes around, opens my door, and offers me his hand. I put mine in his and he guides me up out of the car with ease. He holds my hand and my gaze for a while. For a moment, he seems to relax and turn into his old self again. But he lets me go just as quickly and slides back around the car.

He pulls out of the driveway as I climb my porch steps. I look out into the sky. It's gray, cloud-covered and depressing but it is December. *So, no surprise there.* It's cold out but we haven't yet seen the first snow fall.

I watch as Jason's silver caddy pulls in. Hannah jumps out and runs around to the driver's side. She leans in the window, obviously giving Jason a kiss. When she backs up, she is handed several items through the window. She heads towards me on the porch but she's carrying so much that I can barely see her face.

"We got hair, makeup, jewelry and breath mints." She says excitedly as she walks past me.

I open the door for her and look back to the driveway, but Jason is already gone. I follow her inside and up the stairs. She starts spreading out the hair stuff, makeup and jewelry. I pull the garment bags with our dresses out of my closet and hang them. I sit our shoes next to them as well.

"Are you ready?" Hannah asks, plugging in a hair curler.

"Sure." I say as happily as I can.

Apparently, she is taking the dance very seriously. Maybe I would to if I was going with someone special. *Oh well.* I refuse to ruin Hannah's mood with my sour attitude.

I take a seat on the stool that she placed in between us. I promised to let her do my hair and make-up for the dance tonight.

"Ok, so Jason is going to pick us up in about four hours." Hannah says. "That should be enough time to get ready." She adds calculatingly.

"Ok." I say with a giggle. "Thanks for getting ready with me!" I add.

"Of course." She says. "Where is Morgan? I thought he'd be here." She asks with astonishment.

"Honestly, I don't know. I haven't seen him since lunch." I answer with disappointment.

"I'm totally surprised that Caleb didn't ask you to the dance." She says genuinely. "Every time I go over, he asks about you. Then looks all sad. He's clearly, totally into you. I just don't get it." She says confused.

I think about it while she works on my hair. I'm just as confused as she is. He drives with me everyday, eats lunch with me, sleeps in my bed. I don't understand what's holding him back.

I simply shrug my shoulders at Hannah because I don't know what to tell her about Caleb. Maybe he's just not interested anymore.

After several hours we both have our hair and makeup done. Jason will be here any minute, so we have to get our dresses on. Hannah is wearing a beautiful, red, floor length, strapless dress with sequins at the top. She has matching red, peep-toe, pumps and sparkly jewelry. Her hair is up in an elegant braid and bun. She looks like a movie star.

I put on an ivory, floor length, silk, halter gown, that closes just above my naval. It also drops in the back to just above my butt. Needless to say, it shows a lot of exposed skin, especially since I can't wear a bra. With it I put on some nude, close-toe, pumps, and some simple studs. My hair is curled and half-held back by a loose braid. Hannah really knows how to glam it up.

"Hannah, you look amazing!" I compliment her. "Jason is going to lose his mind!" I add, as she smiles.

"Oh, I hope so. I think tonight is the night. I think I'm going to…you know…spend the night with Jason." She says nervously.

"Really? I hope it's perfect." I reply trying to hide my jealousy.

I'm not into Jason or anything, I would give anything to feel so sure of a guy though. But I really hope tonight is everything she wants.

Just then, I hear a knock at the door.

"Come on. That's probably Jason." Hannah says excitedly, rushing to the door.

She flings the door open and Jason is standing there, wearing an all-black suit, and looking extremely handsome. His mouth breaks into a smile at the sight of Hannah. *Rightfully so!* You can see the adoration in his eyes as he looks her up and down. He pulls her into a hug and gives her a tender kiss.

"You look more beautiful than an angel!" He says lovingly.

"You clean up good too." She responds with a wink.

He puts an arm around her waist, and you can tell that she is still blushing.

I look back down the hall towards Alex's empty bedroom. He's late again, if he even bothers to come home. This is not how I pictured winter formal. I thought Alex would be here, giving us the third degree. I thought I'd have a date of my own. Even before my friendship with Morgan heated up, I really thought that at least Morgan would have asked me to the dance, but he never did. I thought things would be different, and I'm disappointed in reality.

"Rose, you look stunning!" Jason says.

He and Hannah had snuck up beside me and he gently put his free arm around my waist.

"Ladies, shall we?" He says smoothly, taking us towards the car.

He opens the front door for Hannah and helps her in carefully. They share a loving look and I feel tears well in my eyes. I already have the rear door open when Jason closes Hannah's. He turns to me, placing his hand on top of mine, on top of the car door.

"He'll be waiting for you." He says softly to me before helping me in the car and closing the door.

My pulse quickens. It's as if they already know what I am going to do. I'm nervous about all the new questions that the answer could lead to.

Once we are in the school. Hannah and Jason hurry off towards the gym and the music. I stop in the hallway, unsure that I am ready for the answers that I wanted so badly. Jason looks back at me before disappearing down a hallway. I walk towards the courtyard to get some fresh air. We just got here but the air already feels thick.

I walk out into the chilled evening air. It's dark other than the white string lights draped from the gazebo, trees, and shrubs. I walk up on the gazebo and look out. It's beautiful in the dark and you can hear the music playing in the gym.

"You look..." He says speechless, as I turn to face him. "Enchanting!"

He stutters out.

Caleb had snuck up behind me and now stands gazing at me only a meter away. But he genuinely looks awestruck which is the reaction I was hoping for. He looks dazzling in an all-black suit with a black tie.

"Thank you!" I say, looking away while I blush.

I turn my back to him to try and focus on the task at hand. A question that could change everything. My heart starts beating harder and I realize I'm nervous.

"Are you alright?" Caleb asks with concern in his voice.

I feel his hand on my lower back, as he moves closer.

"I'm fine, but I need to ask you something." I say while looking into his beautiful gray eyes.

All he does is nod. Almost like he knew this was coming but he also worries what the answer will do.

"Dance with me first." He says pleadingly.

He doesn't wait for my answer before pulling me right up against him. He takes my right hand in his left and places his right hand on my exposed lower back. I rest my left hand on his shoulder.

My skin under his hand immediately begins to tingle, and the heat rises in my cheeks. My pulse quickens and I have to concentrate on my breathing. If he notices my reaction to him, he pretends not to. Or perhaps, he's enjoying it privately.

We sway to the music, our bodies barely an inch apart. I start to feel like it doesn't matter what his answer would be. I look up into his mesmerizing gray eyes, everything else starts to drift away. He takes his hand off my lower back and caresses my cheek. In that moment I'm sure that he's going to kiss me, and my breath catches in my chest. My senses come back to me only for a moment.

"No." I say, pushing him back from me. "I need to know." I add.

"You need to know what?" He asks calmly, with a knowing tone.

"…" I hesitate and say nothing.

"Rose." He says expectantly.

"…krvi čudovište…" I say weakly.

"Yes." He answers even though I didn't ask a question.

I didn't have to ask the question because he knew where our conversation was going. And in that one word answer I could hear a darkness that I never noticed. *He's dangerous!* And yet, his voice is also laced with regret and defeat.

He moves back towards me and tries to touch me, but I can't.

"No. Don't touch me!" I say forcefully.

And even though there is a tremendous ache in my heart, and overpowering hurt in his eyes, I run. I run because he's a liar and for some reason, his lie feels like the biggest betrayal.

I run to the gym and see Jason and Hannah talking to Xander. They smile at me, but I can't bring myself to smile back. Jason and Xander stop smiling as they figure out that I know. Xander begins pushing his way through the crowd to me. I can see that he wants to talk to me, but I just can't.

Despite expecting this, I am so unprepared for what it really means. I take off before he gets to me and find Morgan talking to Tyler next.

"Take me home." I say with panic in my voice.

"Why? What's going on?" Morgan asks with worry.

His eyes are scanning the room in search of the cause of my panic. And in that moment, I decide to forget what Caleb's truth means about Morgan, because I need time to process, and right now, I need a ride home.

"Morgan please?" I plead. My voice deep with desperation.

Morgan says nothing but grabs my hand and begins taking me to the exit. I see Caleb come into the gym on my way out and he stares at me intensely.

"You look amazing." Morgan says, breaking our silence on the way home.

I can't bring myself to say anything in return though. Because although I've chosen to forget his truth, he's still a liar too.

A few silent tears stream down my face. The weight of what I've just discovered crushes down on me.

"Please, talk to me." Morgan says sadly.

I remain silent, aware that he keeps looking over at me. But I have so much to say that I don't know where to start.

"How could you?" I say, with bewilderment.

"How could I what?" Morgan says with genuine confusion.

"How could you lie to me for so long? How could you pretend to be my best friend?" I say sharply.

I can feel the anger in my chest bubbling to the surface. I guess I can't look the other way at his lie. He holds my gaze while still driving.

"I know what you are!" I say bluntly.

Morgan hits the brakes hard. He's breathing heavily, rapidly. He wasn't expecting this.

"You know." He states. "How?" He asks in disbelief.

I let him think about it. I want him to know what it feels like to have unanswered questions. The engine continues to rumble, and it's deafening in the silence. I watch as understanding hits and anger crosses his face.

"Caleb." He says furiously as a statement, not a question.

He turns back to the steering column, looking at nothing. His hands tighten on the steering wheel, making his knuckles go white. I let out a small gasp at his reaction. He looks like a different person right now. I've never seen him this pissed off. He's normally so easy-going.

Briefly, I forget that I'm the angry one. But not for long.

"You don't get to be angry." I say furiously.

He slams the truck into park roughly and looks back at me. I haven't taken my eyes off him. I dare him to act like he's the victim here. His face softens as he focuses on me. The rage in his eyes is replaced by fear.

"I didn't want to lie to you." Morgan says with honesty.

"But you did." I say quickly. The hurt apparent in my voice.

"Alex didn't…" He begins but stops. "No excuses." He adds with guilt.

I'm beyond hurt. My entire world is collapsing around me.

"Why?" I ask puzzled.

"When you were little, it was easier to not tell you since you were growing up away from that world." He begins. "As you got older, finding a way to tell you seemed impossible." He adds. "But we wanted to protect you. We thought not knowing was best." He continues.

"Protect me from what?" I ask eagerly.

"Everything." Morgan says tiredly.

We go quiet as I try to accept everything he has said. I'm assuming his "everything" includes the Lord guy that I have been seeing. His "we" obviously refers to Alex. I knew that they had secrets, I just didn't know to what extent.

He was supposed to be my best friend, maybe even more. Was that even real? I just don't know anymore.

"Did you ever care about me?" I ask, with fresh tears starting to fall.

Morgan moves across the bench seat and takes my hands in his. His eyes are filled with regret and compassion.

"Of course, I care about you! You're my best friend!" Morgan says easily. "I still want to be more." He adds, with hope.

I look into his eyes. I want to believe him, and I think I do. But this is just too much. I'm exhausted. I pull my hands out of his and ignore the look on his face.

"I need some time. I want to be alone." I say, with resolve.

"You can stay at my place. I'll stay with your brother." Morgan offers kindly.

"Thank you!" I say softly.

Morgan puts the truck back in drive and heads towards his place. I stare out the window, as dark shapes rush past.

When he drops me off at his house, I grab my bag and run inside. I tear off my clothes, put on one of his shirts, turn off my phone, lock the door, and crawl into bed. I plan to stay here essentially all weekend, leaving the room only for food and bathroom breaks.

CHAPTER TWENTY-FOUR

Rose

I wake up sometime in the afternoon on Saturday. I don't know the time. I also don't care. I have no intention of facing the world yet. I grab my phone though and bring it in to Morgan's bed.

I want to call Hannah. To tell her everything and have someone to talk to. But she had big plans for last night. She was going to give herself to Jason completely. I can't burden her with my drama, no matter how bad it seems. I let my phone fall to the floor, deciding to keep my misery to myself.

I fall back to sleep in a pit of my own despair.

Morgan

Knock. Knock. Knock.

I grunt and slide off the couch at Rose's house. I heard someone knock on the door. *Maybe it's Alex.* I think to myself. He hasn't been home all weekend. I glance at my phone before getting up. It's after one in the morning on Monday. *Who could that be?* I wonder as I stumble to the hallway.

I don't wonder long. I can sense him before I reach for the doorknob. I throw the door open in anger. It's his fault that Rose won't talk to me.

Caleb stands there, arms crossed, and a bored look on his face. Xander and Jason stand at the bottom of the stairs, but within earshot.

"You've got a lot of nerve, vampire." I say viciously.

Caleb uncrosses his arms and takes a menacing step towards me. He thinks he can intimidate me, but I have news for him.

"You've got no one to blame but yourself." Caleb says through clenched teeth. "She had every right to know." He adds angrily.

"Yes. And I would have told her." I say defensively, taking a step towards him.

"When?" He asks skeptically. "Is that before or after Dalibor was torturing her into submission." He continues, pointedly.

"I would have protected her." I say smartly.

"You would have failed…" Caleb says flatly.

135

I take another step towards him. He's so arrogant. I don't understand what Rose sees in him. I just want to cast a spell of pain on him and see how tough he really is. I clench my fists tight, preparing for a fight.

Caleb and I are staring each other down. Neither of us wanting to show any weakness to the other. Xander quickly glides up the steps and stops between the two of us. He puts a hand on Caleb's shoulder.

"We didn't come to argue Morgan." Xander says calmly. "We came to see how Rose is doing since she won't answer her phone." He adds firmly.

I smirk at Caleb. She trusted me with her whereabouts but not him. *Maybe I still have a chance.* I realize.

"She's not here." I say smugly. "She wanted some space." I add, knowingly.

"And you think that's a good idea?" Caleb says harshly.

"You certainly don't know Rose very well if you think I had a choice." I say crassly. "Besides, she's in a safe place!" I add.

"Why didn't you stop her?" Caleb demands pretentiously.

"Did you want me to tie her up?" I ask, stunned.

"If that's what it took, then yes." Caleb admits. His temper rising.

My dislike for him begins to flair again. I become stiffer, the tension between us is palpable.

"Rose is a person. A sweet, funny, caring person. She deserves to have a choice." I say confidently.

Caleb has nothing to say to that. No smart remark. He's been around so long that he has forgotten how to treat people. If you take away their freedom, you're no better than Lord Dalibor.

"Can you tell us where she is?" Xander asks patiently.

"No." I say, stubbornly. "If she wanted you to know, then you would." I continue.

Caleb steps forward, shaking off Xander's hand. His eyes flash dangerously as he points a finger in my face.

"You can either tell us, or I can make you tell us." Caleb says threateningly. "It's your choice." He adds. "You know what I am. What I am capable of…" He reminds me coldly.

"I do. And soon, so will Rose." I say proudly.

Xander puts himself directly in between me and Caleb.

"We don't want it to be like this. Please. Don't make him do this!" Xander says seriously.

I can hear the desperation in his voice. But I just can't let Caleb know where Rose is.

Xander lets out a frustrated sigh. He was trying to keep the peace but it's pointless. I will never work with the vampire. Especially THAT vampire. Xander turns to leave but stops and catches Caleb's eye.

"He's young. He's Roses best friend. Remember that." Xander says, before he goes down the steps. Caleb tosses some car keys down to his friends. It's his way of telling them to go. That he has business left to do. Caleb stands there, staring at me, a small grin forming as his friends back out of the driveway.

"She won't choose you after this." I say deliberately.

"We'll see." Caleb replies consciously.

Caleb lands a blow to my ribs. I feel the bruising and swelling already. He's strong. I knew he would be. He takes a step back while I try to suck in air. He's holding back, cautious not to lose himself. I can tell.

"It didn't have to be like this Morgan." Caleb says, in a matter-of-fact tone.

"You can't always get what you want." I say, as I stand up straight.

Caleb manages another hit to my stomach, with more force. I double over, winded, coughing.

"Perhaps. But I usually do." Caleb replies pompously.

He pulls me to my feet only to punch me right in the jaw. His hand impacts so hard, my ear starts ringing.

"Come on Morgan. I know I'm a vampire, but you could at least try to fight back." He says tauntingly.

I manage a few hits. One to his jaw, nose and ribs. Of course, he starts healing immediately. I on the other hand will need a few days to recover completely.

As I lay on the porch after enduring several more fists from Caleb, it occurs to me that I need more combat training. Caleb is sitting on the railing, looking out at the night. Small spatters of blood on his shirt and hands are the only evidence of his fight.

"You're loyal. I'll give you that." Caleb says with surprise. "But. It can't beat passion." He adds, heading down the stairs.

"Your affection for her is toxic. She's smart. She will see it." I say, intentionally trying to get under his skin.

He looks back and grins at me as he walks down the driveway. I know he's considering what I said, even if he doesn't want me to know it. The whole time we fought, he stayed in his human form. He maintained control. He didn't want to do something he'd regret, for Rose's sake. He cares more than he lets on.

I stumble back inside to tend to my own wounds.

Caleb

The bathroom fills up with steam as I let the scalding water, in my shower, rinse the blood down the drain. I came home after fighting Morgan.

Xander met me when I came in. He told me that Jason was using magick to locate Rose. He didn't ask about Morgan. I only had a little blood on me though. A combination of Morgan's blood and mine on my shirt and hands. I didn't want to hurt him. *Okay. Maybe I did a little.* I admit to myself. At least I didn't kill him. He thinks he's better than me because I am a vampire. *Maybe he is.* At this point, it's hard to tell. He's going to be sore for a few days. But he will live.

He got a few good shots on me. He has more strength than I expected. Mind you, I wasn't using any vampire abilities. We had a good, old fashioned, fistfight. It didn't solve anything, but it felt good to hit him.

I wanted to get cleaned up before I see Rose. She already thinks I am the devil, let alone if I show up covered in blood.

I turn off the water and step out of the shower. The hot water had felt good. I was hoping it would wash away some of the monster I have become. But that's a high expectation for water.

I wrap a dry towel around my waist and wipe the moisture off the mirror. As I look in the mirror, I can see that people see me as attractive. But I can see how lethal I am and how "toxic" my affection can be. Morgan sees it too. He doesn't want me to have her, but I don't think I can stay away.

"Hey. Jason found her." Xander says, from the other side of the door.

"Where?" I ask, opening the door.

"She's at Morgan's place actually." Xander says tiredly.

"Of course, he couldn't just tell us." I say incredulously. "Well, I'm going to go see her." I add resolutely. "You guys should stay back and get some rest." I continue, noting his condition.

"Are you sure?" Xander asks apprehensively. "Can you stay in control? I know how she makes you feel!" He adds, rationally.

"I'll be fine." I say calmly. "Besides Jason needs some rest. Morgan had some pretty powerful magick protecting Rose. He's probably drained." I add considerately.

Ok. Goodluck! I hear Xander relay in my head, as he turns to leave.

I throw on some clothes and head out. It's after three but I need to see her. I need to explain myself.

Rose opens the door, looking less than pleased to see me. Before I can say anything, she tries to slam the door shut. I quickly slide my foot in the way. She angrily steps away from the door. I go inside even though my intrusion only seems to ignite her anger more.

"Why are you here? Don't you sleep?" She asks with annoyance.

I take her in. Her hair is messy from sleep and she's clearly wearing a man's shirt. That is it. She is so beautiful, even when she is furious.

"No. I don't much. And I wanted a chance to explain." I say, trying to ignore the way her clothes have my blood pumping, so that I can give her answers.

"I don't care. Leave." She says stubbornly.

There's a pain in my chest from her words. I watched her at her pond, I would check on her in her room at night, leaving the window open as a sign, and I kept an eye on her from the shadows. But she will never know. She doesn't want to. I look at her disbelievingly. She's already forgiven HIM, but she won't even give me a chance. I feel my control slipping away. I step towards her, knowing my features have become darker, more menacing. She steps back from me as I see fear in her eyes.

"Give me a chance." I plead with her.

When I look her in the eyes, all I can think about is her skin against mine, and the warmth and sweetness of her blood. It takes all my restraint to keep myself in check, when I'm around her.

Her reserve softens as we keep eye contact. I can feel the passion and intensity between us. I know that she can too.

"I can't do this right now." She says reluctantly, crossing her arms.

I can hear the devastation in her voice. My desire to kiss her is unbearable. To feel her affection for just a moment. But I know if I do, I won't stop there. Instead, I do nothing. Which probably makes me seem cold and heartless. But it's the opposite.

She takes a deep breath and I hear her shudder. My presence is upsetting her. That's not what I want. I know then that I should leave. She's not ready for this talk.

"I know it's not worth much. But, I'm sorry." I say honestly, as I leave. Perhaps she will forgive me one day.

Rose

It has only been a few hours since Caleb came by, but I had to get ready for school. Last week and all. Seeing Caleb in the middle of the night, had been so hard. When he looked me in the eyes, I felt like there was so much left unsaid. Maybe it was just wishful thinking though.

When he's around, it's hard to breathe and my heart flutters. His gaze always feels so intense, but he never touches me or tries to kiss me. One minute, I'm sure he wants me. The next he's cold, indifferent.

I want to be with someone who knows what they want and shows it. *But a part of me wishes that was him.*

I managed to avoid almost everybody all weekend minus Caleb's little visit. I decide to call Hannah and ask for a ride today. When I turn my phone on, I am bombarded with missed calls and texts. I don't bother to check them. I don't want to talk to any of them. The only person I want to talk to is Hannah.

Oddly, I don't have a single missed text or call from her, which is weird given what her plans had been for Friday night. I try calling her three times with no answer. *Where could she possibly be?*

I have no choice but to send Morgan a text asking for a ride to school but by the time he gets back to me, I know I am going to be late. Which is better than trying to avoid Caleb, Xander and Jason.

I pick up my bag and go wait outside. I twist my hair between my fingers and I quickly notice how cold the weather is. I know the snow will be coming soon and I hate snow. It's cold, wet, and a real bitch to walk or drive in. Oh well, I can't control the climate.

Finally, Morgan's truck pulls in. When he hops out, I can't help but notice how tired he looks. He still comes around to help me into the passenger's seat though which is very kind, but I feel bad because he looks so exhausted, and it looks like he has bruises on his face. He closes the door behind me and climbs back into the driver's seat.

He hasn't said "hi" yet, so I'm guessing he feels as awful as he looks. We pull out and he heads for the school. I nervously glance over at him on the way to school and I see a piece of cloth wrapped around one of his hands, but I don't know why.

"Morgan, what happened to you?" I ask, concerned.

"Nothing, I'm fine. I just didn't get much sleep last night, but it's nothing to worry yourself over. I promise." Morgan says easily.

"What about your hand?" I ask curiously.

"I…Burnt it on some hot coffee this morning." Morgan says uncomfortably. "I promise you, I'm fine." He adds, convincingly.

"Sure." I say not buying the lie. *Obviously.*

I know there's more to it, but Morgan is very stubborn, and I know he won't tell me anything until he wants to.

He looks at me and gives me a small smile but it's sincere. I decide not to push the subject anymore and we drive the rest of the way in silence.

When we arrive at the school, Morgan drops me off at the front door. I know he is going to skip school today and hopefully he'll use that time to sleep. He needs it.

I walk to homeroom in a sullen mood and take my seat next to Tyler, he always saves me a seat now. Class is dull as per usual, I'm not really paying much attention. My eyes keep wandering over to where Hannah always sits and now it's just an empty desk. I'm a bit pissed that her so called friends, the popular snobs, haven't asked me about her absence. Not that I have an answer for them, but they don't even acknowledge that she's not here.

I can see Tyler watching me out of the corner of my eye, but I refuse to talk to him. He's friends with Morgan, Caleb and the guys, so who knows what he is or if he knows everything.

I return my attention to the window. I watch as the sky turns black, the clouds roll in on an aggressive wind, and I start to feel a bit edgy.

As the sky starts rumbling and flashing, I hear a vibration near my foot. Of course, it's only my cell phone so I pull it out and look at the caller.

I don't doubt that my jaw drops a few inches because I'm shocked. It's Hannah calling me, during class. I quickly get up and walk past the teacher to the door. As soon as the door is swinging shut, I answer the phone. Nothing can prepare me for what I hear.

"Rose...Are you there?" Hannah sobs into the phone.

It's Hannah's voice but she's crying. I can hear the fear and inevitability in her voice. It awakens a fire in my stomach to hear my friend so upset.

"Hannah. What's wrong?" I ask worried.

"Oh Rose, I tried to tell him he has the wrong person. He won't listen, he..." She quickly says before she's cut off.

Hannah is cut off before she can finish her sentence. She is clearly hysterical and I'm beginning to feel the same way. Now I know something is wrong.

I can hear the phone being shuffled around and Hannah's cries falls into the background. I'm obviously being handed off to someone else. The next voice I hear chills me to my core!

"Hello Ana!" The familiar voice of Dalibor says.

The man from my nightmares is now on the other end of my very real phone call. Even worse, this psycho has Hannah. I know I have to remain strong and fierce.

"Look Lord crazy, I'm not Ana and you've taken my friend. I don't know what the hell you expect from me?" I say angrily.

"My darling Roselyn, you will be what I want within a few years. However, I have been made aware of the company you're keeping, and I don't like it. So, consider your Hannah to be my insurance policy." Dalibor says with a laugh.

I hear Hannah make a small scream and then we're disconnected. I figure the bastard probably hung up on me. I'm staring at my phone in shock and disbelief, the halls are deserted so I am completely alone. I just can't accept that some psycho from my dream is real, and that he is the one responsible for my friend's disappearance.

What am I going to do? I feel like I have no one to turn to. I can't believe this. My world has become pure chaos.

My thoughts are put on hold when I hear an exceptionally loud rumble and a series of flickering ceiling lights. I tear my eyes away from my phone when I hear a multitude of screams from a class on the other level. The screaming doesn't subside. They continue to scream like they're being torn apart.

The door to my home room flies open behind me and in a blur, I feel an extremely warm hand grab my arm. They're already dragging me down the hallway, half running when I recognize the person. It's Tyler and he seems to be glowing slightly. We're nearly to the stairs when students start coming out of their rooms in a panic. Some look scared, others are running and some just stand there looking confused. I'd probably be doing the same if Tyler wasn't pulling me along.

Finally, I pull free of Tyler's grip, he's a lot stronger than he looks. Shockingly so in fact. I follow him down the stairs and abruptly stop. We are at the bottom of the stairway now and he looks up it. Concern, all over it.

"Tyler, what the hell is going on?" I ask demandingly.

"There isn't time to explain right now." Tyler says. "I will carry you if I have to." He adds.

I don't follow anything he says. It's like he was expecting this to happen, whatever it is. *Was that why he watching me in class?* I don't have a chance to say anything else because his hand is back around my arm and he's staring intensely up the stairs.

"Rose, we have to go…NOW!" He says urgently.

He's dragging me down the hall again but not before I glance up the stairs. Then I see what he's pulling me away from. Black clouds of fog are billowing down the stairs. The screams sound like they're coming from inside it. The mass rolls down the stairs and when it hits the floor, I see shadowy arms reaching out, and grabbing at everything and anything.

I recognize the situation. I had been in a similar one when I dreamt of my mother. She had told me to run and she had been engulfed in the fog and shadows. I turn on my heel and start running beside Tyler. No more resistance. He let's go of my arm when he realizes we are on the same page now. The only reason I'm following him is because I hear my mom's voice in my head telling me to run. I didn't doubt her then, I won't doubt her now.

When we come to the end of the hallway, Tyler grabs my arm and pulls me in the cafeteria doors. Tyler runs back to the doors with a mop and shoves it in the door handles as he backs up. He doesn't take his eyes off the doors as he stands level with me.

We both move back more as the fog comes up against the doors. I can see a frightening skull shape in the glass square of the door. The doors bump back and forth threateningly as it tries to enter. I hear as the mop begins to splinter at the center. We're trapped and the fog will eventually come in.

"Tyler, the mop isn't going to hold." I say hysterically.

We're both standing on the far side of the room with our backs pushed up against the shatter resistant glass. It's the only obstacle that stands between us and the courtyard which we can take at least to the gym.

"I know." Tyler says thinking. "We have to break the glass. I have to get you to the gym." He says.

We both turn our backs anxiously on the fog and start observing the glass for a weakness. It's quite obvious that neither of us like having our backs to the doors. The fog and whatever is inside of it, is still trying to break through the doors. I'm becoming frantic and I pick up the chair and throw it as hard as I can at the glass. It does absolutely nothing, no scratch, crack, or single mark showing trauma. We'll need an axe and more time to break through it, and we have neither.

Suddenly, the mop gives in splintering into pieces. The pieces of wood go flying in different directions and the doors fling open. The fog barrels in. It starts creeping towards us and all I can do is stare in horror.

Just when I think it's all over and that we are goner's, I feel Tyler put his arms around me and cover my head with his. It's a comforting gesture but I don't see how it's going to help us. The fog sounds like a tornado in the small cafeteria, wind is whipping my hair around my face, but I know it is close.

"Rose, keep your arms across your chest and close your eyes. DO IT NOW!" Tyler yells.

I do as he says but I don't have time to register what he's planning. It doesn't matter. Before I know it, we are moving backwards at an absurdly impossible speed. I realize we're going to hit the impenetrable glass and brace myself just as we do. I'm amazed as I hear it crash to the ground and shatter around us. It can't have been possible. I look at Tyler.

"It can't be possible?" I say in shock. "What are you?" I ask fearfully.

"Later!" Tyler says quickly.

I steady myself knowing we still have to run. Tyler looks at me only long enough to ensure that I have no injuries from the broken glass. He slips his hand on my back and ushers me towards the gym.

We run across the courtyard, and I'm majorly shaken at the fact that Tyler had thrown our bodies at the glass, and we'd busted through it without being harmed in the process. It's another incident that appears to have been humanly impossible. I don't care much at the moment, the only thing that matters is that we are putting distance between us and the fog. We're both running so hard but only I can't stop myself from running straight into the gym doors. Tyler stops on a dime and catches me as I bounce back from the collision with the doors.

The force of the impact seems to have given me a nose-bleed, but that is the least of our problems. After all, the fog is still coming. Tyler wrenches the door opens and leads me inside and behind the bleachers as the door closes behind us. He sits me down and gazes deeply into my eyes.

"Rose, stay right here. You'll be safe I promise." Tyler says. "DO NOT MOVE!" He adds seriously.

He jumps back up and runs out the opposite door. I don't know why he thinks I'll be safe in here, but he hasn't led me astray yet. I oblige him. He saved my neck, so I owe him my trust.

For several minutes I sit on the floor behind the bleachers. I have my knees pulled up to my face and I hug them tight. The gym door we came in begins to rattle and I fear that the hinges will break for sure. I'm terrified because I am all alone this time, Tyler isn't here to help me. Tears begin leaking down my cheeks and I'm suddenly very tired. It doesn't alarm me, I have been running for my life, or so it seems. My legs feel like jelly and my chest hurts with each breath. I know I don't have it in me to run again, this is where it ends. *But what is it?*

I accept my fate, life or death. With that thought planted snugly in my brain, the darkness begins to swallow me up and I do what most girls will do in my situation. I faint.

CHAPTER TWENTY-FIVE

Rose

I'm surrounded in darkness and silence when I come to. I keep my eyes shut because who knows what I am going to see when I open them. The silence is deafening now. I don't hear any students running and screaming, neither do I hear any sickly whispers, that had been coming out of the fog. *Is it over? What happened?*

I don't hear the doors banging, as the fog tries to get in. I'm afraid that the fog has gotten in and is right in front of me. Waiting for me to look so that the creatures can pull me in.

I work up the courage and open my eyes but as soon as I do, I am hit by a wave of nausea. It rolls over me and disappears in an instant. I know that I wasn't hurt so my best guess is that I am coming down from my adrenaline rush.

I reach my hands out and feel the surface that I am resting on. It's most likely a bed, at least, it feels like one. Even with my eyes open, all I can see is darkness though. There are pillows propped up behind my back, keeping me upright. It's a large bed. I can't feel the edges with my hands.

I rack my brain of my final memories. The last thing I remember was being in the school gym, hiding behind the bleachers. There was screaming. *So much screaming!* Tyler had just left me, and he said I'd be safe. But he jumped through glass without a mark on him. *What is he?*

Suddenly, I realize that I am in Caleb's bed. The bedding is made of silk. How did I not notice that before? *How did I get here? Why am I here?* I have so many questions. Then it dawns on me. *Caleb isn't human!* What does he want from me? *Am I in danger?*

I don't think Caleb wants to hurt me, but I don't even know him. He slept in my bed all those nights, and I never even knew what he was. For all I know, he might be waiting for something. *This maybe!*

I can see a glow where the curtains meet, falling from the canopy, now that my eyes are adjusting. I consider opening the canopy, but I can hear light footsteps coming in my direction. It's him. *It's Caleb!* But is he alone or is that Dalibor guy with him? For all I know they are working together.

My pulse quickens, and my heart starts beating hard. The footsteps slow outside the canopy. They know that I am awake. I tremble slightly out of fear.

The curtain is thrown open so quickly that I am blinded by the light flowing in, and I can't make out who is standing there. I rub my eyes, trying to refocus, but it doesn't matter because they speak.

"It's good to see that you've finally come to." He says affectionately.

I recognize the voice as I begin to focus. I see Caleb, now sitting on the side of the bed and watching me thoughtfully. At first, I'm filled with relief but within seconds I'm overcome with fear and disbelief. I want to forget my anger and hug him, but I can't.

"Caleb…" I say as my heartbeat quickens. "Please…What…" I stutter.

"Rose. Don't worry. You're safe now." Caleb says reassuringly.

I don't feel safe. Possibly because he's a liar. I stare at him with distrust in my eyes. And he can see it because he's careful not to reach out to me.
"I need to know what you saw. What happened in the gym?" He asks anxiously, ignoring my glare.

There is so much to say and I don't know where to start. And I'm not just talking about the events that happened at the school. How about the fact that he betrayed me, and I'm devastated? How about that this whole ordeal is insane, and I still can't believe it. I'm starting to feel sick again because I'm overwhelmed.

"Caleb, I don't want to talk to you." I say stubbornly.

The anger that I feel towards him, outweighs my fear of him right now.

When he looks at me, I see sympathy in his eyes and it's real. There are moments where he seems to care about me, I know that, but it doesn't change facts.

"I know." He says with remorse. "But you need to." He says in a matter-of-fact tone.

"Do I?" I ask, my voice filled with sarcasm and anger.

At-the-moment, it's easy for me to forget what he is, and to treat him like any other boy who betrayed my trust.

"Rose…" Caleb says, slightly annoyed.

I climb off the bed, careful not to have any physical contact with him. I turn and give him the meanest look that I can manage.

"I want to leave. Where's my phone?" I say forcefully.

"Stop acting like a child." He says, his temper rising.

His temper isn't the only one rising. He has no right to speak to me that way. I didn't ask for this. *Any of this.* I roll my eyes and make for the door hastily.

"Bite me." I say rudely, forgetting exactly who I am talking to.

Caleb leaps up, pinning me against the wall beside the door. His hands are around my wrists and he has them pushed against the wall, on either side of me. There's a silver flash in his eyes, and for a moment, he looks dangerous.

"Don't tempt me!" He says threateningly, through gritted teeth.

I turn my face away from him with a quivering lip. Exposing my neck may not have been the smartest idea but I just can't bear to see him like this. As the hunter. And I'm the prey.

Just then, the door opens and Xander moves swiftly through. His presence seems to calm Caleb and he releases his grip on me.

"Sorry!" He says, taking a step back from me without making eye contact.

"Is everything ok?" Xander asks pointedly, looking from me to Caleb.

"Yes." Caleb says with a sigh.

Xander looks at me and I simply nod. I don't speak. I don't trust my voice not to betray me. And I don't want them to know exactly how scared I am. *Especially Caleb.*

Xander looks back at Caleb and they seem to have a conversation without speaking. I watch as anger passes through Caleb's face, to frustration, to understanding and eventually defeat.

Caleb walks smoothly passed Xander, without even a look back at me. Xander turns his attention back to me, and I release the breath that I didn't know that I was holding.

"Are you alright?" Xander asks me, compassionately.

"I'm fine." I say tiredly.

It's a lie of course. I'm anything but fine. I mean physically I'm fine but emotionally I'm drained. I start to wonder if Caleb would have bit me, he seemed pretty serious.

"He would never hurt you." Xander says, seeming to read my mind.

"I don't know about that." I say disbelievingly.

"He wouldn't!" Xander says again seriously.

Xander takes a seat on the edge of the bed. With one last longing look at the door, I take a seat next to him on the bed.

"Please forgive Caleb. Sometimes his emotions get the better of him." Xander tries to explain. "And for someone of his…maturity, he can still be impulsive and insensitive." He adds.

"Whatever." I say, pretending it doesn't matter.

But it does matter. It matters a lot. My heart is breaking. It was bad enough when I realized he lied to me, but now, it's like he never cared about me. *And I cared about him.*

"Not whatever, Rose. It matters." He says, defending his friend. "This is new to us too, and he's trying." He adds.

I give him an incredulous look. Surely, he can't be referring to my life being turned upside down in comparison with anything.

"You were supposed to know, Rose." He says.

"I was supposed to know what?" I ask with confusion.

"That we exist!" He says sadly.

I suppose that if I had known about the existence of vampires, halflings, enchanters etc., discovering what I was would have been less traumatic.

"Well, Alex and Morgan never gave me that option." I say, with a stray tear making its way down my cheek.

Alex and Morgan lied to me too. Longer. I'm upset with them too, but for some unknown reason, Caleb's lie hurts more. Right now, I would forgive Alex flat out, if it meant I could have my brother back.

"I know that they lied to me too. And I am upset with them, but it hurts less somehow!" I say, confused. "I know it sounds stupid." I add.

"It doesn't sound stupid, Rose. You and Caleb have a special connection, and you feel his betrayal deeply." Xander says knowingly. "Just know that he hates himself for lying to you. He never wanted to." He adds truthfully.

"I just can't forgive him yet. Everything has changed." I say decidedly.

"We just want to protect you. Please let us!" He says sweetly.

Protect me? Protect me from what? Dalibor already has Hannah. My brother is broken. And my relationships are on the rocks before they even begin. What's left to protect? *My life is in ruins.*

"I need a minute." I tell Xander.

"Of course." Xander says, with an understanding nod.

Xander reluctantly rises from the bed and leaves the room. Giving me some privacy. I need to collect my thoughts and sort out my feelings. But it all feels like too much. The weight of my reality is crushing me. I can't breathe. I need air. It's not that I don't believe them, I just don't want this.

I carefully open the door and peak out. No ones in the hall. They've left me alone. *It's now or never!*

I sneak up the stairs and creep to the front door. The cold air hits my lungs like a knife but I find myself running and I don't stop. *I'll never stop.*

Caleb

I can't believe what I did and said to Rose. She probably thinks that I am such a monster. *Maybe I am.*

"You're not. Maybe a bit brooding though." Jason says with a smile, as he takes the seat next to me. He read my thoughts.

"Don't be so hard on yourself." Xander says, coming into the kitchen. "She doesn't think that. Though that wasn't your best self." He adds with a sympathetic grin. As he too joins our conversation.

The three of us are close. We've been around one another for so long so that sometimes we can hear each other's thoughts, if our guard is down.

"I know." I say, discouraged.

I'm disgusted and ashamed with my own behavior. I can't believe I let my emotions get the best of me. I know better than to use physical force on someone undeserving of it. Not to mention, I probably scared her with the "bite" threat. I didn't mean it though. I was just frustrated, and I let it get to me. She has a way of getting under my skin, but I would never hurt her. I only hope she knows that. I care so much about her. It's just hard for me to show her because I worry about losing control of myself with her. Being inhuman isn't always easy. I fight my basic instincts every day, and with her they're stronger.

"Where'd Tyler get to?" I ask curiously.

"He went to find Morgan and fill him in." Xander informs me.

Tyler really came through today and we owe him, so I try not to hold his friends against him. We have no find out why he is here though. But, I'm fairly certain that had he not been there, Dalibor would have gotten Rose. So, he can't be working with him.

Suddenly, we hear the floor in the living room. Seconds later, the door shuts. *She ran.*

"That must have been Rose." I say, detached.

"Where does she think she's going?" Xander asks, bewildered.

"Well someone better go get her." Jason says with a sigh.

CHAPTER TWENTY-SIX

Rose

The black Mercedes pulls up and slows to a crawl beside me as I walk down the road. I hear the window go down, breaking the silence.

"Where are you going?" Caleb asks curiously.

"I don't know. Anywhere but here!" I say hopelessly.

I don't dare look at him because I know if I do, I will break down.

"We need to talk." He says seriously.

"I don't want to!" I say defiantly.

"It's freezing out." He says, hoping that will change things. "At least let me drive you home." He adds sensibly.

I'm shivering now because it is freezing out, but I still don't want to get in the car with him. So, I keep walking stupidly.

Caleb stops the car abruptly, putting it in park. He uses his vampire speed to come to a stop in front of me. I look straight into his chest, refusing to look into his eyes. My heart rate quickens, I don't think I'll ever get used to his speed.

"It's not safe for you to be out here alone." He says reasonably. "Please get in the car." He adds, his patient demeanor faltering.

"I'll take my chances." I reply heartlessly.

Caleb steps to the side, allowing me to pass. I'm caught off guard and stand frozen with my arms wrapped around me for warmth.

"I understand that your angry Rose, but I'm not the only one that lied to you. I don't see you running from him." He says heatedly.

He's talking about Morgan of course. And he's not wrong. I'm taking the fact that he lied to me for a lot longer, much better. I stare at the road, at a loss for words.

"You can't even look at me. Do you hate me that much?" He asks, and I can hear his voice fall.

"I don't hate you." I say calmly.

I risk looking over at him only to see that he is watching me. There's a look in his eyes that is something I've never seen before. *Loss!* Our "relationship" has changed and we can't go back. *We both know it!*

"I just can't forgive you!" I say, with a broken heart.

"Maybe not today. But one day hopefully you will!" He says defeated. "Will you please come back with me? There's a lot to discuss!" He adds.

The feelings of sadness and loss in his eyes disappear and seem to be replaced by a lack of emotions. Perhaps it is a "vampire" thing, or maybe he's trying to pretend like his heart doesn't hurt as bad as mine does.

Whatever his reasons, I nod and head to the car. He's right, there is a lot to talk about!

CHAPTER TWENTY-SEVEN

Rose

Xander and Jason are already sitting in the living room when we get back, and the fire is lit. They obviously knew we were coming. *I have to learn how they do that!*

I go straight for the fireplace and start warming myself. Caleb stays at the furthest spot from me and leans against the door frame, near the front entrance. Not that I'm surprised.

"Ok." I say with a deep breath.

I turn my back to the fire and look from Jason to Xander.

"You're not human." I say bluntly.

I'm not saying it to be rude, after all, I am also not human. I am only trying to be direct so that we can discuss the important things.

"No. We're not." Xander answers simply.

"Why don't we make this easy." Caleb says quickly. "Xander is a muški melez which is a male halfling. Jason is a carbonjak or an enchanter. And I am a…" He adds, but I cut him off.

"Krvi čudovište…vampire." I finish his sentence sadly.

He has said this before in the dream, and I didn't believe him then. We make eye contact for a minute but he's unreadable. It's like he has completely shut-off all emotions. He looks away, breaking our gaze.

"Yes. I am a vampire." He says bitterly. "Your best friend Morgan is also a carbonjak or enchanter." He adds childishly.

"And Tyler?" I ask, trying to ignore Caleb's attitude.

"We think that he is a vucodlak, or a werewolf." Jason volunteers.

I go quiet, trying to process and take it all in but it's a hard pill to swallow. I mean, surely, they understand how ridiculous this all sounds. I turn and look back at the fire, no one says anything.

"So…What am I?" I ask reluctantly.

As much as I want an answer, it makes it all too real. I won't be able to unhear what they tell me I am. But it could give me the answers I need.

"You are a ženski melez. A female halfling." Xander says gently.

"I'm a what?" I ask, bewildered.

Having a name for it only makes in more puzzling. I don't know what exactly it means for me.

"A halfling." Xander says again.

"I'm a halfling. What does that mean?" I ask, cluelessly.

"It means that you're a mix. Part vampire, part enchanter, and something special. This means you will have a range of abilities and you will be very powerful one day." Xander answers knowingly.

"Most ženski melez are hunted and killed before they can reach transition or maturity. This is what we're trying to keep from happening. There are a lot of bad people who want to hurt you or control you." Caleb adds casually.

Not that I'm not grateful for their protection but I can't help but wonder why they're protecting me. There has to be more to the story. I turn back and stare at the fire, allowing the warmth to calm my nerves. I breathe deeply as I try to make sense of everything they've said.

After several minutes of silence, I turn around.

"Ok." I say with finality.

I watch as Xander and Jason let out a small breath of relief. I look over to see if Caleb is also relieved. But for some reason, he is laughing and shaking his head.

"What's so funny?" I ask indignantly.

"You are!" He says without hesitation.

I'm hurt and taken aback with his tone. He's resentful, that much is clear. I just have no idea what's going through his head right now.

He looks directly at me, the intensity in his gaze has me slightly flustered. He takes a couple steps towards me before he speaks.

"Not an hour ago, you said you couldn't forgive me." He says furiously. "Now, you learn what we are, and you just say ok, like it's a normal Monday." He adds.

"What do you want from me?" I respond heatedly.

My hands are balled into fists at my sides, anger courses through my veins. Caleb is acting as though Xander and Jason aren't in the room. The thought of them being present while Caleb yells at me causes heat to rise in my face, and only angers me more.

"I want a chance…" Caleb says, his voice softening.

He looks at me with a longing look. His feelings are obvious at the moment. He seems unconcerned to be expressing his feelings in front of Xander and Jason. I on the other hand am very uncomfortable to have our "almost relationship" issues on display. And to be honest, I don't know what to say.

"I…" I start to say.

Bang. Bang. Bang. Suddenly there is a loud and confident pounding on the door. Caleb walks around the corner and we can hear him open the door.

"Can I help you?" Caleb asks, with annoyance.

"I want to see Rose!" Morgan says adamantly.

Caleb must have gestured into the house because Morgan comes rushing in and comes straight to me. He pulls me into a tight hug just as Caleb comes back into the room. He resumes his place holding up the wall, looking as unimpressed as ever. When Morgan pulls away, it's only to arms length because he keeps his hands on my shoulders.

"Are you ok?" He asks, with concern all over his face. "I talked to Tyler." He adds somberly.

"I am." I say, sparing him my dramatics.

"No thanks to your cover up!" Caleb says spitefully.

Morgan's hands drop from my shoulders and he takes a few steps towards Caleb. This seems to be exactly what Caleb wanted, as he remains leaning, looking unconcerned and smug as ever. I grab Morgan's arm to stop him before he does something stupid.

"I know what I am." I say, pulling him back to look at me.

"You do?" He asks skeptically.

My admission seems to have pulled Morgan's attention away from Caleb, at least for now.

"You know everything?!" Morgan asks, with relief.

"Yes, I…" I start to say, eager to not have secrets between us.

"She hardly knows anything. You've kept it all secret!" Caleb says hatefully.

He stares at Morgan with rage in his eyes. He's not even trying to restrain himself now. He's got his arms crossed and I can see his muscles straining. He may not be restraining his words, but physically, he's just keeping the vampire from showing.

"Alex and I did what we had to." Morgan says back to him, through clenched teeth.

Caleb rolls his eyes in response and leans back against the wall nonchalantly. The dislike they have for each other is clear.

"We have more important things to discuss." Xander says, trying to diffuse the situation.

"Hannah." Jason says with concern.

He's one hundred and ten percent right of course. During the whole situation with secrets being revealed, I completely forgot about Hannah.

"Some guy has her?" I say rattled.

All of the guys heads shoot towards me. I don't know who he is but judging by the look on their faces, I don't even need to say his name, he's real and he's bad news.

"Are you sure?" Caleb asks. A look of concern crossing his face.

"Yes. I was in class and I received a call from Hannah's cell. I went out in the hall to answer it and Hannah was hysterical." I begin ignoring my fear.

"Then we got cut off because some guy named Lord D-something…" I say pausing, as I watch understanding cross his face.

I'm suddenly reassured that this Lord guy is real. I don't know which is worse. Knowing that this crazy guy has Hannah or knowing what Caleb is.

"Lord Dalibor. Unfortunately, I know him." Caleb says sadly. "What'd he say?" He asks.

"Well, he called me Ana and wouldn't accept that my name is Rose. He said he doesn't like the company I've been keeping but I don't really understand that. Also, he kidnapped Hannah as an insurance policy of some sort. I don't know what he wants." I say, exhausted.

"He wants you Rose!" Caleb says honestly.

I don't have the slightest understanding of why someone I don't know would want me, but I know that this is going to be a situation that I am going to have to handle.

"But why does he want me? Where the hell is Ana?" I ask confused.

"I'll explain that later. Tell me what happened after he called." Caleb says urgently.

Things are starting to come together but the facts are still screwy. I'm tired of this puzzle.

"I don't understand?" I say to no one in particular.

All the guys are silent for several minutes and I can tell that they are thinking everything through.

"This can't be happening." I say mostly to myself. "Where is Hannah?" I ask. Though I am not sure I want an answer.

Caleb looks at me with hurt in his eyes. His answer is clearly not going to make me happy.

"There's nothing we can do about Hannah without putting you in danger." Caleb states sadly.

"Well, doing nothing isn't an option." I say angrily. "She's my best friend Caleb and she would do everything she could if the roles were reversed." I explain.

His somber look and light sigh inform me that I'm not going to like what he has to say.

"I understand how you feel Rose. The problem is that Lord Dalibor is strong and smart. He's been around for a very, very long time. Our plan is to hide from him and avoid his allies at least until you come into your power. A confrontation before then will likely kill us all. There are few who can overpower him and I'm not one of them." Caleb says sadly.

"So, we find someone who can and then we save Hannah?" I say.

"There has to be something we can do?" Morgan contributes hopefully.

Caleb sighs in frustration and his eyes briefly close. I know he's trying to be patient but it's obvious that our persistence is defeating him.

"I wish it were that easy Rose, but who we need is an original and we don't know where anyone resembling an original is. Not to mention where Dalibor is. It's not in the best interests of your survival for me to take you right to him. Don't you get it?" Caleb says sharply. "The incident at the school was child's play to him. He was testing the strength of our resistance and nothing more." He adds.

"What do you mean? What was that fog stuff at the school?" I ask.

"It's called the dark shadows and it can be lethal if that's the intention. The fog itself only disorients people, it's what is hidden in it that you have to worry about." Caleb says seriously.

"You mean the shadow figures? I saw them. What do they do?" I ask.

"They're captured souls of everyone he's ever killed, and they have to obey him. They can mutilate a body to the point of making them unrecognizable, the likes of which the human world rarely sees. Or they can observe and be relatively harmless. That's what they did at the school, fortunately." Caleb says with relief.

"How do you figure that's a good thing?" I ask.

"Rose, half the student body went into the fog. They could all be dead, but no one was even hurt. Since humans can't see the creatures lurking in the fog, they chalked it all up to a freak storm. They're clueless. The mortal world remains blissfully ignorant to reality and our existence, yet again." Caleb says resentfully.

"Ok, fine! I get it. Ignoring your downward talk of humans, you're trying to prove that Lord Dalibor is all powerful and can't be defeated. Point taken! Now hear this. I won't do nothing and let Hannah get hurt. So, what are we going to do?" I demand.

I glare at Caleb, daring him to contradict me. He simply looks at me showing a mix of pride and annoyance with my attitude. I don't care as long as he understands that my choice is final. We're still locked in an intense gaze when Xander clears his throat.

"I have an idea if anyone's interested." Xander asks.

CHAPTER TWENTY-EIGHT

Caleb

I can feel all eyes on me as I fume and glare at Xander. I don't want to leave Hannah with that psychopath, but the alternative would put Rose in danger. Rose probably thinks I have no heart right now, but I do. I just want her to be safe. I need her to be safe.

Rose walks right up to me and takes my hands. I can feel the hard face façade I had on, softening with her gaze.

"Please. We have to try!" She begs me to understand.

In the background, I can see a look of hope on Jason's face. Xander's too. My brothers! Maybe not by blood but by choice. I look away from Rose to stop myself from kissing her. She has that effect on me and that's when I realize that we are going after Hannah.

"Okay. Xander let's hear your idea." I say grimly.

Rose wraps her arms around me automatically and pulls me into a hug. She pulls away quickly when she realizes what she's doing. She's been careful not to touch me since she figured out what I was.

"Thank you!" She says sincerely, before returning to Morgan's side.

"Ok…So back on topic, what's your plan?" I ask.

"Well, it's not so much a plan yet as a step in that direction. You probably remember when Caleb entered your dream." Xander says to Rose, carefully.

Before continuing, he glances at Morgan, gauging his reaction. I watch as he grimaces slightly upon learning this, and it makes me smirk. I look at Rose. She's blushing and refuses to make eye contact with me. Probably because she asked me to take off my shirt, not knowing it wasn't just a dream.

"Well, it's called dream walking and you're capable of it also. So, I was thinking that maybe you could enter Hannah's dream. Any information she can give you might help us to find a weakness in his plan. It might help us get her back, it's at least worth a shot." Xander finishes.

I'm kind of amazed at his plan or step as he calls it. It's very clever and sneaky. It sounds pretty good, assuming Rose is comfortable with dream walking. It's a little more complicated than closing your eyes.

"Alright, what do I need to do?" Rose asks without hesitation.

She has made up her mind. She wants to try to save her friend, no matter what. That's one of the reasons I admire her, she's loyal. That's not an easy trait to find.

"Well, first we need something with Hannah's DNA, blood works best but a hair will do. Then we do some minor mixing and say a chant that sends you on your way. I'll spare you the details for now." Xander says.

"Ok well, I know I can get the hair if I go to her house. Blood would be impossible. So, what do I mix the hair with and why? I want to hear the details now." She says impatiently.

"Don't freak out. We have to mix the hair with some blood, and you have to drink it." Xander says carefully.

"Ok, I probably shouldn't have asked. If it gives me the opportunity to see Hannah, then I'll do it." She says adamantly.

Xander smiles at Rose in a show of support. She doesn't know it but she's helping us to help Jason, and that means a lot. *To all of us!*

"You truly are a melez at heart Rose. I'm impressed and I'm glad we got to you in time. I've had to watch a lot of our kind die and I didn't want the same fate for you." Xander admits.

I'm sure she is nervous and a bit scared, but she doesn't let it show.

"When do we do this?" She asks fearlessly.

CHAPTER TWENTY-NINE

Rose

A week goes go by and the snow begins to fall heavier. Ice crystals glisten in the trees, and most of the animals and birds have gone into hibernation or have flown south. The days are short, and the nights have grown longer as though darkness is threatening to engulf the world.

School finishes for the winter break but it hardly seems important compared to everything that's happening. Of course, the boys made me go. They spoke about how school is important, but I'm thinking it had more to do with them knowing where I was at-all-times. It was less time for me to get in trouble anyway.

Now, it's winter break though and I don't have to take part in the ordinary school routine. It'll be Christmas in a few days. Not that my freedom feels much different these days.

Although Morgan seems relieved to have me knowing the truth now. It hasn't made him open up any. When I ask him when we're going to go after Hannah or where he's going, I get the same answers, "soon", "it doesn't matter, I'll be back soon", or "don't worry about it".

Caleb is even worse. It's like he, flat out, doesn't want to be around me. He stopped coming in my room. Now when Morgan is MIA, Caleb sits in his car in my driveway. *What the hell?*

I told myself that if something doesn't change by Christmas, I'm going to have to do something drastic. I miss Hannah. If she were here, I could talk to her about everything. She'd understand how lost I feel, but also how relieved I am. I know she's still alive, I can feel it.

It's an evening in late-December now, two days before Christmas. The snow is already quite deep and it's still coming down in blankets. The snowplows are working overtime to keep the roads drivable. Usually today would be a special day, a celebration for us. Its Alex's birthday but things haven't improved with him. He's still god-knows-where eighty percent of the time, and the other twenty percent he stays locked up in his room drinking. Hell, his boss came by to check on me because of Alex's strange, erratic behavior. Surprisingly, he rarely misses work, but they have noticed the change. The more time that goes by the worse things get. Alex looks deathly ill and I'm worried about him, but he won't even speak to me anymore. I don't know what to do.

Morgan left last night and he hasn't come back yet, but he will. He claimed that he had stuff to do but he won't tell me what he's up to. He's very secretive, even though, the secret is out. I thought the transparency would be a good thing. *Apparently not!* He leaves at night a lot, but he always returns. That's when you can see Caleb outside, sitting in his car.

I find myself uninterested in life, but who could blame me. I'm just going through the motions.

Today is different though and I know it's going to be bad. *It's my intuition telling me.*

I'm sitting on the couch, reading a book to kill time. Caleb is no longer parked outside. He went home a few hours ago. *Not like it makes a difference.*

Finally, I hear the roar off an engine pull in and a door slams, but the vehicle stays idling. It can't be Morgan. Just then, Alex walks through the door looking grim. The circles under his eyes are darker and more sunken. He smells like he just went swimming in booze and his eyes look dead. He stares at me on the couch and I'm too stunned to say anything.

"Rose…It's my birthday!…I'm going to the bar…Don't wait up for me." Alex says flatly.

He turns on his heel and goes right back out the door. I hear the car door slam again and the roar of the engine fades into the distance. I'm still sitting on the couch, frozen in place. He hasn't spoken more then a word to me in so long, I'd almost forgotten what he sounds like. Now he decides to talk to me?…On his birthday? I didn't even wish him a happy birthday. I was too stunned.

I turn back to my book but this time, I'm staring at the words blankly. I'm not really reading it. I'm more confused than ever. Should I go see him or should I leave him alone? *I don't know.* He didn't exactly invite me. I'm torn between these two options when I hear the roar of another engine. This one sounds louder though, so I know its Morgan. *Perfect timing!* He'll know what I should do. I put my book down and face the door waiting for him to come in. He finally does and he looks beat up. He has bruised knuckles, a small cut on his cheek and a tear in his shirt. Not to mention the snow stuck to his pants all the way to his knees.

"Morgan, what the hell happened to you?" I say in shock.

I rush to his side to comfort him even though he doesn't expect it. I watch as he awkwardly kicks off his shoes and rubs his ribs. It's clear that his visible injuries aren't all there is.

"I'm sorry Rose but I really don't want to discuss it. I just want to sit down for a while." Morgan says avoiding my question.

"No. Absolutely not! You're going to go to my room, strip down to your shorts, and let me take care of you for a change. No buts!" I say forgetting how tired I am of his secrets.

He looks at me as though he's angry and about to argue when his expression softens, and he looks happy now.

"Ok, you win. I'll meet you up stairs." He says without a fight.

Morgan heads upstairs and I go to the kitchen to grab an ice pack. I head upstairs and get a washcloth warmed up before I go in my room. Morgan is lying in my bed on his back wearing only his boxers. There are a few bruises on his torso but they're mainly small. There is one big bruise on his rib cage, and it looks painful. I gently get on to the bed and place the ice pack on his ribs. He winces at the weight but doesn't say anything. He closes his eyes and I lean over his face to clean the cut. I dab gently with the cloth hoping I don't hurt him too much.

"Alright Morgan, I'm not going to pester you about what happened to you right now. Just remember that someday you're going to owe me an explanation." I say kindly.

"Mhmm." Morgan replies.

Morgan grunts in agreement with me but he doesn't say much because he seems to be quite comfortable now.

"So, you just missed Alex. He spoke to me." I say randomly.

"What'd he say?" Morgan says very alert.

Morgan's eyes are wide open now and he's paying close attention to what I say. Figures that he wants a play by play of my day, but he won't tell me who unleashed a whooping on him.

"Well, he said it's his birthday, he's going to the bar and I shouldn't wait up. He sounded strange when he said it too. He was sad and his voice was strained." I say.

Morgan doesn't even appear to be the tiniest bit excited about Alex's proclamation. His expression seems sad and pained and I fear that he knows something that I don't.

"Should we go see him?" I ask curiously.

"No. If he wanted us around, he would have invited us." Morgan says.

It's disappointing to hear him say this but I suppose he's right. I guess I had been expecting Morgan to be more upbeat about this new development. Now I just want to work things out with Alex, but I don't want to ruin his night either. I really want to go.

"Well, maybe he'll like the surprise visit?" I say hopefully.

"Rose please just trust me! It's better if we don't go." Morgan says seriously.

"But…" I start to argue.

"No buts' Rose, just promise me you'll stay here." Morgan begs me.

"Fine." I say annoyed.

I grab a book off my night table and swap it for the cloth. Morgan's cut is clean so he's good now and I don't feel like playing nurse anymore. Morgan closes his eyes and I start reading the book to entertain myself. I'm annoyed that Morgan doesn't want me to see my brother. Especially since I have already lost Hannah. First, he keeps things from me and now he's keeping me from my brother. *Not cool.*

A few hours later Morgan is passed out beside me and I'm halfway through my book. I look around my room and see his pants on the floor. I have a horribly stupid, yet incredibly tempting idea. I could always take the truck and go to the bar alone. Morgan is out cold, he'd never know.

I slip gently off the bed and creep over to his pants. I pull the keys out of the pocket and quietly head towards the door. I sneak down the stairs and slip on my boots and jacket, and I grab my cell off the hall table.

As soon as I get outside in the dark, I have the ominous feeling of being watched. I head towards Morgan's truck and have to heave myself up. After all, I'm fairly short and Morgan's truck is jacked up.

I quickly pull out of the laneway after hastily buckling my seatbelt, and head down the road. The bar is about twenty kilometres from our house and it's on the out skirts of town. I know I'll get there before last call and probably before Alex leaves, but I'm wracked with guilt. I've taken Morgan's truck without permission and without a licence, and without even bothering to leave a note in the event that he wakes up. Then again, he neglected to tell me that I'm not entirely human my whole life, so we'll call it even.

Like ninety percent of all drivers, I'm going slightly over the speed limit. I realize that this is a dangerous and reckless idea considering its dark, snowy, and as far as I can see I'm the only vehicle out. I still feel like I'm being watched, or I guess it would be followed now, since I'm travelling at about one hundred kilometres an hour down the dark road. Unfortunately, I'm not paying much attention to the road, I keep thinking about Morgan and the way he looked when he asked me not to go see Alex. There was an underlying message in his look, and I didn't understand it until now, he thinks Alex is dangerous.

I'm about five kilometres out from the bar now when something darts in front of the truck. I can barely see because of the darkness and snow and usually I wouldn't care. This truck will demo anything that gets in its path but at the last minute it looks like a person. *I freak!*

I slam on the breaks and start skidding but the person just stands there. I'm starting to panic now, and everything feels like it's in slow motion. I know the truck won't stop in time, so I do the one thing you're not supposed to do, I swerve. I'm not an experienced driver though and I end up turning the wheel too hard to the right and the truck begins skidding sideways off the road. I feel the tires hit the gravel and then the truck is rolling sideways. As the truck flips my head smashes into the window, shattering the glass. The windshield explodes and I try to cover my face with my hands. The airbag deploys and it feels like a car just hurled itself into my face. The truck finally comes to a stop, upside down, against a tree. I can't see very well, there is dirt, dust, and snow everywhere, but I can see the person still standing on the road. All I can see from my position is their shoes and that doesn't exactly help me to identify the person.

My heart is pounding and with every beat I think it is going to burst. The feet start moving in my direction. I swear I'm having a stroke or something as I watch them come closer. I suppose it's like watching a shark's fin come towards you, it's like being taunted about impending pain.

I scream when I hear what sounds like a gunshot go off. *Stupid me*! It's actually just the passenger airbag popping out. When I look back out the person appears to be gone. I quickly look everywhere I can see, and I start crying because I'm afraid this person is dangerous. They would have already helped me if they were good. I know in my head that they wanted me to crash and they must have been the one's following me because they give me the same creepy feeling that I've been getting.

I have to get out of here, I need to get to the bar, and I am less than five kilometres away.

I look around but I can't see my cell phone. God knows where it got to in the crash, with all the windows busted it could be anywhere. I look around again to make sure I'm still alone, then I play with the seatbelt buckle trying to get it to let go. It's harder than you think when you're upside down.

The buckle finally comes apart and I come crashing down. I land head-first and then slide my back across the broken glass sitting on the roof of the truck from the windows. I feel a burning sensation in my back and quickly lean to the side while I slide my hand down my back to where the pain is. I feel the sharp, jagged edge of the small piece of glass that is lodged in my lower back. I try to grab it unsuccessfully and end up cutting my hand. I cry out in pain and hope that the person doesn't hear me and decide to come back. I try to remove the glass again because I want to get it out before I hit it on something, and it goes in further.

I grab the glass again and pull as hard and fast as I can. It comes out and I strangle a fresh scream. I sit there crying for a minute. I can feel the wetness of the blood coming from the wound where the glass had been. I hope I'm not going to die from blood loss. I carefully crawl across to the only window not blocked by the tree or snow. I slide out of the broken window and take a deep breath of the night air. I can't see anyone and that only sets me on edge. Where did that person go?

I'm sore, dizzy and confused, not to mention terrified. I'm still bleeding quite badly, and I know I need to leave to get help. I don't want to be here if that weirdo does come back.

I start walking in the direction I had been to the bar. My walking is unstable, and my vision keeps blurring but I have to make it. I keep forcing myself to walk even though every step hurts. I've been walking forever it seems and I still can't see the bar. I grow weaker with every step and it's then that I realize that I'm not going to make it. I collapse on the side of the road and start to cry. I'll probably freeze to death over night but I'm just so tired. I lay in the snow for a while and then the world goes black.

When I finally come to, I'm lying on my back staring up at the starry sky with the occasional snowflake landing on my face. It's so beautiful that for a moment I forget about my accident. Nothing else matters except the stars twinkling down on me. I hear movement behind me, so I try to sit up and look but pain shoots through my entire body. I quickly realize that I'm still bleeding but not as badly. I manage to roll onto my stomach and see behind me.

At the time no one is with me, I'm alone but I've been moved. I'm no longer lying at the side of the road, but rather I'm on soft grass with a light coating of snow. I know exactly where I am now, the pond of angels, my pond. The thing that frightens me is that I have no idea how I got here. When I passed out, I was alone, on the road.

I crawl on my belly a few feet to the edge of the water. Despite the freezing cold temperature, the water remains unfrozen. I put my injured hand in the icy cold water to rinse the blood. The gash isn't so bad when red liquid isn't gushing from it.

I pull my hand back to me and try to raise myself onto my feet but it's a waste of energy, I simply can't stand. I'm still dizzy and now I'm feeling quite nauseous, maybe I've lost more blood than I'd thought. Reluctantly, I try again because it's not like I can stay here all night. Its freezing and I really need to see a doctor.

I lay sprawled out on my belly and that's when I hear them. Heavy footsteps are crunching in the snow towards me. I start trembling in fear, is it the same person who made me crash? Have they come to finish me off? Are they the one who brought me here? I'm petrified that this might be the end. Even Caleb's protection is useless against my own stupidity. I wonder how long it'll take for someone to notice that I'm gone.

Morgan

I wake up in the dark, so I know it's really late. My body aches all over from the beat down I got earlier. I look beside me, but Rose is gone. I sit up quickly and flick on the lights, but the room is empty aside from me. I listen to every noise hoping she's in the kitchen or the bathroom, even though my gut's telling me that she's gone. I suppose she could be with "him", since her bed was occupied tonight. I don't think she knows that I've been well aware when he's in the house. I can always sense him now. He doesn't even try to hide his presence anymore. It's almost like he wants everyone to know when he's here. *I hate vampires!* I've only met a handful and I don't like them, including Caleb. I'm sure it's a mutual feeling.

I jump off the bed and grab my shirt off the floor, and then I pull on my pants and socks. I reach into my pocket and pull out my cell phone, but I freeze. My keys are gone. It dawns on me. She's not with Caleb but I know exactly where she went. She just had to go spend tonight with Alex, after I asked her not to. I should've known better with her. I pull out my phone and dial Tyler's number. If Rose found Alex, I need to hurry but I'm going to need help.

"Tyler, its Morgan. I need you to come to Rose's now!" I say urgently before I hang up.

I head downstairs and sit impatiently on the couch. I keep dialling her cell phone, but she isn't answering. This is bad, very bad. She's in serious danger, I can feel it. My instincts are usually right. I should've known better than to try and hide something from her again. Now I might be too late. I see headlights dash across the wall through the window, and I bolt out of my seat. Every second I waste puts her in greater danger. I grab my coat and dash out the door before Tyler can put his car in park. I jog towards him and he looks at me with concern when I jump into the car.

"Morgan, what's going on?" Tyler asks, with confusion.

"It's Rose. She took my truck and went to see Alex." I say.

"Ok. So why is this a bad thing?" Tyler wonders, skeptically.

"Alex isn't Alex anymore. He's been possessed. By a wraith." I say.

Tyler looks at me with a mix of confusion and curiosity.

"Are you sure? I thought the wraiths have been extinct for centuries." Tyler says.

"So, did I. But I can guarantee that's what has gotten to Alex." I say confidently.

"Ok, what do you need me to do?" Tyler asks.

"Change form. See if you can find her." I say thoughtfully. "I need to borrow your car. I'm going to need Caleb's help even if I don't want it." I say reluctantly.

"You got it!" Tyler says.

Tyler gets out of the car and I switch seats. I hear the familiar crackling of bones signalling that he's changing, and then I see him take off into the woods. I don't have the time to just sit around so I take off towards Caleb's house.

After about ten minutes I pull up and practically run to the door. I knock twice not wanting to wait for someone to answer. As the door opens, I feel a wave of pure hate go through my body. I know then that Caleb and I will be face to face. My senses are right, he's standing there looking smug as usual and he doesn't say anything.

"I wouldn't be here if it wasn't important." I say gravely.

I hate how he just stands there looking at me like I'm nothing more than a bug that needs to be squished.

"Rose is in trouble." I say honestly.

Finally, that seemed to wipe the smile off his face. I'm guessing that he's no longer feeling like the big bad vampire. I can see it in his eyes, he's scared. He hesitantly motions me inside and I step in, but the door remains open. I see Jason and Xander come in from the other room and they're listening intently.

"Where is she Morgan?" Caleb asks calmly.

"I can't be sure. She took my truck while I was sleeping, likely to see Alex." I say.

"But Alex isn't Alex anymore!" Caleb states.

"How do you know that Caleb?" I ask curiously.

"I can sense him Morgan." Caleb says smugly.

"I know it's crazy, but he's been possessed by a wraith, I'm sure of it." I say.

"I believe it Morgan, I've felt it. We have to find her, now." Caleb says urgently.

Just then Caleb grabs my arm and pulls me forward so hard that my arm feels like it might snap. There is a loud thud and some bones cracking where I was just standing. I turn around to see Tyler almost back in human form. I don't bother to thank Caleb. I don't really want to and fortunately we don't have time anyway.

"Tyler, did you find her?" I ask.

"No but I found your truck. It's upside down and totalled by the woods. She must have rolled it and she's been hurt. There's quite a bit of blood leading away from the accident but then it just disappears." Tyler says.

"He's already got her!" I say helplessly.

I don't know what to do now, all hope seems lost. She's probably dead or gone. I fall into a pit of my own sadness and I let Caleb take over the situation.

"Alright Tyler, sorry bud but you got to change back. You and I will go on foot and Xander, Jason and Morgan can follow in a car." Caleb suggests.

I'm being motioned back out the door towards the car and I see Caleb and Tyler take off in a blur. I know they will find her. I only hope we're not too late. *I can't let her die, I love her!* Now I know that's what has been bothering me. I'm in love with Rose and I need to tell her before its too late.

We take off with a jolt, Xander's driving. I guess he's the best one to do so with his heightened reflexes. I don't have the luxury of being selfish because this is for Rose. If we can save her, I promise there will be no more secrets, no more lying. I will even try to be friendlier with the vampire. I swear on my life to make her happy!

CHAPTER THIRTY

Rose

I'm still on my stomach and I desperately want to get to my feet so I'm not so vulnerable. It's just not happening though. The snow is starting to burn on my bare hands, and I can hear the crunching of footsteps come to a stop behind me. I can see and smell the bits of blood sprinkled on the snow from me. It looks harsh against the white snow.

Finally, whoever is here with me comes to a standstill in front of me. I recognize the person's black shoes and blue jeans. It's the same person who caused my accident. I'm too terrified to look up because I don't want to see who my killer is going to be. I remain on my stomach with my chin in the snow staring at the shoes as they walk out of view. I hear them stop beside me and I'm afraid of what comes next. I wait for pain, but it doesn't come. At least, none that I don't already feel. It's only a matter of time before they get on with their plan.

"Rose, your kind is quite pathetic." The voice says, unrecognizably.

The voice is raspy, hollow, and devoid of all emotion but there is something familiar about it.

"What do you want from me?" I say through my tears.

"Well personally, I want you dead, quickly, slowly, I have no preference as long as it ends you. However, I have orders." The voice replies.

Whoever this is, it's clear that they couldn't care less about me. I am lower than dirt on their scale, they see me as nothing more than an annoying inconvenience. I know this isn't Lord Dalibor because he wouldn't take orders from anyone, more than likely they work for Dalibor.

Finally, I muster up the courage and strength to roll onto my back. They're twirling a dagger in their hands and it gleams in the moonlight. I look up to the hooded face.

"No, it can't be." I say as barely more than a whisper.

This can't be real. It must be a bad dream. Maybe I'm in shock or something but this just can't be happening. When I look at their face, I see my brother, but the eyes are not his. His color is off and there are dark,

167

sunken grooves under his eyes. It's obvious that he is dying from the inside out. I don't want to believe it, it's not fair.

"Alex!" I cry out.

"I'm sorry dear but Alex is otherwise detained at the moment. I assure you he can see everything though." The voice says teasingly.

This thing that is inside Alex is taunting me, trying to torment and scare me as much as possible. It's working. I'm still in shock because it just doesn't seem real that this is Alex, he would never do something like this. I don't understand.

"What are you talking about? You're Alex!" I say pleading with him.

"I promise you sweetheart that even though I look like your brother Alex, inside I most certainly am not." It says reassuringly.

It's starting to become clearer now. I have no idea how it's possible for this to be Alex but not be him. I suppose anything is feasible in the other world.

"Where's Alex? What have you done to him?" I ask, concerned.

"Oh, he's still here. He's kind of like a hostage in his own body right now. Trust me sugar, he's just as annoying as he was months ago when I snatched him." It says, bragging.

"Oh my god. It was you all along!" I say after figuring it out.

The beast simply laughs, relishing in the fact that it had me fooled for so long.

"Of course, it was me you dumb girl. I had to endure hell before I could fully control this puppet. He found out that excessive drinking could slow me down but eventually his own body turned on him. He's dehydrated, starving, sleep deprived but he's still putting up quite a fight. Of course, once I'm gone, he won't last long." It says happily.

"Let him go! You've got what you want." I beg.

"Hardly. How is it you can possibly know so little. I want Alex, Rose. I feed off his suffering and it makes me stronger. When I finish him off I'll be even stronger. So you see? You're nothing but an errand to me. My Lord requested you and freed me from my grave. I owe him." It says.

The beast paces by my feet, toying with the dagger. He seems very impatient and wants nothing more than to kill me. I assume he's been instructed to keep me alive or I'd already be dead. I have to do something. I can't just wait.

"So. What are you waiting for? Why don't you just take me to him and be done with it?" I ask curiously.

"Oh you stupid girl, you have no idea what torture awaits you. My Lord has sent another to relocate you, that's why I'm waiting." The beast says, annoyed.

Negotiating will be pointless. This creature has no heart. I feel the fire inside me fighting its way to the surface. I desire to kill this thing inside my brother. First Hannah and now Alex, I want revenge. I pull myself into a sitting position and stare at the Alex imposter. I can't hurt my brother, I won't. There must be something I can do though.

"So, you're Dalibor's errand bitch eh? Now I get it." I say rudely.

I watch as the creature grits Alex teeth and I can sense the anger and resentment flowing through his veins.

"I'm no one's bitch girl. I do what I need to survive and that's it. You best learn some respect and call him Lord, or your pain will be that much greater." It answers angrily.

"Sure, whatever." I say, disrespectfully.

I know I've struck a nerve. If being a teenager is good for anything its pissing people off. The Alex wanna-be jumps down beside me and puts the dagger to my throat. I know I'm playing a very dangerous game with an even more dangerous opponent, but I don't know what else to do.

"I could kill you right now, do you understand?" The beast says, threateningly.

"Of course, I understand you idiot, but you won't because you're afraid of him." I reply.

"My orders are not to kill you but that car accident you had was a nasty one. I think I can add a few lacerations and chalk them up to the accident." It says with a smirk.

Now I am afraid. I haven't considered all its options and I definitely didn't think of them. He's leaning over me twirling his dagger. I can see in his eyes that he is deciding where to stab me. He looks demonic and I have to fight to remember that my brother is still in there somewhere. Trying to fight him physically would be futile so for now I guess I'm kind of at his mercy.

He brings the blade down in the blink of an eye across my right leg. I scream in pain, but it doesn't help, he seems to enjoy it. I feel the burning on my leg as moisture soaks my pant around the cut. I'm in so much pain that all I can do is cry.

"Oh, I'm sorry, did that hurt? Maybe now you'll keep your mouth shut and hold your tongue. If not, I can always cut it out but let's do another one to ensure that you understand the severity of my threats." It says enjoying my suffering.

This time he raises the dagger straight up and I watch him do it. I can tell by his stance that he's planning on stabbing me this time, not just cutting me. I don't know where he's going to do the damage, but I don't want to either. I close my eyes and try to prepare myself for more pain, although it's already unimaginable. Before I feel the dagger pierce my flesh again, I hear a strange growl and I can't help but open my eyes. I see the sharp knife plunging towards my stomach and I'm unable to keep from screaming.

"NO, PLEASE!" I scream.

There's a loud thud above me and something grazes my side, but it doesn't feel like the knife. I open my eyes again and look around. No one is standing above me anymore, but the Alex imposter is circling with a werewolf. I know it's Tyler and I can't let him hurt my brother.

"Tyler don't, Alex is still in there." I yell to him.

The werewolf looks from me to Alex and continues growling at him. The creature begins laughing hysterically as though he knows he's in no immediate danger.

I hear a whoosh through the air and when I turn my head Caleb is kneeling beside me and looking me over.

"Rose, are you ok?" Caleb asks me, full of concern.

"I think so, but you have to help Alex." I say, pleading with my eyes.

I hear a strange crunching sound and look over to see Tyler's wolf form being thrown towards me. Caleb grabs me in a flash and pulls me back. Tyler's limp body lands where I was not two seconds ago. He's breathing but he isn't moving. I glace over at Caleb in surprise.

"Well, it looks like this is my exit, but I'll leave you a parting gift dear Rose." The beast says smartly.

The creature laughs and raises the dagger with both hands. I realize what he's going to do too late. Alex forces the dagger deep into his own chest and drops to the ground. A shadowy form raises itself from Alex's body and looks over at us. It has yellow-orange eyes and I understand why I saw a flame in Alex's eyes that day.

"NO!" I yell. "Alex?" I try to call out.

I scream for my brother and manage to barely get to my feet. I stumble across the gap between myself and Alex and I drop to my knees by his side. Tears are already pouring down my cheeks, they're warm and salty.

"Alex, please don't leave me." I cry, begging him.

I sob and Alex opens his eyes slightly, the wound in his chest is hemorrhaging blood around the dagger.

"Rose, I'm so sorry. I thought I knew best, but I was wrong. Can you ever forgive me?" Alex asks.

"Of course. I love you! You're my brother." I say easily.

"I love you too." Alex says softly.

His eyes close and his breathing stops. I know he's dead. He's gone. *I'm alone!* I cry harder than I've ever cried for anything. It's not fair that he's been taken from me.

I hear Morgan arrive through the trees and I assume that Xander and Jason are with him. I don't bother looking, I'm too busy leaning across Alex's body wishing he'll come back. I feel a warm hand go across my shoulder and I look up. Morgan's looking back at me with teary eyes. I burrow my face into his chest and let it all out. I know he won't ask me to stop. He gently lifts me to my feet and motions for me to go with him. I walk blindly wrapped in Morgan's arms and praying this is all a nightmare, but I know it's not. It's real. It's all real. I hear shuffling noises behind us, and I know everyone is helping to carry the dead or the wounded but they're not far.

I vaguely remember getting into Alex's car but as soon as it starts, I pass out. I'm too exhausted emotionally and physically, especially from my massive blood loss.

When I come to, I am in Caleb's bed again and Morgan is lying beside me watching. No one else is with us which I'm grateful for. If I look as bad as I feel, a blind man won't want me.

"Hi Rose." Morgan says softly.

"Hi Morgan." I say sadly.

"How are you feeling?" Morgan asks.

I look down and I have bandages all over my body. I also notice I am in my pajamas but that's the least of my worries. They're certainly taking good care of my injuries. I don't feel much pain.

"I'm ok I guess." I reply.

"I'm so sorry about Alex." Morgan says honestly.

"I don't blame you, there's nothing any of us could have done." I say.

We both go silent. I know Morgan feels the loss of Alex as well. He's like part of our family after all. The thought of family makes me think about everyone oddly enough.

"Morgan is everyone ok? Tyler?" I ask.

"Yes, everyone is fine. Tyler has a few bruises ribs, but he heals quickly." Morgan says.

"Ok." I say, feeling reassured.

I lay my head back and feel myself drifting off to sleep again. I know the truth and I've seen it. I believe and I accept it, at least I'm trying to. Alex is gone, it's just me. *I'm scared.* What's going to happen now?

ABOUT THE AUTHOR

Erica Richer is determined to give her readers an intense, emotional journey by writing about strong, passionate characters. She is new to writing novels but wants everyone to experience a book that they just can't put down.